DOWN TO THE WIRE

David Rosenfelt

St. Martin's Paperbacks

Please e-mail David Rosenfelt at dr27712@aol.com with any feedback. Your comments are very much appreciated.

This is a work of fiction. All of the characters, organizations, and events portrayed in this novel are either products of the author's imagination or are used fictitiously.

DOWN TO THE WIRE

Copyright © 2010 by Tara Productions, Inc.
Excerpt from *On Borrowed Time* copyright © 2011 by Tara Productions, Inc.

Cover illustration by Pete Garceau

For information address St. Martin's Press, 175 Fifth Avenue, New York, NY 10010.

Library of Congress Catalog Card Number: 2009041135

ISBN: 978-0-312-35680-4

Printed in the United States of America

St. Martin's hardcover edition / March 2010
St. Martin's Paperbacks edition / February 2011

St. Martin's Paperbacks are published by St. Martin's Press, 175 Fifth Avenue, New York, NY 10010.

10 9 8 7 6 5 4 3 2 1

For Debbie

IF YOU'RE A CORPSE, you should get your name in the paper.

That's what Chris Turley always thought should be the bare minimum. But this particular corpse was going to get shut out, at least from Chris's paper, the *Bergen News*.

Chris watched as the poor guy, covered with a blanket, was loaded into the coroner's van. It was a rather unglamorous way to go, knocked over like a bowling ball by a speeding Toyota whose driver didn't even have the decency to hang around afterwards.

Chris was standing, and the victim was lying, on Grand Avenue in Englewood, New Jersey. It was a mostly commercial area, and there would not have been many people around when the accident took place. Chris imagined that the driver might have gone on to Route 4 and then exited the area, to avoid detection and capture, though there were certainly no pursuers to evade.

The police were not releasing the victim's name, pending notification of his family, assuming he had a family. By the time the name would be made public, it would be past the deadline for Chris to file his story.

That meant that the only chance the deceased had to get his actual name in the paper would be if he turned out to be a person of status, unlikely in this Englewood neighborhood, or if the police were to eventually catch the perpetrator. If the victim were not already dead, Chris would not recommend that he hold his breath waiting for the arrest to be made.

Chris had a mental game that he played with himself whenever he covered an event of any kind. He tried to imagine what would have to happen to turn it into a Pulitzer Prize–winning story. Since it was two o'clock in the morning in thirty-degree weather, he wasn't much in the mood for mental game playing, but as he had to wait for the police briefing anyway, he gave it a shot.

Turning this pedestrian, hit-and-run-of-the-mill death into a Pulitzer would take some doing. The corpse would have to turn out to be a nuclear scientist and the hit-and-run driver would have to be a KGB agent. And not just any KGB agent, but Vladimir Putin himself. And since the KGB was known not to exist anymore, he, Chris Turley, would uncover through his investigative reporting that the agency had been resurrected, and was in cahoots with Al Qaeda.

And then the Pulitzer committee members would come crawling and the Nobel people would be on all fours right alongside them. And the Oscar, Emmy, Grammy, and Golden Globe lackeys wouldn't be far behind.

Of course, at times like this, Chris told himself he wasn't in this for the glory. He became a journalist to protect the people's right to know. It would just be nice if along with that right to know came an obligation to care. Because the truth was that no one was going to pay any attention at all to his story about an anonymous man killed by an anonymous driver on Grand Avenue in Englewood at two o'clock in the morning.

It was 3:30 by the time Chris filed his story back at the newsroom. Even at that hour, with only a skeleton night staff on duty, the place had an energy level that Chris always noticed. It was true of every newspaper office Chris had ever been in; there was a busy, bustling quality that was tangible, even when there was no business or bustling going on.

The story would be in the online edition almost immediately, so that when the Pulitzer judges woke up they would have no trouble finding it.

Now, if the police would only catch and arrest Vladimir Putin. . . .

"WHAT TIME DID YOU get back here last night?"

The questioner was Dani Cooper, the paper's entertainment editor and resident gossip columnist.

"Close to three," he said.

"I just missed you," she said. "I left around two thirty."

He smiled. "Why so early?" It was a significant part of Dani's job to hit the late-night New York hot spots and then write about celebrity sightings. She also would have been responsible for hitting the New Jersey hot spots, but unfortunately, New Jersey was a hot spot–free zone.

She shrugged. "It was a movie premiere, and the film was so bad that nobody wanted to hang around late at the party afterwards. You should have come."

"To the bad movie, or the dreary party?" Dani was always inviting Chris to things, and couching it as a work function, not a date.

"It wasn't that bad," she said. "I got plenty of stuff to write about."

Dani managed to be constantly upbeat, without falling into the dreaded "perky" category. Part of this was because it's tough to categorize a five-foot-eleven woman as perky, but mostly it was because she combined her natural optimism with an obvious intelligence. She felt that at any one moment in hers or anyone's life there were good and bad things going on. She made a conscious effort to focus on the former, while remaining realistic about the latter.

"Maybe next time," Chris said. Even though he didn't have a girlfriend at the moment, one thing Chris's life was not lacking for was female companionship. As a good-looking, single, heterosexual thirty-something he was doing reasonably well in that department. Dani was definitely someone he found attractive, but he just felt that to start a relationship in the newsroom was to invite disaster. They flirted occasionally, nothing serious, and nothing he planned to act on.

"Yeah, right," she said, knowing better. "Good piece you wrote, though. What a way to die, lying there on a cold street, killed by a son of a bitch who didn't even have the decency to stop."

Chris could hear the anger in Dani's voice, and though he had heard it a number of times before as she railed against some injustice, it always surprised him. "What would you do if you got your hands on that guy?" he asked.

"They would need dental records to identify him," she said, and then smiled.

The phone rang and she picked it up. "News desk. Cooper here." She listened for a moment, then asked who was calling. After hearing the answer, she handed the phone to Chris.

"Who is it?" he asked.

She smiled. "A concerned citizen."

Chris took the phone and said, "Turley."

The male voice on the other end said, "Mr. Turley, is this really you?"

"I'm afraid so."

"I'm a big fan of your work. Your writing is terrific."

"Thank you," Chris said. "How can I help you?"

"Actually, I think I can help you. I've got a pretty big story for you to write about."

Chris frowned for Dani's benefit as a way of telling her that he was talking to a loser.

"Really?" Chris asked, trying to sound interested. "What might that be?"

"It's about corruption by a high-level government official. And I can prove every bit of it."

"I'll need specifics," Chris says.

"I've got them. When can we meet?"

"Why do we have to meet?" Chris asked. "Why don't you just tell me about it?"

"I've got documents; we definitely need to meet," the man said. "It will just take a few minutes." When Chris hesitated, he continued. "Believe me, Mr. Turley, this will be worth your while. I wouldn't waste your time."

"Okay. You want to come here?"

"No. I don't want to be seen there. I want to do this anonymously."

Chris rolled his eyes for Dani's benefit, but decided he might as well find out what the man had to say. They finally settled on a park in Teaneck, across from a small medical office building, at 2:30 that afternoon. Chris knew where it was because he had been to an orthopedist in that building for a basketball-related knee injury. "You won't be late, will you?" the man asked. "I'm a little nervous about this."

"I'll be there," Chris said, and then hung up. "Thanks a lot," he said sarcastically to Dani.

"Sorry, but when he said it was a concerned citizen I thought he was joking, and that he was a friend of yours," Dani said. "I guess not, huh?"

"No, but don't worry about it. Maybe it'll turn out to be something."

Dani nodded. "Right. I mean, this is how Watergate started."

"No, Watergate started with a break-in at Democratic Party headquarters."

"But Deep Throat was also a concerned citizen," she persisted.

He shook his head. "No, Deep Throat was the number two man at the FBI."

"You're not going to give an inch on this, are you?"

He smiled. "I'm not planning to, no." This back and forth was typical of the banter between them, with the only difference that this time he seemed to come out on top. It was a small, and rare, victory.

Chris spent his lunch hour doing what he'd done on at least five lunch hours in the previous month. He went car shopping with his friend Craig Andrews, going to showrooms and checking out the latest models.

Craig was a midlevel city bureaucrat with the official title of deputy commissioner of housing and development, and would jump at any chance to get out of the office.

Craig and Chris had been friends for almost five years, ever since Chris wrote a favorable article about a piece of legislation that Craig, then a city councilman, was supporting.

Craig had called to offer his thanks, and in the ensuing conversation discovered they had been hanging out at the same sports bar for years without having ever met. Except for the fact that Craig was a Jets fan and Chris was a Giants fanatic, they learned over time that they shared pretty much the same view of everything.

Actually, what the two men did on that lunch hour wasn't actually car "shopping"; it was more like car "looking." They didn't have the money to buy the kind of cars they would want, not even close, but they did buy lottery tickets every week, so it couldn't hurt to be prepared.

Chris sat in the driver's seat of a Porsche, and for a few brief moments was imagining himself out on the open highway. When he got out, Craig came over and said, "What do I have to do to put you in this car today?"

"Steal it," Chris said.

After a solid hour and twenty minutes of deflecting the questions of actual car salesmen, it was time for Craig to go back to the office and Chris to meet the corruption whistle-blower.

"You want me to come with you?" Craig asked. "In case he's a psycho killer luring you into a trap?"

"What would you do if he was?"

Craig shrugged. "Probably nothing. I've got to be back for a three o'clock meeting, and besides, psycho killers intimidate me."

"I thought women intimidate you?"

Craig nodded. "And pushy salesmen and people who walk around wearing army fatigues. But psycho killers are the worst."

Chris laughed. "Go to your meeting. I'll get by without you."

"Any chance you'll tell me what kind of political corruption you're investigating?" Craig asked. "I'm asking because I'm political, and someday I hope to be important enough to be corrupt."

"I don't even know," Chris said. "But when I find out, you can read about it in the paper."

"And some guy just called you out of the blue?"

"That's right."

Craig was barely able to conceal his surprise at this, mainly because he knew his friend was lying. He could never reveal how he knew that, but the deception was worrisome and confusing. Why would Chris suddenly become secretive and distrustful, particularly on a matter like this?

There was no way for Craig to raise these questions, so he dropped the subject entirely. As they were walking out, Craig looked back at the sports car they had just been admiring. "You think either of us will ever get one of these?"

"If we did, what would we have to look forward to?"

Craig shrugged. "I'd think of something. See you later."

THE PARK WHERE CHRIS was to meet the tip-ster occupied close to half a square block near the center of town.

It wasn't really a park, since the accepted definition for "park" includes some usage for recreation. This was more of a grassy area, with a few tables. The closest it came to recreation was some recreational drug usage after dark.

Since the temperature was in the forties, there weren't too many people hanging around outside. Walking towards the designated meeting place, Chris could see about fifteen people, and he realized that he had no way to know who the "informant" was. Hopefully the man would know Chris, since he claimed to be a fan of his work.

Nobody seemed to be looking around for him, and most people were in small groups. One man sat at a table talking on his cell phone, but he didn't seem to be waiting for someone.

Chris looked at his watch and saw that the time was 2:28, which is how he later was able to be accurate about what time it was when he heard the noise that was so loud it felt like his eardrums were going to explode.

In the moment, his mind could not process what could have made such a noise, or why he was thrown against a fence by the power of it.

Chris landed on the ground and turned to look towards the street, where it seemed the sound and force had come from. In what appeared to be almost slow motion, the left half of the medical center building had turned into a fireball and was crumbling before his eyes.

He could see patches of flame within the structure and became aware of the sound of screaming. He couldn't tell whether those screams were coming from the building or from horrified onlookers.

Chris struggled to his feet, relieved and a little surprised to discover that he was not hurt. He ran towards the building to see if he could help in any way. It was too soon for the fire department to be on the scene, and no one else was doing anything.

Chris reached the front of the building on the side that was still standing. He was hesitant to go in, since it seemed quite possible that the remainder could fall at any time. Then he heard screaming that he was sure was coming from the interior, and after looking around and seeing no one else helping, he went inside.

The interior was filled with smoke and dust, and it took a while for him to get used to it and become able to see. He was not used to physical danger, and it took a conscious effort to quell the panic that he was feeling. He walked slowly, deliberately, very conscious that every step he took towards the interior of the building meant that was another step he would have to take getting out.

His eyes watering from the smoke, and wary of falling debris, Chris headed for the sound of the voices. He was less than thirty feet into the building when he found five people, two men, one woman, and two young children, huddled in what appeared to be the doorway of a doctor's waiting room, but which no longer had walls on two sides.

One of the men was bleeding pretty badly from a head wound, and the others seemed to have some injuries, as well, though Chris certainly did not have the time or ability to assess them.

"We've got to get out of here!" Chris screamed, in a near panic that the rest of the building was going to come down on top of them at any moment.

The people seemed to be in a state of shock and did not respond. "Can you walk?" he yelled.

Again, there was no answer. The children were crying, and the adults seemed paralyzed with fear. At that moment they were probably the only people in the country more frightened than Chris, but at least he remained capable of turning that fear into action.

"Let's go!" Chris grabbed the two children in his arms and started to move towards the entrance. The adults were not following, so he turned and screamed, "Come on! NOW!" and this seemed to penetrate. They started to follow him as he carried the children out.

When Chris reached the street, he ran into a group of four firemen who had just arrived. He gave them the children and ran back into the building. The adults were heading towards the front but moving slowly, and he literally herded them along, yelling at them to move quickly.

They finally got near the entrance, where more firemen were waiting for them. Chris pushed the adults out and then followed. He fell to the ground, gasping for air, and was grabbed by a fireman and half carried, half dragged across the street. He was aware of more screaming coming from the building behind him, but was unable to do anything about it.

The paramedics were already attending to the more seriously injured and Chris was left to lie on the cold ground, for the moment unattended. He was about halfway to breathing normally when he watched the remainder of the building come crashing down to the ground.

And then the screaming stopped.

CHRIS SPENT AN HOUR answering questions from detectives and fire officials on the scene.

He was in a makeshift triage area, where doctors and paramedics were examining and stabilizing the victims, and then determining to which of the waiting area hospitals they needed to be sent. It was by its nature semiorganized chaos, though the emergency responders were clearly competent and professional.

When the paramedics got around to checking out Chris, they recommended that he go to the hospital to be examined further, but he had no intention of following their advice. He called into the office and learned that the media was reporting that the explosion was already being considered a criminal act, not an accident, such as a gas leak.

This was without question the biggest story that Chris was ever involved in, and everything else was a very distant second. No one could report it like he could, because no one had lived it like he had. He was not going to sit around in a hospital while competitors ran off with his story.

Chris didn't announce to anyone that he was leaving, he just blended into the chaotic background. He also didn't bother asking any questions to fill in the gaps of his knowledge; back at the office they would know the pieces that he didn't, mostly from watching television coverage.

Lawrence Terry, the managing editor of the paper, was waiting for Chris when he got back. This was an event in itself; the seventy-year-old rarely ventured to the newsroom anymore. He was inching more and more towards retirement, mainly since the business was inching more and more towards something he no longer wanted to be associated with.

Chris's relationship with Lawrence was a complicated one. Lawrence and Chris's father, Edward Turley, had been very close friends, having met while covering the Vietnam War for their respective papers. On those rare occasions that neither Lawrence nor Edward were off reporting on some international crisis, or uncovering shocking revelations back home, Lawrence was a frequent visitor at the Turley house.

Actually, Chris's recollection was that Lawrence was there as often as Edward. Edward treated his home as a stopping-off point between assignments, and by any standard, he viewed husbanding and fathering as part-time jobs.

Five years ago, Edward had succumbed to a combination of alcohol and cigarettes, not necessarily in that order. He suffered a massive heart attack in the produce aisle of a supermarket, grasping and pulling down a display of melons as he fell to the floor, a rather ignominious end for such a larger-than-life figure.

Since then, Lawrence smoothly assumed the mantle of old-school lamenter-in-chief for the media business. All the so-called star journalists of today did was read words off a TelePrompTer, Lawrence would say. They read the news, they didn't live it. Not like he and Edward.

But the truth was that the business was passing Lawrence by. He knew it, and it galled him. His peers were all far younger and he was having trouble maintaining his relevance. Of course, he was at an age at which for most people relevance was not a concern, since they were retired.

Chris had called ahead and told some colleagues what he did after the explosion, and they in turn had filled Lawrence in. So Lawrence didn't need to be brought up to date, and he didn't want to burden Chris with unnecessary conversation. Stories should be written when they were as fresh as possible.

"You feeling okay?" Lawrence asked. "Not hurt?"

"I'm fine," Chris said.

"We've already got the nuts and bolts of the story covered," Lawrence said. "You need to go at it from the personal, emotional side."

Chris nodded. "That's what I was thinking."

"Good," Lawrence said. "Knock the sucker out of the park."

And Chris sat down at his computer to do just that. When he finished, he looked up and saw Dani standing there. "I hear you did pretty good today," she said.

He shrugged, but couldn't resist a smile. "Just another day at the office."

"Can I read your story?" she asked.

"Sure," he said, and pointed to it still on the computer screen.

She read it slowly and carefully, and when she finished, she said, "Wow. Can I tell people I knew you when?"

"When what?"

"When you were just a normal person."

"You think I'm going to change?"

"Chris, everything is going to change."

ONE REPORTER'S EYEWITNESS ACCOUNT
OF A NIGHTMARE
by Chris Turley

I am not a hero. I'm just not the type. I have lived thirty-two years without displaying any physical courage at all. So let's get that straight going in.

But I was across the street from the medical center this afternoon when it exploded. The force of it, even from a distance of a hundred feet, was unlike anything I have ever experienced. And very much unlike anything I want to experience again.

Because I was so close, even as I write this I know very few particulars of what happened and why. I reacted in the moment, with no real understanding of what was going on.

The left side of the building, as I faced it, crumpled to the ground within seconds. The right side, perhaps even sixty percent of the building as a whole, remained, stubbornly refusing to give in.

It was from that area that I thought I heard screams, though because the explosion had dulled my hearing, I couldn't be sure that the voices were not from people with me on the street.

Never having been in war, and war is the only comparison I can make, I was not prepared for the chaos around me. But I had to do something, even though every instinct told me to run away.

I went to the building and confirmed that the terrified screams were coming from inside. I ventured in, going through a front door and façade that remained perfectly intact, as if it had not gotten the memo that the rest of the building was . . .

IT'S RARE THAT A story comes out just right the first time; usually it's a process of rewriting and editing. But Chris's story was approved almost without any changes at all, such was the vivid power of his words. Of course, stories are almost always written to match up with available space, but that was not a consideration this time. For a first-person account of such an enormous event, Chris would have all the space he needed.

Eleven people died in that building and another seventeen were injured. Chris wrote about five of them in his story, the five he rescued, but ironically didn't even know their names. In a way, their anonymity was appropriate for the story; Chris's rescue efforts were a human reaction to other humans in trouble. Personal knowledge of who they were, or a personal connection to them, was not necessary in any way.

When the story was put to bed, Lawrence called Chris into his office, where he poured him a drink. To Lawrence, a drink was scotch, and the only choice offered was for it to either be on the rocks or with water.

Chris hated scotch, but saying no to Lawrence was not a consideration, so it presented him with a dilemma. If he took it with water, it diluted the taste, which was a good thing. However, it increased the size of the drink and made it last longer, which was quite a bad thing.

On this particular occasion, he opted for the scotch on the rocks, mainly because he needed something to calm his nerves quickly. He had acted instinctively after the explosion, but the enormity of what had happened was finally starting to hit him hard. As he drank from the glass, his hand shook.

"You sure you're okay?" Lawrence asked.

"I'm fine. Why?"

"You look like you're enjoying that scotch. Usually you drink it like it was medicine."

Chris laughed. "So why do you always give it to me?"

"Because when I die, I don't want your father coming up to me and saying, 'Why the hell did you give my son a fucking Kahlua and cream?' "

"I like Kahlua and cream."

"Quiet," Lawrence said, looking skyward. "He can hear you." Then, "But I'll bet he's proud of you today."

Talk of his father often made Chris uncomfortable, especially when it was Lawrence doing the talking. Lawrence had an uncompromisingly positive view of Edward, a view which much of the rest of the world did not fully share. Edward had taken a scorched earth approach to journalism, and his unwillingness to take his foot off the throat of his "victims" often provoked fear and hatred, albeit with a healthy dose of grudging admiration.

"I was in the right place at the right time."

"That's what good reporters do," Lawrence said. "They make sure they're in the right place at the right time. That's what your father did with Hansbrough. You did good, but your life will never be the same again."

"Why?" Chris asked.

"Because the world is about to know your name. It's not going to be easy to handle."

"Then can I have another scotch?"

Lawrence laughed. "That's a good start." He got up to pour the drink when his phone rang, and he answered it. "Terry."

He listened for a moment, frowned, and held the phone out for Chris. "Shit. Here it goes," he said.

"Who is it?" Chris asked.

"The *Today* show."

FOR THE MAN WHO would soon be known as "P.T.," things were going perfectly.

He had arrived at Simmons Crystal and Glass, a large factory in Edison, New Jersey, an hour before closing time. He had pretended to be a vendor, hyping a new type of glass-making machine that produced a more durable product than the kind they were using.

It was the fourth time he had been in the building; the first three amounted to crucial scouting missions. Nobody paid him much attention, since vendors wandered in and out of there all the time. But none had ever been there for a reason anywhere close to this important.

Of course, all he knew about glass he had learned in the last two months, through the magic of Google. And the wondrous machine he bragged about did not even exist. But it got him in the door, and though his halfhearted efforts were brushed off by the purchasing manager, he couldn't have cared less.

P.T. hid in a storage room until a full hour after closing, then carefully made his way onto the factory floor. He knew from his research that there would be no one around, and that the security guard made his rounds every half hour. That would give him twenty-five minutes to do what he had to do, which was more than enough time.

The first thing he did was disable the security cameras, which for P.T. was the easiest part of the operation. He did it in such a way that they would restart when he left and no one would ever know they had been off.

P.T. then quickly went to the enormous crystal ball being assembled in its own room near the back of the factory. It was an extraordinarily impressive piece, twelve feet tall and six hundred pounds of fine crystal. He detached four of the panels, then opened his briefcase and took out four clear, odorless packets, each weighing more than three pounds. They were connected by remarkably thin, clear fiber-optic wires to a device no larger than a small computer chip.

The difficult part was in attaching the packets to the inside of the detached crystals without damaging the elaborate laser lighting mechanisms inside. He had to be incredibly careful; he was placing them where they could virtually never be detected, yet if he made the slightest mistake it would be immediately noticeable to everyone.

P.T. knew that even with all that was to follow, with all the precision maneuvers he would conduct, this would be the most difficult. In fact, it was the only thing that had the slightest risk of failure. If he erred, he would still be able to compensate, but it would be a setback. And he hated setbacks.

But things went off without a hitch, and twenty-five

minutes later, P.T. was driving home. Alone in the safety of his car, he spoke the first words he had spoken in hours.

"Happy New Year."

THE VISITS WERE MORE for him than for her.

Logically, there was no getting around that. Harriet Turley had been in the Eddings Nursing Home for Women in Teaneck for three years, which meant that she had literally outlasted more than seventy-five percent of the people who were living there when she arrived. Of course, that would depend on one's definition of "living."

Chris had always known his mother to be a forceful, independent woman with a razor-sharp mind, one of the few people who could hold her own in a conversation with Chris's father. The probing, badgering style of questioning that Edward Turley used in his interviews often carried over into his private life, but Harriet could stand toe to toe with him.

Most memorable for Chris was the time he sat unnoticed, at the top of the stairs in their house, as Edward and Harriet argued in the kitchen below. The subject was not memorable, something about the way Harriet had dealt with Chris's fourth-grade teacher about some difficulty he was having. But Edward was criticizing Harriet's handling of it, and she was giving better than she got, letting him know in no uncertain terms that as long as he was going to be a relatively absentee father, she was going to call the shots.

"You're entitled to your opinion," she had said in a calm voice. "But I am making the decisions."

Chris often thought that if his interview subjects could have watched her in action, they wouldn't have been nearly as intimidated by Edward and his type-writer, and in later years his camera and microphone, as they always seemed to be.

But Harriet's mind had gradually been erased, over a three-year process that Chris watched with horror and Harriet initially cloaked in denial. For at least the past two years, she had displayed a decreasing recognition of Chris when he arrived for a visit, and by this time the frequency of her awareness of him as her son had dipped to less than five percent.

But even though Harriet had no recollections of his visits five minutes after he left, it was still far more than obligation that brought him there three times a week. He loved her deeply; she was the only person he could count on every day of his life. And even though her own life might be coming to an end, he wanted to hold on to her as long as he could.

She was also a link to his father. Sometimes, in her more lucid moments, she would talk about Edward as if he were still there, as if they still shared a life to-gether. A few months before, she had even referenced a rare vacation that they took as a family, talking about it as if it were yesterday, although it was twenty years ago. They had gone to Hersheypark, the amusement park in the Pennsylvania town famous for its chocolate factory.

"Remember how your father took us to a restaurant at the corner of Chocolate Avenue and Cocoa Street?" She laughed at her own recollection, and Chris was stunned by it.

"And then we toured the chocolate factory, and I ate all those free samples," he said. "I was sick for a week, but it was still the best time I ever had."

But she didn't answer. As fast as her lucidity had appeared, just as quickly it was gone, and her blank stare returned.

The few times that Harriet was in touch with her memories, she always talked about times when they were together as a family, when Edward's presence made her feel safe and happy. The irony, of course, is that her relationship with him was always distant and sporadic; it was on Edward's terms when Edward's work permitted.

But Chris would never correct her and would just let her ramble, hoping she would hit upon a memory that they could savor together.

Most of the time Chris just talked to her, talked as if she could process and understand what he was saying. So that day he talked about the building explosion and the rescue of the people. She seemed to listen intently, but had no response.

"And tomorrow morning I'm going to be on the *Today* show," he said. "They're putting me up in a hotel tonight in the city and sending a car for me in the morning."

She seemed to smile slightly at that, so he continued. "I don't think Dad was ever on the *Today* show, was he? I'll ask the people here to bring you over to the television so you can watch me."

He looked at her and saw that her eyes were closing. She did that more frequently every week; she just fell asleep in the middle of a visit. He thought that was a good thing and hoped she could have coherent, pleasant dreams.

"I wish Dad were here to see me on the show," he said, basically to himself. "I think he would have been proud of what I did."

And then he kissed her on the cheek, and thought he saw her smile.

And then he left.

"P.T." PICKED PARAMUS PARK out of a hat.

He felt that an operation like this called for a randomness; a total lack of bias. His selections were not intended to make a point, nor to demonstrate a pattern. It was as much a moral as a tactical decision. While he didn't want to do anything that could be predictive of future actions, he also felt that fairness was best served by impartiality.

The Paramus Park mall was only one of many shopping centers in the Paramus/Teaneck/Ridgewood area. Certain others, like Riverside Square, were more upscale, and therefore might have been better suited to P.T.'s needs. But he picked Paramus Park, and Paramus Park it would be.

He parked his car behind a gas station adjacent to the shopping center on the Route 17 side and walked across a field to the other side. The lot was close to full, as he knew it would be on a late-November evening. The pre-Christmas rush was getting longer and longer; soon it would start at Labor Day.

P.T. knew where the security cameras were; he had scouted them on previous trips. He made sure that his face was not turned towards them, and with a windbreaker and hood on, there was no way he could be identified. The closest they would come would be the Syracuse logo on the chest of the windbreaker, if the cameras were capable of picking it up. He didn't much care either way. He never went to college; he was self-educated.

P.T. identified eight cars to choose from, all of which were Toyotas, since he had randomly chosen the Toyota brand that morning. From that group, two were left unlocked, which made the decision process easy. The coin came up heads, which meant he would go with the beige Toyota sedan.

After a quick glance around to make sure that no one was approaching or watching, he climbed into the backseat and waited. The car was not parked near a light pole, and the darkness was perfect for his purposes. He just hoped that only a driver would return, without additional passengers. That could get a little messy.

P.T. didn't even know if the driver would be a man or a woman, nor did he particularly care. The end result would be the same.

After about twenty minutes, he saw a man heading in the direction of the Toyota, and P.T. sensed that this was it. The man wore what looked to be an expensive coat and carried three shopping bags. P.T. hoped he would put them in the trunk rather than the backseat, but again, the end result would be the same.

The man walked to the passenger side of the car, but rather than heading towards the trunk, he opened the rear door.

That decision probably hastened his death by thirty or forty seconds. The moment he opened it, P.T. fired a small dart gun into his neck. The poison rendered him unconscious in less than a second, and killed him within ten seconds of that. It was unlikely that the victim even had time to register what was happening, and that was how P.T. wanted it. He had no interest in causing unnecessary suffering.

The man slumped forward towards the car, and P.T. grabbed him and pulled him into the backseat. He took the keys, which the man conveniently had in his hand, got into the front seat, and started the car. He drove it slowly and cautiously out of the parking lot and on to the highway, then made a U-turn back to the area where his own car was parked.

Once there, P.T. moved the man's body into the trunk of P.T.'s own car. He turned off the victim's Toyota, but left the keys in the ignition. He also left the shopping bags in the car; it would be up to the guy's family and friends to figure out how to divvy them up. P.T. didn't have to worry about any fingerprints, since he had worn gloves the entire time.

Leaving the dead man's car behind, P.T. pulled away and drove down Route 17 to Route 4, then headed east. He had another hour of work ahead of him, which he wasn't looking forward to. But he really had no reason to complain; things had been going just as he had planned for all these years.

"Thanks, pal," P.T. called back to the body in the trunk. "You did good back there."

"IT'S A PLEASURE TO welcome Chris Turley of the *Bergen News*," said Matt Lauer.

The introduction followed a three-minute piece on Chris's heroics after the explosion, so it was not necessary for Lauer to once again tell the audience who Chris was or why he was there. The interview was taking place during the first hour of the four-hour show, which was a testament to the importance it was given by the show's producers.

"Before we begin," Lauer said, "I just want to say that Chris's father was Edward Turley, who could accurately be called a legend in journalism." Then, to Chris, "He was certainly one of my heroes."

Chris smiled. "We have that in common."

"And speaking of heroes, how does it feel to be one?"

"Believe me, Matt, that's not how I see myself," Chris said.

"But that's how everyone else sees you. According to the authorities, five people are alive today who wouldn't be if you hadn't rushed into that building."

"I'm certainly glad for that."

"What were you doing there?" Lauer asked.

"I was actually meeting someone about a story I was working on. I was waiting for him, and all of a sudden I was thrown to the ground. Things happened pretty fast after that. I heard some people yelling, and I tried to find them."

"Did you realize when you went in that the rest of the building might come down?"

Chris shrugged. "I'm not sure. There really wasn't time to think about much of anything."

"Well, there were a lot of other people on the street, and none of them ran in."

Chris smiled. "They're probably smarter than I am."

Lauer announced that after the commercial break they would be going live to a hospital room, where they would talk to three of the people that Chris saved. This would give Chris the opportunity to have a strained and embarrassing conversation with them, which he dreaded.

It turned out to be as bad as he feared. Two of the adults who he'd rescued were there with one of the children, and they took turns thanking Chris and praising him for his heroism. There was pretty much nothing for him to say, other than that he was glad they were recovering well.

The segment lasted for five minutes, but it felt like five hours, and when it ended and they went to a break, Lauer apologized. "These things are always awkward," he said. "But the audience loves them."

Chris left the studio and went back to the office to write a follow-up piece on the aftermath of the explosion. When he got there, he was met by the man in charge of the online edition of the paper, Scott Ryder.

"What time you think you're going to be ready with the story?" Ryder asked.

"Maybe an hour and a half," Chris said. "Why?"

Ryder smiled. "Because yesterday we had five times more hits than our site has ever gotten in one day. And everybody was there to read your piece. The site almost crashed; so today we need to be prepared."

"So you're finally earning your money?" Chris asked. Chris and Ryder had become friends since Ryder's arrival at the paper three years ago and often played basketball together. Ryder's job, while not considered particularly important when he took it, had dramatically increased in significance as the Internet caused major and ongoing changes in the newspaper business.

Ryder smiled. "It had to happen eventually."

"You'll be working at *The New York Times* by next week," Chris said.

"Only if you go with me."

Chris had become a mentor of sorts to Scott in his time at the paper, especially coaching him on how to deal with Lawrence. To Lawrence, this computer stuff was somewhere between incomprehensible and evil, and Scott was initially a little thin-skinned about Lawrence's criticism and dismissive attitude.

Since Chris's piece ran, there was a general feeling of euphoria in the newsroom. It was rare that the *Bergen News* was in the center of any kind of major story, and everyone seemed to be relishing it.

At one point, Cynthia Harden, a young reporter whose lack of seniority forced her to cover whatever no one else wanted to, let out a scream. "Chris, Chris! Check this out!"

Chris went over to her desk and she pointed to her computer screen, which showed the front page of the *San Francisco Chronicle*. "They picked up your story! On the front page! And that's not all; you're everywhere."

He smiled. "From sea to shining sea." It was a prime example of a truism of the media world that Chris had never really gotten used to; bad news was good for business. It just felt a little off-putting that everyone was so clearly enthused when so many people had died.

Chris went home early. He lived in a garden apartment in Hasbrouck Heights, one of forty-five absolutely identical units, which were structured so that each had its own parking space right in front of the apartment. With no lobby or common area, it was possible to live there for years without having any more than a nodding or waving acquaintance with your neighbors, and Chris was living proof of that.

He lived modestly, a lifestyle that was dictated by his salary at the paper. He had legal control of a very substantial amount of money that Edward had left to Chris's mother, but though it was to revert to him when she died, he didn't feel he should touch it while she was alive.

It was impossible to tell how many phone messages Chris had, because the machine had reached its capacity sometime the previous day. The *Today* show had sent a car to pick him up at the hotel at 5:30, and lack of sleep and the excitement of the day had left him exhausted. He decided not to listen to the messages until the next morning.

He put a frozen pizza in the oven and had just sat down in the living room to watch a Knicks game when the phone rang. He saw by the caller ID that it was his friend Kip, a corporate lawyer with an office in Newark. He debated for a moment about whether to answer it, and decided he would.

"Hello?"

"Hello, is the hot-shit hero there?"

"You're talking to him."

"Yeah? Well, how come I'm not sitting with him?"

"What does that mean?"

"Does the phrase 'birthday party' ring a bell?"

Chris literally smacked himself in the head. "Damn, I forgot." It was Kip's thirty-first birthday, and while that would ordinarily not be the occasion for a party, Kip had survived a bout with melanoma earlier in the year. His recovery was truly a reason to celebrate, and they had planned a big party at the Crows Nest, their local bar and hangout.

"That's really nice," Kip said, twisting the knife. "Heartwarming, actually. Craig remembered and showed up, but he's a good friend."

"Kip . . ."

"He asked where you were," Kip said, "and I told him probably at a heroes' convention."

"I'll be right there."

Chris turned off the oven, threw out the pizza, and drove the ten minutes to the bar. There were about sixty people there, and when he arrived the party was in full swing.

Chris knew maybe half of the people, but he no sooner walked in the door than one hundred percent of them stood up and cheered. It was a standing ovation at a birthday party, not exactly standard procedure for someone whose birthday was six months ago.

The rest of the evening was like hanging out with sixty Matt Lauers, as everyone felt compelled to ask him endless questions about the explosion, its aftermath, and how it all made Chris feel.

Chris sat down at the bar and the rest of the partygoers all faced him and started asking questions. "Were you ever scared?" asked one woman who Chris did not know.

"I don't think so. Although I did piss in my pants," Chris said, smiling to show that he was joking.

After a few more questions, Kip stood up on a chair in the back of the room and said, "What is this? A press conference?" He pointed to his own chest. "Birthday boy? Remember?"

Chris laughed and tried to redirect attention to Kip, but he had to admit to himself that it was feeling pretty good. There was something to be said for being the recipient of hero worship, and though Chris was notorious for leaving parties early, this time he hung out to the bitter end.

Late in the evening, in one of the rare moments when Chris was sitting alone, Gail Edmonds came over to him. Gail and Chris had had a relationship that lasted for almost two years, which for Chris was an eternity.

"It's been a long time, Chris."

"I saw you here two weeks ago," he said, although he wasn't sure that was true. He used to come to this bar more frequently, but in the last year his appearances were far more spread out. It was a pattern he had chalked up to advancing age and approaching maturity.

"I mean, it's been a long time since we were together. What ever happened to us?" she wondered, wistfully.

"You dumped me," he said. "As I recall, you sent me an e-mail to that effect."

She smiled. "That was in another lifetime."

"It was six months ago," he pointed out.

"But you weren't a hero then, you were just Chris."

"Does that make a difference?"

"Of course."

"Had I known that, I would have become a hero years ago."

"I always knew you had it in you," she said.

He smiled, kissed her on the cheek, and walked away to talk to other friends. A number of single women showed him an inordinate amount of attention, but though he had ample opportunity to do otherwise, Chris opted to go home alone. He needed the time to decompress and think about all that had transpired. It seemed amazing that the explosion had happened less than forty-eight hours before; it felt more like a month.

As he was leaving, Chris's good friend Craig came over and walked with him to the parking lot. Craig had been with Chris at the car dealership just before Chris went to his meeting near the medical center. "I guess I should have gone with you," Craig said. "Women would be throwing themselves at me, too."

Chris laughed and shook his head. "I don't think so. You don't have the look."

"Did you ever meet with that guy who called you? The informant?"

"No. I don't even know if he showed up," Chris said.

"So you never found out what he was going to tell you?"

"No," Chris said and then shrugged. "Maybe he'll call back."

"Maybe," Craig said. He wanted to ask more questions about it, but decided he couldn't take the chance. "Have a good night."

"You, too."

As Chris drove home, he reflected on an enjoyable, eventful day. Lawrence had said that his life would never again be the same, and at that moment Chris thought he was going to be right.

And at that moment Chris was fine with that.

"HELLO, MR. TURLEY, REMEMBER ME?"

The voice was that of the man who Chris was going to meet in the park across from the medical center. "We were supposed to meet the other day."

"Of course I remember you. Were you there when the building blew up?"

"I got there a couple of minutes after it happened. I even saw you come out of the building with those people. You were amazing; I was afraid to go near it."

"I'm just glad it worked out."

"Well, I'm not sure I'd say it worked out all that well. A lot of people died that day."

Chris was simultaneously annoyed with himself for saying something insensitive and with the man for calling him on it. "You're right about that. It was terrible."

The man's voice suddenly got more cheerful. "So when can we meet?"

"Well, I'm going to be busy on this story for a while . . ."

"So you're blowing me off?" the man asked. He seemed to have a tendency to change moods on a dime.

"Of course not. It's just that my time is limited. Can this wait for a while?"

"I'm afraid not. It's all going down Saturday night."

"What is?" Chris asked.

"That's what we were going to meet about. Come on, don't you think that in a way you owe me? I'm the reason you're a big star; if it wasn't for me, you wouldn't have been anywhere near that building." He didn't say this in a challenging way; it was more like he was trying to cajole Chris into giving in.

"I'll tell you what. Give me the information over the phone, and if it's as good as you say it is, I'll make the time to follow up on it."

There was a pause of about ten seconds before the man said, "Fair enough. You got a pen?"

"Of course."

"Do you know the Claremont Hotel?"

"In Woodcliff Lake?" Chris asked. It was a very fashionable hotel on sprawling grounds, with one of the best golf courses in New Jersey.

"That's the one. Mayor Stanley is giving a speech there that evening, and he'll be spending the night in one of the bungalows. Bungalow number sixty-two. He'll be registered under the name of Alan Sloane."

Chris started taking notes as he thought about Alex Stanley. Stanley was the mayor of Englewood, and while most New Jersey mayors went no further in their political careers, Stanley was expected to be the exception. Young and charismatic, he was already being groomed for a run at Congress, in a soon-to-be-vacated seat in northern Bergen County.

He was also a champion of moral values and had

directed his police force to be aggressive in ridding his city of "the sex trade that is contributing to an ongoing moral decay in our great country."

Chris had covered Mayor Stanley's news conferences on a number of occasions, and even interviewed him once. He found him to be bright, engaging, and arrogant and came away convinced that Stanley was going to be a force to be reckoned with.

"Why should I be interested in this?"

"Well, for one thing, at around midnight he will also have cocaine and a hooker in the bungalow with him. She goes by the name of Charity."

Chris felt a jolt of excitement, and he immediately underlined the information about the hotel that he had jotted down earlier in the conversation. "How do you know this?"

"That's not important, and it's not something I'm going to share with you."

Scandal stories like this were not the kind Chris liked to cover, but in the past he'd always just been following up on them. He'd never been in the position of breaking one before. And Stanley was important enough so that, if this were true, it would be a major story. Stanley's public moralism would provide the additional element of hypocrisy that would make the whole thing even juicier.

"When I asked why I should be interested, you said 'for one thing,' and then you told me about the drugs and the hooker. Is there something else?"

"You're pretty sharp," the man said.

"What else is there?"

"Well, this particular hooker charges three thousand a night, which is pretty steep on a mayor's pay."

"Obviously 'Charity' is not her real name. But why should I care about that?"

"The only way he can afford her is because he more than triples his salary by taking bribes."

Chris wrote down "bribes" on his notepad. "From who?"

Another long pause and then the man said, "I think I'll wait on that. If you break this story, I'll call you back and tell you the rest. Maybe you'll even meet with me." He laughed.

Click.

Chris looked at the phone in surprise at the hang-up, but just shrugged and smiled. "Don't count on it, buddy."

Chris googled "Claremont Hotel" and "Woodcliff Lake" and got the hotel phone number. He never called information anymore, not since they eliminated the human beings on the other end of the line. For some reason he was much more comfortable typing into a computer than talking to one.

Once he got the number, he dialed it and asked for Alan Sloane.

It took the operator about fifteen seconds to say, "Is Mr. Sloane a guest?"

"Yes, he is. I believe he's in bungalow sixty-two."

Again, there were a few silent moments before the clerk said, "Oh, I have it. Mr. Sloane will not be checking in until Saturday."

"Sorry, my mistake."

"No problem. Have a lovely day."

"Thank you. You, too."

Chris hung up, a little surprised that at least one part of the story had checked out. Of course, it didn't prove much; Alan Sloane could really be Alan Sloane, and he could be a car salesman coming for a golfing vacation.

Or he could be Alex Stanley, mayor of Englewood, coming for an evening of sex and cocaine, paid for by money he took as bribes.

Chris smiled at the possibility. Wouldn't that be something? Could he be that lucky twice in one week?

CHRIS WAS A BASKETBALL JUNKIE.

He liked to watch it, to read about it, and to discuss it endlessly. But most of all, he liked to play it.

He was on teams in three separate leagues, each of which played one game a week. A backup point guard for Syracuse back in the day, Chris had lost at least a step, but still had more than enough talent to be the best player on each of his teams.

Just six hours after he spoke to the informant, Chris was playing for an industry team made up of print reporters from local Jersey papers. They were playing a team of Bergen County cops, which meant they were in for a rough evening under the backboards. Which further meant that Chris was planning to do a lot of shooting from the outside.

It was considered a friendly game, as were most of the games in this particular league. Most of the players had been in the league for a number of years, and they all knew one another.

But that friendliness sometimes had a way of disappearing during the game, especially when it was close. And this game was very close, mainly because three of the leading members of the usually superior police team had to work overtime.

Thomas Oswald, CEO of a local software firm, had been reported missing. His car was found adjacent to the Paramus Park shopping mall two nights ago, with gifts that he had purchased still inside. There were no real leads so far, and the police were using an enormous amount of manpower on the case. Playing on the police basketball team was not considered a valid reason for avoiding overtime.

With his team down sixty-two to sixty-one, and just four seconds remaining, Chris saw an opening down the lane, drove to the basket, and got fouled. He went to the foul line to shoot two shots, with the game's outcome obviously hanging in the balance.

As he stood on the foul line waiting for the ball, Jonathan Novack, a local detective, walked over to him. Chris knew him only as "Novack," as did everyone else. Though he'd played against the guy for seven years, he didn't have the slightest idea what his first name was. He only knew that Novack couldn't go to his left and was not above throwing elbows around under the basket.

"You make these two shots," said Novack, "and I'm going to plant half a kilo of heroin in your locker. You'll spend the next twenty years as the highest-scoring convict in New Jersey state prison history."

Chris laughed, though Novack certainly wasn't smiling when he said it. "And what if I miss?" he asked.

"You will never get another speeding ticket again."

Chris nodded and stepped up to the line. He made both shots without even hitting the rim, and as his team finished celebrating on the court, Novack came over to him and shook his hand.

"You decide who you're going to make your one phone call to?"

Chris smiled. "I was thinking maybe your wife."

Novak shook his head. "You just dug your grave a little deeper."

He started to walk away, but turned when Chris said, "Hey, Novack, you got a second?"

"What for?"

Chris hesitated for a few moments, wanting to avoid making a mistake that he would regret.

"Hello?" Novack asked impatiently.

Chris decided there was more upside in confiding in Novack than in not doing so. He walked over to him and talked softly. "What do you think of Alex Stanley?"

"He's my boss's boss's boss."

"I didn't ask for his corporate ranking. I asked what you thought of him."

"He's a scumbag shithead. Or maybe a shithead scumbag; I always get them confused."

"If I got a tip that you could use to nail him, would you be interested?"

"Nail him for what?"

"Drugs, solicitation of prostitution, and bribery."

"If you're bullshitting me, I will staple your ass to your face." Novack said it with a wistful half smile, as if he were hoping to get the chance to do some ass stapling.

The idea of getting his ass stapled to his face was a disturbing one to Chris, so he made sure to qualify his comment. "I'm not sure the tip is good, but it'll be easy to find out. And if it's not good, neither of us have lost anything."

"Can you be in my office at nine tomorrow morning?" Novack asked. "I want my partner to hear it; he hates Stanley more than I do. And I'll ask him to bring his staple gun."

Chris nodded. "I'll be there; but we'll have to move quickly. This is supposed to go down on Saturday night."

Novack smiled. "The sooner the better."

Jonathan Novack was that rare man who was completely happy with his life, with no real ambition other than to preserve the status quo. As the lead detective in the department, he had significant autonomy to pursue the cases he wanted in the manner he wanted to pursue them. That is not to say that he wasn't subject to the whims and idiocies of the brass, but he had long ago learned how to successfully navigate those minefields.

Novack's personal life was going swimmingly, as well. Divorced three years ago by his wife Cindy, he had pretty much refused to accept that verdict, and kept hanging around the house. The split actually created a new dynamic between them; her ability to throw him out of the house when he drove her crazy provided the release valve she and they needed.

Even Cindy would admit that their relationship had

never been better, but remarriage was not a consideration, as both of them were wary of screwing things up.

Although Novack was content in all aspects of his life, that didn't prevent him from being cranky and irritable. That was simply his nature, and everyone around him had learned to ignore it.

But the prospect of catching Alex Stanley in something like this warmed his heart, even though at this point he viewed it as unlikely. He mentioned the situation to Cindy when they were having dinner that night at the Coach House diner on Route 4, which is where they ate at least sixty percent of their meals. He had no reluctance to confide in Cindy; she was pretty much the only person in the world that he completely trusted.

"Now you're targeting the customers of prostitutes?" Cindy asked, knowing that Novack always focused on what he considered more substantial crimes than that.

"If a law is being broken, it's my job to enforce it, not to question it."

"That's bullshit," she said.

He nodded. "Yes, it is."

"You're pursuing this because he's the mayor."

"No, I'm pursuing this because he's the mayor and he's a hypocrite. He makes judgments about how people live their lives."

"And then fails to live up to those standards himself?"

He shrugged. "Yes, but it's the judgments I don't like. Do you know there are people in this world who think that because we're no longer married, we shouldn't sleep together?"

She smiled. "Maybe they have a point."

"No, they don't. They do not have a point. They are pointless. Never forget that."

Chris was at Novack's office as promised the next morning, though he was slightly uneasy with what he was doing. Alignments with the police were not something that reporters entered into casually; there was a tension between the two sides that did not generally yield productive partnerships.

But in this case, Chris felt that he could control the situation, and in fact bringing the police in might benefit him greatly. He also knew from experience and reputation that Novack could be trusted, which made his decision that much easier.

Novack brought his partner, James Willingham, into the room for the meeting. When Willingham shook hands with Chris his expression looked as if he had just found a roach in his cereal; this was clearly not a guy who liked journalists. "He wanted to see what a real-life hero looks like," Novack said.

"No problem," Chris said, "and after this is over, I'll give you both autographs."

"That's great," Willingham said. "Except for defense attorneys, newspaper reporters are my favorite people."

"So tell us how we're going to take down Stanley," Novack said.

"Before I get into that, you'll need to agree to two conditions."

Willingham frowned. "Here comes the bullshit; let me go get my shovel."

Chris ignored him. "First, I'm to be on the scene when all this goes down. And second, I'm the only media person you talk to about it, at least until I've gotten a chance to write the story and a follow-up."

Novack shot a quick glance at Willingham before answering. "Yes to the second part, and maybe to the first. It would depend on the legalities, and if there is danger involved."

Chris nodded. "Fair enough." He then proceeded to describe what he was told by the informant, without embellishment, and Novack and Willingham were quiet as he did so.

When he finished, Novack asked, "And you confirmed that an Alan Sloane is registered for that night?"

Chris nodded. "In that bungalow."

"That doesn't mean shit," Willingham said.

Novack nodded. "Right. Unless, of course, it does."

"True," Willingham said.

"It's inspiring to hear two law enforcement professionals in action," said Chris.

"Here's the thing, Chris," said Novack. "We can't just go barging into a hotel room because somebody we don't know called and told you there would be bad things going on in there. We need probable cause that a crime is being committed."

"What if I go in?"

"Then there would definitely be a crime, except you'd be the one committing it."

"So you don't want any part of this?"

"Can we have the court reporter read that back? Because I don't recall anyone here saying that. We just have to make sure, and I mean make sure without any doubt, exactly what is going on in that room before we join the party."

"How do we do that?" Chris asked.

"You don't," Willingham said. "We do."

"Don't forget my conditions. It's not illegal for me to be there, nor is it dangerous."

Willingham nodded. "You'll be there, but as an observer only. And if we decide to call it off, it's off. Understood?"

"Understood," Chris said.

"I'll call you tomorrow morning at ten and tell you where to be and when to be there," Novack said. "But for now you have to leave it to us. And not a word of this to anyone."

"I'll be at my office," Chris said, and wrote down his phone number. "But tell me, what do you guys think about this? You think it could be legit?"

"If it is, hero, you're having a helluva week."

NOVACK WAS TAKING NO chances with this one.

His instinct was that Chris's information was going to prove accurate, but an even stronger instinct, a self-preservation one, told him to make sure he was completely covered before proceeding.

The key step for Novack and Willingham to take would be to bring Chris's story to Captain Mark Donovan, their immediate superior. Novack was concerned about doing so, because Donovan was widely known to be a shrewd department politician who sometimes found it difficult to look past his next promotion.

While an attitude like Donovan's would usually leave someone like Novack pissed off and annoyed, it strangely didn't do so. Donovan avoided this antagonism by basically being up-front about his ambitions, and by demonstrating a healthy respect for Novack's superior instincts as a cop.

Complicating matters was that Novack knew that Donovan, like every other police captain in the area, was already under tremendous pressure to find Thomas Oswald. The businessman still had not been heard from, no ransom had been demanded, and while the police would not say so publicly, they held out little hope that he was still alive. That he had vanished into thin air from a crowded parking lot, however, was causing considerable nervousness on the part of the public.

Willingham was positive that Donovan would tell them not to go anywhere near Mayor Stanley. His reasoning was that if they didn't nail Stanley in the process, the mayor would exact revenge by turning Donovan into a school crossing guard with a defective whistle. But Novack, while recognizing that possibility, thought that Donovan might very carefully go along. If Stanley were taken down, then whoever took his place would owe Donovan big-time. That would make it a very hard temptation to resist.

Knowing he would have only one shot with Donovan, as soon as Chris left Novack he went to his buddy on the vice squad, Detective Sammy Garcia. Garcia was tied into pretty much everything that went on in the city, and Novack wanted him to use his informants to determine if a high-priced hooker named Charity could be identified.

"I'll see what I can find out," said Garcia.

"You think you can do it?"

Garcia shrugged. "Probably. Not many girls around here work the expensive hotels. If she's from the city, that makes it a little more difficult. But not impossible; it'll just require a few more phone calls."

"I need it right away," Novack said.

"Who's the john?"

"Alex Stanley."

Garcia's face lit up at the prospect of bringing down the mayor. Like many cops, his dislike of Stanley was more economic than personal; the mayor had played hardball with the police union during the last contract negotiations, and they had walked away with only a two percent yearly raise. The problem was that no one had told the gas companies and supermarkets that their costs could only go up by a similar amount.

"Get the hell out of here," Garcia said, smiling. "I've got some calls to make."

Within an hour, Charity was identified and it was confirmed that she had an appointment on Saturday at midnight at the Claremont Hotel.

Novack and Willingham were convinced; this was the real thing.

Donovan fired questions at Novack and Willingham for an hour and a half that afternoon. From the moment he heard the details from the detectives, it was obvious he relished the idea of taking down Stanley. But that wasn't the issue; the issue was whether or not they could be certain they would be successful. Because failure would represent a total, career-killing disaster.

Donovan had two main concerns that had to be satisfied before he would authorize proceeding. First, they had to be absolutely positive that when they broke into the bungalow, Stanley would be in the process of doing something illegal. Second, they needed to be sure that they had the legal authority to enter the room uninvited. In order for them to do so, it was essential that they have probable cause that a crime was being committed.

Donovan called Alice Zimmerman in the prosecutor's office and laid out the situation for her, without mentioning the fact that the mayor was the target. Her response was encouraging; she said that if the informant's tip was corroborated by the fact that he had the correct name of the guest in that bungalow, and if vice had independent evidence that the woman was a hooker, then her arrival at the bungalow, as predicted by the informant, would provide probable cause.

Once the police entered the room and determined that a crime, in this case prostitution, was being committed, then they had the right to search the room for weapons or illegal substances. Taking no chances, Donovan asked Zimmerman to provide the opinion in writing and to fax it over, and she promised to do so.

Once he was off the phone, Donovan had Novack and Willingham take him through their plans for that night. He wanted to make sure nothing was left to chance, and though it took a while, they demonstrated that they had thought through every eventuality he could come up with.

"What about the reporter?" Donovan asked.

"Our deal was that he could be there when it went down, and would have an exclusive on the story."

Donovan shook his head. "No good. The guy's too well known right now after his hero act at the medical center. If he shows up, people might come over to him and start a commotion. That's the last thing we need."

Novack nodded. "He'll stay in the van until we've made our move. Once that happens, we could have George Clooney with us and nobody will be paying any attention to him. The shit will already have hit the fan."

"I don't want it blowing back on us."

Novack smiled. "It won't." Of course, he had no way of knowing that for sure, and he wondered how Donovan would deflect the blame if things went south. It would be a neat trick, but he had little doubt that Donovan could pull it off.

EXCEPT FOR A PLANE CRASH, there is probably nothing more difficult to investigate than a bombing.

The reason is obvious; the devastation is usually such that virtually all trace evidence is obliterated. Even a fire frequently exempts some random areas from destruction; a bomb rarely plays such favorites. It's also a complicating fact that the perpetrator doesn't have to be near the scene at the time of the explosion.

That's not to say that there isn't a lot to be learned. Investigators can usually determine the exact area in which the bomb went off, and that in itself can be revealing. Additionally, residue and fragments can be found, which usually will reveal the type of explosive.

It was up to FBI Director Jonathan Kramer to decide who would be the point man for the FBI in the bombing investigation. It was easily the most important decision Kramer would have to make on the case, since he believed in allowing the lead investigator significant autonomy.

The reason for giving that autonomy was twofold. First, it invariably resulted in a more successful investigation, since he would only choose an experienced professional. Second, it insulated Kramer from blame if things went bad. If things went well, there were also fewer barriers for him to grab his share of the credit.

While the decision was important, it wasn't particularly difficult. Kramer's first call, less than an hour after the bomb exploded, was to FBI Special Agent Nick Quinlan at the Chicago office.

"Have you been watching television?" Kramer asked.

"The Weather Channel," Quinlan said sarcastically. He knew full well why his boss was calling. "I like it because it has a lot of highs and lows. I find that exciting."

"Get your ass on a plane."

"My wife's birthday is Saturday," Quinlan said. "We've got tickets to the Bulls game."

"My eyes are filling up with tears. Now get your ass on a plane."

Nick Quinlan was as good as it gets at bombing investigations. He didn't sift through the rubble, looking for clues. He wouldn't know a clue if he fell on one; that was best left to the forensics people. But once the information was fed to him, there was no one better at tracing it back to the source.

Quinlan was known by people who worked for and with him as two people, Quinlan 1 and Quinlan 2. Quinlan 1 was gregarious, open, and sensitive to the needs and concerns of others. Quinlan 2 was icy cold and intense, his anger and displeasure manifesting itself in biting sarcasm and logical badgering.

No one on his staff could predict with any accuracy which Quinlan would be present at a particular moment, but once Quinlan 2 made his appearance, the word spread among the group like wildfire, and everybody who could do so left the scene.

Both Quinlans shared a laserlike focus on work, which meant solving cases and chasing down criminals. His success rate was among the highest of all agents, past or present, and he was held in such esteem by fellow agents that he received the biggest of compliments; he became a verb. When wanted criminals who evaded capture for a long period of time were outsmarted and finally caught, they were said to have been "Quinlaned."

Quinlan's permanent base was the Bureau's Chicago office, but even before he got Director Kramer's call, he had started packing. Two and a half hours after the call, he was on a plane to Newark Airport. The investigation would be in his hands, and no expense or manpower would be spared. Whoever did this had to be taken off the streets immediately.

An agent was waiting for Quinlan with the case file when he arrived at the airport. Quinlan then headed straight for the Newark office, closed the door to the office he'd be using, and started to read. It was his style to absorb all available factual information before he would listen to opinions from other agents.

The file showed that on-scene investigators had determined the point of origin within hours of the explosion. It was on the second floor of the east end of the building, with one of two possible doctors' offices being the exact location. The bomb was a powerful type of plastic explosive, clear, odorless, and very difficult to detect. It was also a mixture of the type that investigators hadn't seen, which meant that the perpetrator knew exactly what he was doing. And based on the damage, the amount used was probably the size of a shoe box.

There was no reason to think that it was the work of a suicide bomber, so the device was probably detonated from a remote location, possibly by cell phone. In fact, at that point there was no reason to consider this the work of an ideological terrorist at all, since no group had come forward to claim credit. That did not conclusively rule out such a terrorist group, but it made it far less likely.

Quinlan was not about to jump to conclusions about the perpetrator; he or she could be anything from a terrorist to a disgruntled patient to a random lunatic. The grievance could be real or imagined. Quinlan's approach was not to try to anticipate the evidence; he would just let it lead him to where he was supposed to go.

There were no early breaks in the case, so on his second day, Quinlan set in with his team to do the painstaking work of interviewing victims and bystanders, checking building records, doctors' office visits, etc. Most of that work would be done by agents under him, and Quinlan would be called in only if that initial work turned up something which seemed to be of some significance. But Quinlan would read all the reports with a fresh eye, just in case something was overlooked.

Quinlan and the task force formed under him for this investigation set up shop in the Federal Building in Newark. When he was inside the offices, however, it was the same as being back in Chicago, as they seemed to have been constructed to exactly the same specifications. The only really noticeable difference was that nobody wondered when the Cubs would win the World Series.

Quinlan's team numbered twelve agents, but more would be available on a moment's notice if needed. He had worked with most of them before, since traveling around the county troubleshooting was his specialty.

Two days into the investigation, an agent Quinlan had brought with him from Chicago, Frank Serrano, knocked on Quinlan's door, even though it was always open. Quinlan had specifically requested Serrano to be assigned to this case; he trusted him and totally respected his judgment.

Both agents generally found themselves thinking on the same wavelength, which was amply demonstrated by the fact that Serrano had recently married Quinlan's first wife, Kate. Since Quinlan was currently on number four, he hadn't had a problem when Serrano approached him about it.

"You sure you're not upset?" Serrano had asked.

"Of course not."

Serrano remained dubious. "You sure?"

"Hey, I'm not gonna have to give her away, am I?"

The wedding went off without a hitch, and the couples remained good friends, though these days Kate was probably pissed off with Quinlan for dragging her husband to New Jersey.

"You got a second?" Serrano asked from the office door.

"Sure."

"We got a list of all the patients for each of the doctors on the second floor of the building. It goes back five years."

"Good." Quinlan had specifically requested that the patient list go back that far, in case someone had felt that the doctor had committed malpractice and damaged their health. Of course, to retaliate by blowing up the entire building would have been evidence that it was their mental health that was in question. "What kind of doctors are they?"

"*Were* they," Serrano corrected. "They were both killed in the explosion. One was an orthopedist, the other an eye doctor."

"Any interesting names on the list?"

"I just looked at it quickly; not much that jumped out at me."

"Nobody named 'Mr. Mad Bomber'?" Quinlan asked. "No bin Ladens on the list?"

Serrano grinned. "No. But that reporter, the one who saved the five people, was a patient of the orthopedist."

"Maybe he was coming or going that day, and that's why he was there."

Serrano shrugged. "Probably."

"Talk to him," Quinlan said. "Talk to everybody."

CHARITY ARRIVED AT THE hotel promptly at 11:45.

She drove up in a Mercedes sedan and was as fashionably dressed as any of the guests returning for the evening. Nobody could have guessed why she was there or who she was going to see.

On the other hand, she could never have imagined that the man who opened the car door for her and gave her a valet ticket was actually a vice squad officer. And she certainly had no idea that when he helped her out of the car he attached a tiny microphone to the inside of her coat.

The maneuver was entirely legal. The police had identified her as a prostitute, and had good reason to believe that she was at the hotel to conduct business. If she went to the bar, had a drink, and then left, that would be that. If she did something else, like plied her trade, then the microphone would be activated and ready to record it.

Charity went through the lobby, out the door, and past the pool to the bungalows. It was clear to the numerous officers watching her that she knew her way around the place quite well; this was obviously not her first visit.

The bungalow the mayor was occupying was the farthest from the main lobby, which made it easy for the police van to be parked along the back road, about forty yards from the bungalow. It was painted the same color as the hotel vans, with HOTEL CLAREMONT emblazoned on the side.

While Chris was in the van, as promised, for the moment he might as well have been home on his couch. Also in the van were Novack, Willingham, and two technicians, which made it quite crowded, and they positioned Chris on a bench from which he could not see out the window. Since the officers would be listening to the goings-on in the bungalow through headsets, he wouldn't be able to hear anything, either. So all Chris could do was watch the officers as they monitored the situation. It was not the vantage point that he had planned on.

Charity reached the bungalow door and knocked and the door opened within ten seconds. One of the technicians, watching with night-vision goggles through the tinted windows, said, "She's in."

Novack and one of the other techs each had on a pair of headsets and they huddled over a console, listening intently. After about thirty seconds, Novack said, "What the hell is going on? I can't get anything."

The other technician looked over and turned a knob on Novack's console, which prompted him to say, "Got it." After another couple of minutes, he said, "I don't believe this guy. He's telling her about the damn speech he gave."

"Can you turn up the sound so I can hear it? Or give me a headset?" Chris asked, but nobody in the van bothered to answer him. Chris was annoyed at the treatment he was receiving, but wasn't about to do anything that might mess up the operation. It would remain Novack's show until the mayor was in custody.

It was another ten minutes, during which Novack complained repeatedly of inaction, before he seemed to tense up and hunch over the console. "Bingo," was all he said.

"They getting to it?" asked Willingham.

"Oh, yeah." Then, "Call Donovan."

Willingham called Donovan on his cell and then put Novack on the phone. Novack assured him that there was no doubt about what was going on. "Wait until you hear the tape. We put it on eBay and we can retire."

Donovan was quite happy not to hear the tape and that he'd avoided being on the scene was by design. If things went well, he would have no trouble claiming credit. If they went badly, he would be nowhere to be found.

"Any mention of drugs?" Donovan asked.

"No, but you don't have to talk about them to use them. And it doesn't even matter if he's using, as long as they're in his room."

Donovan gave the go-ahead, though it was not an enthusiastic one. Whichever way this went down, somebody was going to get stomped on.

Novack put down the phone, barked a command into an intercom, and everything swung into action. He and Willingham burst through the door of the van, with Novack yelling to Chris, "You stay in here."

There was no way Chris was going to do that, and he ran out the open van door after them. He could see up ahead that nearly a dozen officers had encircled the bungalow, waiting for Novack and Willingham to get there. Everything remained eerily silent.

When Novack reached the bungalow, it signaled the end of the silence. He pounded on the door. "Police! Open up!"

The only way the occupants would have had time to obey would have been if they were standing inside with their hand on the doorknob. Novack gave them no more than five seconds and then signaled to two officers with a large battering ram to knock down the door.

They did so, with a noise that Chris thought he could have heard if he had been at home, twenty miles away. Officers rushed into the room, guns drawn and screaming, and Novack and Willingham followed. Mixed in with all the male yelling was a woman's voice, screaming obscenities at the top of her lungs. Charity was clearly pissed off at being interrupted.

Chris stayed behind, peering in and trying to find out what was going on, but there were too many police officers milling around. When he moved closer toward the door, an officer blocked his way.

Other hotel guests walked over to see what the commotion was and the night scene was now brightly lit by the colored lights of arriving police cars. After about ten minutes, the noise level had considerably abated and ten minutes after that, Chris could see a man being led out, in handcuffs, a blanket over his head. Chris got a shot of it with his cell phone camera.

That, Chris thought, had better be Mayor Stanley.

The man was put into a car and driven away, with Willingham next to him in the backseat. Novack came out moments later and looked around until he saw Chris. "In the van," he said, and Chris followed him there.

True to his word, Novack described for Chris exactly what happened in the bungalow. Mayor Stanley and Charity were naked in bed, in the middle of a sex act that was regretfully aborted when the "guests" arrived, but which was captured for posterity by a police photographer. On the desk was an assortment of drugs and drug paraphernalia, and Novack was quite certain that the mayor would test positive for a number of them.

Novack was clearly delighted with the results of the evening's work, and he told Chris that the highlight was the mayor repeatedly yelling, "You work for me! You work for me!" at the officers.

"What did you say?" Chris asked, searching for details for the story.

Novack smiled. "I said, 'Not anymore, Mr. Mayor. Not anymore.'"

Chris stood up and extended his hand to Novack. "Great job, man. Thanks."

"You must be kidding; you did it. And if you ever meet your informant, buy him a beer on me. It doesn't get much better than this."

Chris went back to the office, where a roomful of people were waiting for him, having held the morning edition up to include the story. He'd pretty much written it already, at least in his head, so it did not take long.

Scott Ryder was one of those waiting, since the story would go into the online edition immediately. "I hope this is good," he said. "My bedtime was three hours ago."

Chris smiled. "It's better than good."

The only difficulty Chris faced in writing the story was in making it journalistically dispassionate, so as not to reveal the glee he was feeling at his good fortune. He also was feeling a weird sort of power, knowing that he was in the process of dictating what everyone would be talking about starting the next morning.

Once it was filed and put to bed, Chris had a little time to reflect on the evening's events. The funny thing was, he realized, that it would have been a huge story no matter how it turned out. Had Charity actually been a librarian there to read poetry with the mayor, and had the strongest thing in the room been Diet Coke, the break-in would have still been page one.

Novack and Donovan's asses were on the line, but Chris would have come out fine either way. The media thrived on bad news, and once the operation had commenced, there was certainly going to be bad news for somebody.

SEX, DRUGS, AND HYPOCRISY: A POLITICAL CAREER COMES TO AN END IN BUNGALOW 62.
by Chris Turley

I was at the Claremont Hotel in Woodcliff Lake last night after midnight when Mayor Alex Stanley was led from his bungalow to a waiting police car. He had a blanket over his head to frustrate photographers, but they haven't invented a blanket strong enough to ward off the media storm that is sure to drive him from office.

Twice this week I have uncharacteristically managed to be in the right place at the right time. But this was no happenstance; it was an anonymous tip from a caller to me that set the sting operation in motion.

And let there be no doubt about it; this was not a case of innocent people being victimized, like those that happened to be in the medical center when the bomb went off. This wound was self-inflicted, by a man who may have just been shown to be an unworthy champion of moral values, a man widely considered to have a bright political future, but with a hidden need for the very things which were certain to destroy that future.

There will be speculation of a police vendetta against the mayor, but in my view nothing could be further from the truth. I went to them with evidence that a crime was about to be committed, and they uncovered probable cause that my information was correct. Not to have pursued the matter would have been to abdicate . . .

ANY MEDIA PERSON WILL tell you that there is more than one sex drive.

There is the traditional one, which everyone knows about, and which people strive to satisfy, with varying degrees of success. And then there is the other one, the insatiable need for people to read about other people's sex lives, the more sordid and humiliating the better. The latter is a satisfaction that can be achieved without having to take anyone to dinner first.

Chris's story about Alex Stanley's arrest was a media explosion that actually rivaled the medical center detonation. The New York and national media descended on Englewood Town Hall the next day like vultures, and the twenty-four-hour cable news networks talked about Stanley's fall from grace and the medical center twenty-five hours a day.

Of course, they couched the new story in terms that made their reporting seem more noble, citing Mayor Stanley's betrayal of the public trust. Newscasters all over the dial shook their collective heads sadly at what the mayor's poor family must be going through.

But the bottom line, and all the media really cared about, was that he was caught with a hooker and enough drugs to qualify the hotel room as a pharmacy, and the one thing the public could trust was that the media would milk it for all it was worth.

With Stanley released on bond and not communicating with anyone, and with the police refusing to comment on an ongoing investigation, Chris effectively became the center of the story.

He was there when it went down, which was a monstrous journalistic coup. Novack also kept feeding him small tidbits of information, which allowed him to keep the story current for several days.

Chris tried to stay out of the limelight as much as possible, not because he didn't enjoy the attention, but because he recognized that overexposure was not in his best interest. He spent long hours in the office, working the phones as always, but mostly waiting for his informant to call back. The man's information had proven stunningly reliable, and Chris hoped there was more where that came from.

Chris could even feel the difference in the office. People with whom he routinely traded good-natured insults were treating him more deferentially, recognizing that he had outgrown the small paper. It wasn't a change that Chris necessarily welcomed, and it made him feel slightly uncomfortable.

He was at his desk late in the afternoon when Bruce Harlow stopped by. Harlow was what was called a contributing editor, which basically meant he wrote op-ed and feature pieces, mostly for the paper's Sunday edition. He also had the freedom to write elsewhere, be it books or magazines, as long as he didn't work for a competing newspaper.

Bruce and Chris had known each other for about eight years, having met when both were speaking on a panel at a symposium in Manhattan. Chris had introduced Bruce to his father, and the result was a collaboration on Edward's autobiography, which Bruce was to ghostwrite.

Though Bruce put in almost a year of his life researching the book and doing interviews, Edward changed his mind and decided he didn't want it written after all. It had created a major rift between the two men, and for a while Bruce considered a lawsuit.

Bruce and Chris had never really talked about any of it, both realizing instinctively that it would not be helpful to their friendship. Edward died about six months after the book was finished and Bruce could technically have published it, since Edward was no longer around to object. But he didn't, and Chris had appreciated that fact.

Chris felt that Bruce was correct in the dispute, and had expressed that view to Edward, though he was obviously not persuasive enough to get him to relent. But Chris was still glad that Bruce honored Edward's wish by not publishing it posthumously.

"How's it going, hero?" Bruce asked.

Chris smiled. "Just another day at the office." It had been only fifteen hours since the raid on the bungalow, but the intensity of it had felt to Chris like fifteen weeks.

"You doing okay?"

"I'm tired," Chris said. "Saving lives and dodging groupies can be exhausting work."

"Somebody's got to do it," Bruce said. "You know, if you keep breaking these big stories, we could be looking at a bestselling biography for you."

"Maybe. You think Woodward would be available to write it?" Chris asked, as Bruce laughed and walked away.

Dani was another of the colleagues whose attitude towards him did not change at all. She was, however, amused at his sudden fame and told him that before long she might be including him in her celebrity coverage.

"In fact, I just got a call from the Paramount publicity department," she said. "There's a premiere tonight, and they want to know if I can bring you along."

"Why?"

"Well, it's not that they want your opinion of the film, believe me. If you're there, they'll get more press coverage, and the movie will benefit."

"You've got to be kidding," he said.

"If I'm lyin', I'm dyin'," she said.

"If I'm lyin', I'm dyin'?" he repeated. "Is that a hip expression?"

She shrugged. "Must be. My niece says it all the time."

"How old is she?"

"An old seven. Chris, you need to face what's going on here. You are smack-dab in the middle of your fifteen minutes of fame. Now's the time to milk it."

"Milk what? How?"

"How? That's up to you. You can become a talking head on one of the cable news shows . . . you can become a quiz show host . . . you can write your goddamn memoirs for a fortune. You're famous; you can do whatever you want, and people will pay for you to do it. And I'll write about it."

Until that moment, Chris, while secretly enjoying all the attention he had been getting, hadn't really thought about how he might tangibly benefit from it. But Dani was right; the possibilities, while probably not as limitless as she thought, were undoubtedly very substantial.

"What time is the premiere?" he asked.

She did a double take. "You'll go?"

He shrugged. "Why not? Can I bring a date?"

She nodded. "Absolutely. Me."

The movie was a comedy that had two disadvantages: not only was it unfunny, but it was also derivative of at least five other unfunny comedies in the past year. Nonetheless, the crowd roared and clapped with approval at each attempt at humor; this was clearly an audience predisposed to like it. Chris assumed it was friends of the cast and crew, and Dani told him that for the most part he was right.

Chris, and Dani because she was his date, was treated like a VIP. They were taken in a limo to the after party, which was held in a pier down along the Hudson. The studio had spent an obvious fortune decorating the place, and it gave new meaning to the word "ostentatious."

From the moment he walked in, Chris was surrounded by people eager to talk to him and ask for his autograph. He was accommodating, but after fifteen minutes of it, he looked around for Dani, who was off plying her reporting trade. They made eye contact and she came over and extricated him, bringing him to a special VIP section, which was roped off from the peasants.

"Those people are a little nuts," Chris said.

"They're called 'fans,' " she said. "Your fans."

For the next three hours, Chris sat in the roped-off area, nursed a couple of drinks, and watched the people watching him. The stars and director of the movie came over and introduced themselves, and he lied and said they and the film were terrific.

Dani overheard him telling them how hard he laughed at the film and when they walked away she said, "You catch on pretty quickly."

"Everybody's being really nice to me," he said.

"You're the flavor of the month."

At about 1:30, she told him she was ready to leave. "I'll take you home," he said.

When she looked at him strangely, he said, "Date . . . remember?"

"You're obviously an incurable romantic," she said. "But I have to go back to the office and write about this lovely evening."

"Then I'll take you to the office."

"You're on."

He brought her back to the office, and when he pulled up to the entrance of the building, she turned to him and said, "I'd invite you up, but the city desk editor is home and he's very protective of me. He would want to know what your intentions are."

"I understand."

"Thanks for coming," she said. "You made it much more fun for me."

"I enjoyed it. Thanks for inviting me."

She smiled and he kissed her. He didn't mean to; it just sort of happened. It was a long, lingering, great kiss.

When it was over, she said, "Uh-oh."

He nodded and said, "That wasn't one of my intentions. In fact, it never happened."

"Then I've got a great imagination," she said, and then she got out of the car and walked into the building. She didn't look back, but if she had, she would have seen him staring at her the entire time.

"CHRIS TURLEY" GOT OVER two hundred and thirty-eight thousand hits on Google.

The combination of "Chris Turley" and "hero" got more than eighty thousand, and if Chris had time, he would have read all of them. Even though no one saw him googling his name, he still felt a little self-conscious about it. Having said that, he enjoyed and appreciated the fact that search engines were keeping an Internet scrapbook for him.

But Chris was a busy man. He turned in a follow-up piece each day on both the bombing and the mayor's arrest, stories which were subsequently being picked up by the Associated Press and virtually every newspaper in the country.

He also spent an inordinate amount of time fielding media requests, most of which he turned down, accepting a select few. He did an interview with *Newsweek*, and was planning a full hour with Larry King.

Chris even made his first involuntary appearance on the cover of one of the trashy gossip magazines. Paparazzi had obviously snapped a picture of him and Dani leaving the premiere, and according to the magazine, they were planning to marry shortly. Part of the reason for this was that she was pregnant with his "love child."

They clearly had an even wilder imagination than Dani.

The only troubling aspect of all this to Chris was the fact that the informant who alerted him to the mayor's hotel adventure had not contacted him again. The man had said he would present proof that the mayor had gotten his money through bribes, and although Chris had not revealed this to either the police or his readers, it would be another bombshell for him to drop.

But he had no way to reach the man and could only wait and hope for his call. In the meantime, he had plenty to do.

The next day, Chris drove into Manhattan to the CNN studios to conduct the Larry King interview via satellite. It was a solid hour of softball questions from King, mixed in with hero-worship phone calls from the audience. The on-air promotions for the show made it obvious that CNN considered getting the interview to be a coup, coming just two days after the mayor's arrest.

King started the interview with, "I'm not sure I've ever seen a reporter grab national attention quite so quickly. I knew your father, Edward, a great reporter, but where have you been?"

Chris laughed. "I've been working, Larry, trying to write stories and do the best I can. I once read an interview that Dustin Hoffman gave about working in obscurity for years before getting the lead role in *The Graduate*, which made him a big star. He said it took him ten years to become an overnight sensation. It's been like that for me, except he was talented; I was lucky."

"So it's all luck?" King asked, giving Chris a chance to say otherwise.

"A lot of it is, although whoever said 'the harder I work, the luckier I get' knew what he or she was talking about. In my case, at least as far as the medical center bombing was concerned, it was also being in the right place at the right time."

"You were just walking by?"

"No, I was meeting someone across the street. It was pure coincidence."

The rest of the interview was more of the same, with King and the audience offering praise and Chris good-naturedly deflecting it. All in all, not a bad way to spend an hour.

It was on the way home, after just getting through the Lincoln Tunnel, that Chris's cell phone rang.

"Mr. Turley, that was a very interesting interview you gave tonight."

Chris immediately recognized the voice as the informant. "Hello, I was hoping you would call." Then, "How did you get my cell number?"

"Oh, that was easy."

It may have been easy, but it made Chris a little uncomfortable. He decided against pursuing it, because he didn't want to scare the man off. "No problem, I would have given it to you anyway. That was great information you gave me."

"You used it well."

"I just realized, I don't even know your name," Chris said.

"I want to remain anonymous in all this; you can take all the credit."

"So what should I call you?"

The man hesitated for a moment. "You can call me P.T."

"Fine . . . good. You should call me Chris," he said. "P.T., have you got that other information that you mentioned? The evidence of the bribery?"

"Of course."

"When can I get it?"

"I'll get back to you on that," P.T. said. "It won't be long."

"That would be great. Do you have documents?"

"Yes."

Click. He hung up abruptly, as he had the previous time they'd spoken. It served to confirm Chris's impression that he was very nervous, or somewhat weird, or both.

But Chris was quite pleased. The documents, if they were as damning as promised, would not only put another dagger into the heart of the mayor, but would also implicate all those who were doing the bribing in an additional scandal. If he played it right, it could prolong the story for weeks.

Chris had no sooner hung up the phone than it rang again. This time it was his friend Kip, once again suggesting that Chris meet him down at the Crows Nest.

"I've got three women here, I mean great-looking women, who don't believe I know you. They want me to prove it."

"You want me to talk to them?"

"Talk to them? Are you nuts? I want you to get your ass down here. You can have whichever two you want; I'm not proud, I'll take the one you turn down. That's how good a friend I am."

"I can't, Kip. I've got to get a story written and filed tonight."

"What are you talking about?" Kip asked, incredulous. "Has a pod taken over your body? Do you know what you're turning down here? One of them is like six foot forty. I come up to her knee."

"I think I've got a pretty good idea. I'll tell you what . . . ask them if we can do it tomorrow."

"Tomorrow? There is no tomorrow." Then, "How long have we known each other?" Kip asked. "Fifteen years?"

"So?"

"So in all that time have I ever begged you for anything? Never, right? Well, I'm begging now. I'm here at the bar, on my knees, and these three gorgeous women are staring at me like I'm crazy."

"You *are* crazy. Good-bye, Kip."

He hung up, laughing to himself at the situation he was in. Driving home from being interviewed by Larry King, beautiful women throwing themselves at him, considered a hero by millions of people and a top-notch reporter by the rest . . . never in his wildest dreams did he think he would ever experience anything like this.

And the amazing thing was that, if he played his cards right, then Kip would be proven wrong. There would be plenty of tomorrows, and they might even be better than today.

If such a thing were possible.

Nick Quinlan couldn't remember the last time he watched Larry King. In fact, except for sports, he could hardly remember the last time he watched television. But as an FBI agent, it was sometimes necessary to deal with the public, and it was therefore helpful to know what the public was hearing and thinking.

Besides, staying at the Newark Airport Marriott didn't leave Quinlan with that many social options. He preferred airport hotels, as they provided him with the illusion that he could get out of town and back home that much faster. But this time was no different than all the other cases he traveled for; he would leave when the bad guys were identified and captured.

Not a moment sooner.

When someone told him the show would be about the medical center bombing, he decided to order room service and tune in. The information he had been given had proven only partially accurate; the show was totally centered on Chris Turley, and it therefore was divided between the bombing and the arrest of the New Jersey mayor.

Quinlan saw Turley as a guy on a hot streak, and for

all his attempts at modesty and self-deprecating humor, it was obvious he was relishing the attention. And King wasn't exactly firing difficult questions at him.

The show was not particularly informative, except for one comment that Turley made. He said that he just happened to be in the neighborhood of the medical center because he was meeting someone nearby. Since his name had come up on the patient list of one of the doctors, Quinlan had assumed that was why he was there.

This minirevelation now moved his presence there into the area of coincidence, an area that Quinlan generally did not believe in. It was probably nothing, but he made a note to move Turley to the top of the list of people to be interviewed. He was already on that list, but this moved him to a priority position.

It was an interview he might conduct himself. Who knows? He might even prove tougher than Larry King.

IT WAS ALMOST TWENTY-FIVE years ago, but it was still the worst day of Peter Randolph's life.

It was not a recollection he had to summon. Rather it was burned in his mind, always there to provoke sadness and anger. Especially anger.

Peter was only eleven that day when he stood with his father on New Year's Eve, watching his family's home from a vantage point two hundred yards away, near the highway. Except it wasn't his family's home anymore, and hadn't been since shortly after his mother died and his father had lost his job.

Standing there on the grass that day, his father warned him about power, and how it could destroy anyone. And he talked about innocence, and how it really had no meaning, not anymore.

And then, as Peter watched, he saw his father turn and walk away, out onto the highway. Into the speeding cars.

It was almost five years before Peter learned that it was Edward Turley who'd sent his father onto that highway, that it was Edward Turley who wielded the power, and who took away the meaning of innocence.

It took Peter many more years to get his revenge. But he had gotten it, and it felt good.

But now it wasn't enough.

Having filed his story the night before, Chris got to the office at 10:30 A.M. He had a bunch of errands to run and he would have gotten in even later, except for the fact that he received a phone call saying that Lawrence Terry wanted to see him immediately.

It was unusual to be summoned to such a meeting, and Chris hoped he hadn't said anything on *Larry King* or in any of the other interviews that embarrassed Lawrence or the paper. He figured it was more likely that Lawrence was just trying to be paternal, a role he had intermittently assumed since Chris's father died. He of all people should have known that Edward's death did not exactly leave a paternal void, since it was a role that Edward himself filled so infrequently.

In any event, Chris hoped it was too early for Lawrence to make him drink scotch.

As soon as Chris entered his office, Lawrence said, "There are two FBI agents on the way over to talk to you. They'll be here in ten minutes."

"How do you know that?"

"When the call came in, the operator put it through to me. It's standard procedure."

Chris barely had time to reflect on the surprising fact that there was a "standard procedure" at the paper as it related to phone calls from FBI agents. "What do they want?"

"To question you about the bombing. They claimed it's routine."

"So?"

"So you're a journalist. Talking to the FBI is never routine."

"Can't I just tell them what happened?" Chris asked.

"Does telling them include betraying your source?"

"Lawrence, I don't have a source, not on the bombing. I was just there to meet a guy."

"A guy who turned out to be your source on another story. Be careful here, Chris. There's a lot at stake."

"I don't even know his name, or how to reach him. I couldn't give him up even if I wanted to." He saw Lawrence look up quickly at him. "Which I don't," he added.

"You want me to sit in on the interview with you?" Lawrence asked. "Or maybe one of our lawyers?"

"Honestly, Lawrence, I don't think it's necessary. I'll be fine."

Lawrence did not seem fully convinced. "Okay, but if you start to feel uncomfortable, or unsure about anything, you stop the interview and call me."

"Will do," Chris said.

"Someday remind me to tell you about the run-in your father had with the FBI."

"You already have, Lawrence. At least ten times." Edward Turley had broken a story about the inside machinations in the Reagan White House regarding the bombing of the marine barracks in Lebanon. The FBI was assigned to find the source of the leak, but they ran head-on into Edward, who would rather have enlisted in the Lebanese army himself than reveal a source. The Justice Department tried to have him jailed for refusing to cooperate, but negative publicity made them back down.

Lawrence grinned a little ruefully. "I never do get tired of telling those stories."

The intercom in Lawrence's office buzzed and he picked it up and listened for a moment. Then he hung up and turned to Chris. "They're here."

Chris went out to the reception area and brought Agents Nick Quinlan and Frank Serrano back to his office. "Will this be okay?" he asked.

Quinlan, who seemed to be the one in charge, said, "Fine. This won't take long."

"Take as long as you need," Chris said. "I'll cooperate in any way I can."

Quinlan nodded. "Thank you, we appreciate that. How did you come to be in the vicinity of the medical center when the explosion happened?"

"I was meeting someone in the park across the street."

"Who might that be?" Quinlan asked.

"I actually don't know his name. He called and said he had some information for me."

Serrano jumped in at that point. "Information about what?"

"Another story I'm working on."

"So he contacted you anonymously, and you agreed to meet with him?" asked Quinlan.

"Yes."

"Do you often do that?"

"It depends on the situation."

"Who chose the location?" Serrano asked.

"He did."

"Was it a place you were familiar with?"

Chris nodded. "Yes. My orthopedist had an office in the building that was destroyed. He was killed in the blast."

"Did you actually meet the man that day?" Serrano asked.

"No, just as I arrived the bomb went off."

"Have you heard from him since?"

"Yes," Chris said, then added pointedly, "On the other story."

"We'll need to be in touch with him."

"Good luck," Chris said. "I don't know how to reach him, but the truth is I wouldn't tell you how to do so even if I could. Not unless he authorized it. He's a source that I am obligated to protect."

"So your willingness to 'cooperate in any way you can' has its limits?" asked Quinlan.

"Not many, but this is one of them," Chris said.

They spent the next twenty minutes taking Chris through his actions, minute by minute, from the time the bomb went off. He answered their questions truthfully and completely; there was no reason not to.

They thanked him and left, and Chris was surprised

at how nervous and shaken the interview had left him. Talking to the FBI could be a little scary and intimidating, even if you had nothing to be afraid of.

It was just another example of how Chris was not, and would never be, his father. Not even close.

P.T. WATCHED THE FBI agents leave the *Bergen News* building.

He was not at all worried about what was said; Turley couldn't have betrayed him even if he wanted to. But he wouldn't have in any event. P.T. knew that people like Turley had a warped sense of morality; they had no reservations about destroying someone's life, but then they would turn around and pretend to take the high ground by vowing to protect their sources at all costs.

P.T. went home, turned on his computer, and routed a call through to Chris's office. His computer brilliance, he knew, was not a sign of any special genius, but rather evidence of years spent preparing for this moment. He had willed himself to become an expert in many disciplines, knowing each would be needed for the task ahead.

From this computer he felt that he could rule the world.

"Hello, Mr. Turley. You are well this morning?"

"I'm fine, thank you, P.T.," Chris said. "How are you? It's good to hear from you." Chris spoke deferentially;

he instinctively felt the man needed to be treated with kid gloves.

"I'm ready to take you to the next level."

Chris thought that was a strange way to put it. "You mean give me the additional information?"

"Yes."

P.T. told Chris that he would meet him at 7:00 the next morning at a parklike area just off the Palisades Interstate Parkway, near exit three. "Please come alone," he said. "I don't want anyone else to see me."

Chris wasn't sure why it had to be so early, but getting the documents was the primary goal, and he didn't want to do anything to scare P.T. off. He readily agreed to the arrangement, and P.T. again hung up abruptly.

Chris stayed at the office doing work for the rest of the day. None of it was newspaper work; rather, it was answering fan mail. Between e-mail and regular mail, more than twenty thousand people had attempted to contact him in the last week. It was mind-boggling.

At about five o'clock, Dani came to the door of his office. "Quick question," she said. "I was out last night from about eight until eight-oh-five. My phone machine was on, but it doesn't always work. Any chance you called during those five minutes to ask me out?"

Chris laughed and nodded. "I called at eight-oh-three, but it rang three times, so I gave up."

She snapped her fingers. "Damn. I knew it."

He closed the door behind her. "Dani, I've always thought it was a bad idea to have a relationship with someone in the office. And the reason I've thought that is because it is definitely a bad idea to have a relationship with someone in the office."

She nodded. "I can see that, so how about this? We go out, but we never have sex."

"That's your idea of an acceptable solution?"

"Actually, it's me trying to lure you in," she said. "I've never gone out with a real hero. By the time I was old enough to date, Davy Crockett was dead."

"You two would have made a great couple."

"So what do you say?" she asked. "Dinner tonight? I mean, what's the big deal? I'm already having your 'love child.'"

He started to say no, but it didn't come out quite the way he intended. "I'd love to" is what he actually said.

She made the reservation at an Italian restaurant in Ridgewood that was the closest thing New Jersey had to a "hot" restaurant, and for which Chris knew it was very difficult to get reservations. Chris picked Dani up at her house, which was only about a mile from his, and they drove there together.

When they pulled into the crowded parking lot, he asked, "How did you get us in on an hour's notice? Do you know someone?"

She nodded. "Yup. You. I said it was for you."

As they entered the restaurant, Chris could feel everyone staring at him. It was a sensation he was experiencing frequently, but wasn't quite used to yet. Two people came over during the meal and apologetically asked for autographs, allegedly for relatives.

"Are you dealing with all of this okay?" Dani asked. "I mean, it must be a shock to the system."

"That it is."

"But you're enjoying yourself?"

He thought for a few moments. "There are definitely some aspects of it that I could do without, like those people coming over and interrupting our dinner. But basically, yes, I like it a lot. Does that say something bad about me?"

"Chris, I've dealt with a lot of famous people. And in my experience there are two kinds. The ones who like it and admit it, and the ones who like it but pretend not to."

They talked for two hours and he realized that despite working together for a couple of years, they knew very little about each other. Dani revealed, with some apparent embarrassment, that she had earned an MBA from the University of Virginia.

After graduation she went to work for a brokerage house, but "I walked in the front door and out the back. Everybody was just too serious. They acted like they were saving the world when all they were doing was buying it."

"How did you wind up in the newspaper business?"

She shrugged. "I saw an ad for a job as a copy editor on a weekly paper in New Haven. From there it's been a meteoric rise to the top. How did you get here?"

"According to my former shrink, I wanted to emulate my father."

"Was he right?"

"Maybe, but it's probably a little more complicated

than that, because as soon as he said that, I made him my former shrink."

They closed the place down, and it was almost midnight when Chris drove her home. "You want to come up?" she asked.

"Would you believe me if I told you I had to be up really early in the morning?"

"I don't think so," she said.

"It's true. Remember that guy who called in the office that day, when you answered the phone? He was the guy who tipped me off about Mayor Stanley. Anyway, I'm meeting him at seven tomorrow morning for round two."

"Seven?" She looked at her watch. "That gives us plenty of time."

He leaned over and kissed her. "You know something? It sure does."

CHRIS SET HIS PHONE alarm for 6:00 A.M., which gave him three hours of sleep.

He got out of bed and got dressed, and when he was almost finished, Dani opened her eyes for the first time and saw him.

He smiled at her. "You going to get up and make me breakfast?"

She said, "Not in this lifetime," and closed her eyes again.

He went over to the bed and kissed her lightly on the forehead. "I had a really nice time."

"Then get back in bed."

"I wish I could. Believe me, I wish I could."

He left and drove towards the George Washington Bridge, turning off just before he got there onto the Palisades Interstate, a road that runs parallel to the Hudson River, with the first five miles in New Jersey and then on into Rockland County.

When he reached exit three, he got off and drove down towards the area where P.T. said they would meet. He parked in a rest area and walked down a winding path towards the eastern end of the park. There were no other cars around.

There was also no sign of P.T. or anyone else, but Chris was a few minutes early, so it didn't concern him. He continued on the path, turning a corner while looking back. He thought he heard a noise, which could mean that P.T. was behind him, since that was the only direction he could be coming from.

Not seeing him, he turned forward and let out a scream so loud that if anyone was nearby, they would have come running. But the only person around was hanging from a tree, right in front of him, and that person would never do any running, or talking, or breathing, ever again. He was encased in plastic—it almost looked like Saran Wrap—and it was wrapped so tightly around him that it contorted the man's face into a weird grimace.

Chris instinctively ran back down the trail; he just had to put some distance between himself and that horrible sight. He tried to regain his composure and think what action he should take next, but thinking was difficult.

Cutting through the shock was Chris's fear that whoever had done this might still be nearby, and that therefore he was in grave danger. He stopped on the trail halfway back to the rest area and called 911, trying to calm himself down so that he could explain coherently where he was and what he had seen. The operator promised to send officers immediately.

Though he thought that perhaps he should not leave the area where he made his grisly discovery, he felt too vulnerable there, and he ran back to his car. The parking lot was where the police would arrive, and he could lead them back to the hanging body. And that way, if he felt in danger before their arrival, he could get in his car and flee.

Once back at the car and thinking a little more clearly, Chris realized with some horror that whoever P.T. was, he had to be behind this. Either that, or he was the one hanging from the tree.

But if P.T. had murdered that man and brought Chris to this place to discover it, what else had he done? Had he blown up the medical building, after bringing Chris to the scene? And how did the mayor's liaison figure into it?

Two squad cars arrived seven minutes after Chris's phone call, though to him it felt more like seven hours. After confirming that Chris was the one who had made the emergency call, they asked him to describe what he had seen. Based on that description, they called for more backup before asking Chris to lead them back to the body.

He took the four officers down the trail, hoping that the body would no longer be there, perhaps a disgusting figment of his imagination brought on by lack of sleep. It would be embarrassing, but he'd deal with it. Anything so that he wouldn't have to see it again.

But it was still there, swaying slightly with the wind. The officers stopped walking as soon as they saw it, not wanting to get too close and possibly contaminate what was obviously a crime scene.

Two of the officers waited there, while the other two escorted Chris back to the cars. All four had their guns drawn, in case the perpetrator was still in the area. They instructed Chris to sit in one of the police cars; he wouldn't be questioned until the homicide detectives arrived.

Within minutes, the area was swarming with police cars, two ambulances, and a coroner's van. The highway was closed off, even though the body was found at least a quarter of a mile from the road. If the killer was somehow still around, they didn't want him blending in with traffic.

Chris sat in the car for more than an hour, with nobody paying any attention to him. He was okay with that; being out of the spotlight for even a few moments felt like a welcome relief. He dreaded when they would finally come over and draw him back into the ugliness.

The car was running with the heat on and Chris cracked open the window to get some air. He was able to overhear a few conversations among the officers, which was how he became aware that they thought the victim was Thomas Oswald, the executive believed to have been abducted from his car at the Paramus Park mall. He had no idea whether that was true, but hoped that it was not. He wanted it to be P.T., since P.T. was all that connected him to this horror.

The door opened and an enormous man, wearing a suit about three sizes too small, sat down on the seat next to Chris.

"Mr. Turley, my name is Detective Duane Wilson, homicide division. Obviously, we're going to need to talk with you, but it would be easier down at the station house. Would you be okay with that?"

"Yes, of course. Whatever you say."

Detective Wilson was a large man at six three, two hundred and twenty pounds, yet he spoke incongruously softly and slowly. "Fine, thank you. You'll drive with me, and one of the officers will follow us in your car."

Wilson got into the driver's seat and told Chris to get into the front, as well. Once he did so, they drove off, and Wilson said, "You have certainly been a busy man these last couple of weeks."

"I'm afraid so."

"You sure there isn't more than one of you?" Wilson asked, and then smiled silently at his own joke. He was the only one in the car who was smiling.

After driving for no more than five minutes, Wilson received a phone call. He listened for a few moments, said "but, sir" a couple of times, and then hung up. "Change of plans," he said to Chris, obviously not pleased by whatever it was.

"What does that mean?"

"It means you're going to talk to the FBI instead."

Chris was brought to the FBI's Newark office and an agent who didn't identify himself took him into an interview room. Detective Wilson seemed to melt away, not an easy maneuver for a man that large.

As Chris waited in the interview room for an interrogator to make an appearance, he briefly considered Lawrence's suggestion that a newspaper lawyer be present when he talked to the FBI, and whether that would be a good idea here. He decided against it. He could not have been a suspect and certainly nobody had read him his rights.

Quinlan and Serrano came into the room moments later.

"Well, you do get around," Quinlan said, a comment Chris didn't bother responding to. "You okay if we tape this?" Quinlan asked.

"Would it matter if I wasn't?"

Quinlan shrugged. "Not to me."

The interview was meticulous and painstaking, with Quinlan spending more than three hours taking Chris over every aspect of the story a number of times. Chris left out nothing, and told Quinlan about every contact he had with P.T. He did not give the fact that P.T. was a source a moment's thought; this was no longer someone he had any interest in protecting.

"Why do you think he picked you?" Serrano asked.

"I don't know. For all I know, he's the one hanging from that tree. Maybe somebody found out what he was doing and killed him for it."

"When did you speak to him last?"

"Yesterday," Chris said.

"Well, unless you were at a séance, that's not him," Quinlan said. "That guy has probably been dead for a week."

"So you think P.T. killed him? And brought me there to find him?"

"Did I say something to give you the impression we were going to question each other?" Quinlan asked.

"I don't see what harm would be done—"

Quinlan interrupted him. "If P.T. contacts you again, try and arrange a meeting. In the meantime, with your permission, we'll be tapping your phones and tracing calls into them."

"I don't know about that," Chris said, unsure if he should be going along with it.

"We can also get a warrant and do it without your permission," Quinlan said. He didn't even wait for Chris to respond, he just stood up and said, "And I don't want you writing about this yet."

"Why not?" Chris asked.

"Because it wouldn't be helpful to our investigation," Quinlan said.

"I can't make any promises; I have to talk to the managing editor."

Quinlan frowned. "So maybe you can sell a few more papers?" He didn't wait for an answer. "You can go now. We'll contact you if we need to speak to you again."

With that, Quinlan dropped Chris's car keys on the table, a signal that he could drive himself home. Then he and Serrano walked out, leaving Chris with about a thousand unanswered questions.

CHRIS TURLEY HAD NO idea that the FBI considered him a suspect.

It never entered his mind. He was focused on P.T. and his now-certain conclusion that the informant was at the center of this. P.T. had brought him to an obscure location where the body was waiting, just as he had brought him to the scene of a massive explosion moments before it happened.

But what could he have been trying to accomplish? His motive did not seem to be to cause Chris physical harm, since he could have done so easily. He could have lured Chris into the exploding building, or killed him in the same location where he'd left the body hanging.

In fact, one could easily and accurately argue that Chris had benefited from P.T.'s efforts. Certainly it had helped him achieve fame, and even respect.

It simply made no sense.

The fact that Chris was an FBI suspect was not in itself particularly significant, since Agent Quinlan believed everyone was a suspect until proven otherwise. To him, the salient fact was that Chris was at the center of three apparently unrelated acts: the explosion, the mayor's arrest, and the Oswald murder.

To Quinlan, the connection of the bombing to these other two events, through Chris, was a positive development. The fact that it represented a puzzle he hadn't yet solved was not particularly worrisome. The key point was that at least now he had the pieces just waiting to fit together.

The bombing investigation, though admittedly at an early stage, had been going nowhere. That it could now be linked to other events, and to P.T. and to Chris, was a monumental leap forward, even if nothing seemed clear at the moment.

"Everything revolves around Turley," Quinlan said to Serrano in one of their frequent conversations. Quinlan liked to have an agent around who he trusted to bounce ideas off of and to talk things out with. In this case, like many others, Serrano filled that role.

"You think he could be dirty?"

Quinlan shook his head. "I doubt it. But I don't think he just happened to be in the middle of this. He was chosen for a reason."

Since there were three separate crimes so far committed in three separate jurisdictions, there were three law enforcement groups involved. The FBI had taken over the bombing investigation, but the mayor's arrest and the Oswald murder were being handled by different local police agencies.

Agent Quinlan arranged a meeting that afternoon

at FBI headquarters to bring the various investigations together. Detectives Novack and Willingham were there, since they were assigned to the mayor's case, and Detective Wilson was there as the officer nominally in charge of the Oswald investigation.

The purpose of the meeting, as expressed by Quinlan, was a free flow of information between the groups, since on some level the three crimes were connected. The local cops viewed this with more than a little distrust, since in previous experiences with the FBI they had learned that the Bureau agents were interested in information that flowed in one direction only . . . towards themselves.

Quinlan opened the meeting by asking an agent to summarize a report that the Bureau had quickly prepared on Chris Turley.

"He earned a master's degree in journalism and has been a newspaper reporter for nine years," the agent said. "The last seven have been at the *Bergen News*. There has been nothing extraordinary about his career at all, though, of course, the last two weeks have been more than extraordinary.

"His father was Edward Turley, who I'm sure you are all familiar with. He's never been married, dates a lot, definitely heterosexual. No steady girlfriend that we know of, though he seems to have started seeing a woman in his office named Dani Cooper.

"Mother has Alzheimer's and is in a rest home and he visits her two or three times a week. He's never been arrested and hasn't demonstrated any previous behavior consistent with any of this. After the meeting, I'll hand out the full report for you to have."

Quinlan thanked the agent and said to the detectives, "Anything to add?"

Novack nodded. "He's lights out inside twenty-five feet off the dribble and can drive to the basket and score with either hand."

"What the hell does that mean?"

"I play basketball with him."

"So why haven't you removed yourself from the case?"

"Because he's not a suspect. He's an informant."

Before Quinlan could respond, Wilson asked, "You mentioned he had a degree in journalism. Where did he go to school?"

Quinlan turned to the agent who'd prepared the report, who checked his notes and said, "Syracuse undergraduate, Northwestern graduate."

"Why?" Quinlan asked.

"The night Oswald was murdered, the mall parking lot video showed a hooded man walking around. We can't connect him to the car, because the cameras near the car were tampered with. And we couldn't see his face."

"So?"

"But we could see that he was wearing a Syracuse windbreaker."

Quinlan turned to Novack. "Your basketball buddy is a suspect."

Novack shook his head. "I understand why you think that, but it doesn't fit. An apparently normal guy, never been in trouble, decides to go on a killing spree, but stops in the middle to make sure the mayor is caught getting his rocks off?"

"Look, I'm not saying he's my first choice for this . . . not even close," Quinlan said. "Right now I'm looking at this P.T. character. But Turley has turned up everywhere, which makes me suspicious. Now, you'll all remain on your individual assignments, but you'll keep this office informed of any information you develop."

Quinlan could see the detectives starting to react; their natural antipathy to the FBI was kicking in. "Your respective superiors in your chains of command have already agreed to the arrangement, but feel free to confirm that with them."

Confirmation would not be necessary, the detectives knew. No ranking officer in his right mind, when faced with the kind of crimes they were dealing with, would turn down an FBI request for cooperation.

It simply would look awful if there were more killings. And there was one thing everybody in the room could agree on.

There would be more killings.

P.T. WAS DELIGHTED WITH what he didn't see on television.

While there was substantial coverage of the discovery of Oswald's body, there was so far no mention of Chris Turley, P.T., or any connection between this murder and the bombing or the mayor's arrest.

In fact, it was being reported that the body was discovered by a jogger, whose name was being withheld. P.T. wasn't there at that particular moment, but he imagined the only jogging Turley did was in reverse after he saw the hanging body.

The fun part would be in seeing whether or not Turley would write the story himself, revealing his discovery of Oswald's body. P.T. was betting that he would; the chance to stay in the spotlight would be too great to pass up. But either way, the truth would get out; P.T. would see to that.

So much of this was going to play out on television that P.T. wished he could just watch all day. But he had too much to do, and in the process he would create what they would be reporting. In that way, he saw himself as a screenwriter, or TV producer.

He was providing what TV people called "content," and by the time he was finished he would draw a bigger audience than the Super Bowl.

This time Lawrence Terry had no intention of gently suggesting anything. From the moment he got the phone call from Chris telling him what happened, Terry decided to take a more aggressive role in dealing with what was becoming a very difficult and complicated situation.

Waiting for Chris when he got back to the office were Lawrence and Michael Stanton, the chief counsel for the newspaper. Chris was no longer resistant in any way; this bizarre situation had grown to the point where he felt he could use any and all help.

Chris gratefully took Lawrence's offered scotch on the rocks, even though it was only three in the afternoon, and then brought Lawrence and Stanton completely up to date on all that had happened. They quickly came to the same conclusion he had.

"P.T. is dirty," Lawrence said. "The question is, why is he bringing you into it."

"I have no idea," Chris said. "I can't imagine who he is or why anyone would hate me that much."

"Hate you? The guy is turning you into a star. You could hire ten agents and they wouldn't do half this much for your career."

"He's a killer, Lawrence."

"Of course, he's a killer. And he's a scumbag and a lowlife and a roach. But you know what else he is? He's a newsmaker. Not only that, but he's *your* newsmaker. He's *our* newsmaker. When we get the Pulitzer, we'll thank him from the podium."

The lawyer, Stanton, asked, "Did you make any commitments to the police about what you would or would not write?"

"No. They asked me to keep a lid on all of this, but I didn't promise anything."

Lawrence nodded his approval. "Good. And I didn't promise anything when the chief called me."

Chris wasn't surprised to hear that Lawrence had gotten a call, and certainly wasn't at all surprised that Lawrence wasn't impressed or intimidated by it. "You don't think we have an obligation to hold off for a while?" Chris asked.

"We have an obligation to inform the public. Now, show me how someone is going to get killed because of what we report and I'll hold back. But how does the public benefit in this case by being kept in the dark?"

Chris shrugged. "Maybe the police will have a better chance of catching the guy if we stay quiet."

"And maybe they won't. Or maybe they have their own agendas. Michael?"

Stanton thought for a few moments and then said, "There are no legal reasons to sit on the story. This is an event that happened to you, and you are free to write about it."

"I agree that I'm free to do so," Chris said. "The question is whether it's the responsible thing to do."

An agitated Lawrence started firing questions at Chris. "Every reporter worth his salt is going after this story, you think it's not going to come out? Three different sets of cops know about it, you don't think any of them will leak it? Why shouldn't you be the one to write it? You want to get scooped on your own story?"

Chris certainly knew that Lawrence had a point. Somebody would dig out the story; it might as well be Chris.

Lawrence stood up, signaling that the meeting had reached a resolution and was over. "Good. Write the story, but only about finding Oswald's body. Leave out P.T. and the connection to the bombing and the mayor."

"Why are we holding that back?" asked Chris.

"Because you're going to call this 'part one' of the story, and the rest will be in tomorrow's follow-up piece," said Lawrence, smiling. "Which I think we'll call 'part two.'"

"SON OF A BITCH" is what Agent Quinlan said when he saw Chris's story.

He had been told that a great deal of pressure had been brought upon Chris by the local authorities not to write it, obviously without effect. The fact that Chris didn't make the connection to the bomber and the mayor was of small comfort; that would no doubt be included in the promised second part, to run tomorrow.

Not being able to control Chris is what annoyed Quinlan, since the truth was there was no great downside to the story's appearance, at least not as far as tipping off P.T. was concerned. It was clear he could be certain that the police had made the connection between the three events, once Turley found the body. The only difference is that now the public would be aware, which would increase the pressure to catch the guy. It would have no real effect on Quinlan, though, since no one could put more pressure on him than he put on himself.

The other negative was that the story provoked another call from FBI Director Kramer, who was starting to get anxious that there were no breaks in the case.

"They're getting nervous at the White House. You need to send me daily progress reports."

"They'll make for quick reading, because we haven't made any progress," Quinlan said. At this stage, Quinlan could easily fend Kramer off, but it would grow increasingly difficult the longer there was no arrest.

Other media outlets, again trumped by Chris on a big story, were starting to let their collective annoyance show. One commentator compared Chris to Zelig, the character in the Woody Allen movie of the same name, who kept popping up in notable historical events throughout the ages.

Chris had stopped watching any of the coverage and had avoided phone calls seeking interviews. He holed up in his office, even after he finished writing part two of the story. He was nervous about the effect it would have, and not completely comfortable about being the one to reveal P.T. to the world.

Dani stopped by his office. "You okay?" she asked.

He smiled. "Well, there's quite a bit going on."

"I know. The receptionist said she has a hundred and forty-one messages for you."

"I told her not to put any calls through."

"Isn't it possible you-know-who will call?" she asked.

"He's got my cell phone number."

"How did he get that?" she asked.

"I have no idea."

She sat down. "Chris, I assume you've given a lot of thought to who this guy might be. Could it be someone you know?"

"That's another thing I have no idea about."

"Okay. Let's change the subject. What are you doing for dinner?" she asked.

" 'No idea' works for that one, also."

"Then you're coming to my house."

"I don't want to put you to any trouble."

"It's just as easy to order in for two as for one. And you can be the boy and pay, if you want."

The idea of spending the evening with Dani, and not alone, had surprising appeal to him. "You've got a deal." He hesitated a moment, and then added, "Can we make a stop first? There's somebody I really want you to meet."

Chris said, "Harriet Turley, this is Dani Cooper. Dani, this is my mother."

"Hello, Mrs. Turley," Dani said, taking her not-offered hand. "It's really nice to meet you."

If Harriet had any idea who they were, she did not display it. Instead, she sat there quietly with a small smile on her face. Chris had long ago learned that the fact that the smile was always there removed any meaning it might have had. She was not amused. She was not happy. She was a blank slate.

Chris and Dani talked to her for twenty minutes in a manner that never revealed that Harriet was oblivious to what they were saying.

"Your son is famous," Dani said at one point. "You should be very proud of him."

Chris smiled. "But not as famous as Dad."

When they were about to leave, Chris leaned over and whispered something in Harriet's ear before kissing her. When they got into the car, Dani asked, "Why did you bring me to meet her?"

Chris thought for a moment before speaking. "I used to bring a lot of girls home to meet my mother, and afterwards she would ask me if that was the 'special' girl. I always said no, and Mom would tell me that when I found the 'special' girl, I should let her know."

"Is that what you whispered to her before we left?"

Chris nodded. "Yes."

Dani didn't say anything for a while, and Chris looked over and asked, "Am I making you uncomfortable?"

"Uncomfortable? Are you nuts? That was the nicest thing anybody has ever said to me." Then she laughed. "Even though you said it to her."

Chris leaned over and kissed her, and then they drove off.

P.T. had watched Chris and Dani leave the newspaper and get into his car together. He followed them from a safe distance to the rest home, waited until they came out, and then followed them until they parked on a street about a mile from Chris's house.

They got out of the car, walked down the block and into a house, and P.T. noticed that they were holding hands.

There are always surprises, P.T. thought. Just when you think you know everything there is to know about someone, something catches you off guard.

So Chris and Dani were really an item, like that rag magazine had said. Like everything else, P.T. knew he was resourceful enough to turn this discovery into a positive. Of course, it would be a negative for Chris and his lady.

A major negative.

TYING IT ALL TOGETHER IN A HORRIFYING, MURDEROUS KNOT: THE MED CENTER, THE MAYOR, AND THOMAS OSWALD
by Chris Turley

There is a man out there who calls himself "P.T." who has phoned me four times in the past week. I believed he was an informant, and I was across the street from the medical center to meet him when the building blew up. He chose the location for our meeting, but at the time I had no reason to believe he had anything to do with the explosion itself.

Then he provided me with the information that resulted in Mayor Stanley's arrest at the Claremont Hotel. Again, I did not believe him to be anything other than a concerned citizen, exposing government corruption and hypocrisy.

However, under the guise of providing additional details about the mayor, he lured me into the discovery of Thomas Oswald's body. In that one instant, everything changed. It is now my belief that "P.T." was the perpetrator of the medical center bombing and the murder of Thomas Oswald.

I believe he will contact me again, but for now it is my responsibility to state very clearly what I believe:

"P.T." is not finished killing.

EVEN WITH ALL THAT was going on, it was as pleasant an evening as Chris could remember. He and Dani ordered in pizza, then played *Scrabble* and listened to U2 albums. After that, they drank wine and talked, and then after a while they silently put the wineglasses down, went into the bedroom, and made love.

Chris was more than a little surprised at how comfortable things were with Dani. He'd had two serious relationships in his life, each of which had lasted for almost two years, but he couldn't remember ever experiencing a similar level of comfort back then. Yet he literally had been dating Dani for only a matter of days.

When he got out of the shower the next morning, he smelled something in the kitchen and was surprised to see her making breakfast. "Smells good," he said.

She smiled. "They're my famous pancakes."

"How famous are they?"

"Well, they haven't reached their full level of fame yet. It's only the second time I've made them."

She put three of them on a plate and handed it to him. They sat down and he made the mistake of trying to cut into his stack with a fork. It was like trying to penetrate a manhole cover, and he had to make a number of attempts at it before getting the fork all the way through.

She watched him struggle. "Something wrong?"

"No. I've just never had famous pancakes before." He put a piece into his mouth and bit down on it, then paused to make sure his teeth were still intact. He smiled. "Nice and chewy."

"You don't like them?" she asked.

"Are you kidding? They're delicious," he lied.

She went back to the stove to prepare a few more, and he could only hope that they were for her. The doorbell rang and she asked, "Can you get that?"

Chris went to the front door and opened it, but there wasn't anyone there. He looked down and saw, sitting in front of the door, a wrapped gift the size of a shoe box.

The box, left there like that, was highly suspicious, and he just stared at it for a few moments as Dani came up behind him. "Who left that?"

"Someone who didn't want to be seen."

"What should we do?"

At that moment, they heard a phone ring and the box exploded upward. Dani screamed as they both jumped back and saw one of those fake rubber snakes shoot out of the box. The cover fell off to the side.

"Oh my God," she said.

Still a little leery, Chris peered into the open box. Sitting on some tissue paper was a cell phone. As if on cue, it started ringing again. After three rings, he decided to answer it, knowing full well who was going to be on the other end.

"Hello, Chris."

"P.T."

"Chris, I have to say I'm a little upset with you."

"Why is that?"

"You don't know why? Really? Have you read the morning paper?"

"No," Chris said.

"Well, I just finished doing so, and imagine my surprise to learn that you've betrayed a source. Our conversations were to be treated in confidence, yet there they were, for all the world to see."

"Did you kill that man?"

P.T. laughed. "You expect me to reveal more to you? After you've just demonstrated that you have no journalistic integrity? You're no different than your father."

The reference to his father surprised Chris. "How is that?"

"You're about to learn how, believe me."

"I think we should meet," Chris said.

"Finally, something we agree on."

"Good. When can we do that?"

"Very soon, Chris. Very soon. But first you need to experience a bit more. Get a sense of what it was like."

"What does that mean?"

Click.

Chris dropped the phone back into the box and ran out into the street. He realized that the box hadn't burst open until he and Dani had discovered it, yet they hadn't touched it. That could only mean that they were being watched by P.T., and he had seen them open the front door.

There was no sign of him anywhere. He could have been hiding in any one of many places, or he could have been in a car and driven away once he saw the door open, since he could use the cell phone from anywhere.

P.T. was after him in a very serious way; there could be no doubt about that now. And to make matters worse, now he knew about Dani.

And he knew where she lived.

CHRIS HAD HIS CHOICE of police agencies to go to, and he chose Novack.

He had a comfort level with Novack and how he operated, as well as a measure of trust. Chris knew that the information would be circulated and would find its way to the FBI, and that was fine. But Chris was feeling that there were very few things he could control and the choice of who to tell about the latest contact from P.T. was one of them.

Chris called Novack and briefly told him what happened and Novack said that he and Willingham would come over to Dani's house immediately. He told him to leave the box and cell phone exactly where they were, that they would be bringing forensics people with them.

As they were leaving the precinct, Willingham asked, "You gonna call Quinlan?"

"This call is in our jurisdiction, and we're responding to it."

Willingham knew that Novack was being protective of his turf and he felt the same way. "I understand that. But are you going to call him?"

"Absolutely," Novack said.

"When?"

"All in good time."

"Phew, that's a relief," said Willingham. "I was afraid it was going to be all in bad time."

Chris was in front of the house when they arrived. Dani was inside; he had suggested she stay there in recognition of the fact that P.T. likely had been and could still be watching them, and she agreed.

The three of them stayed outside until three squad cars and a forensics team pulled up. Novack sent the officers around to canvas the neighborhood as to whether anyone had seen any strangers and the forensics people starting working on the shoe box and cell phone.

Inside, Chris and Dani told Novack everything that had taken place, without any interruption. When they were finished, Novack asked, "You got here last night?"

"Yes."

"How often have you spent the night here?"

"This was only the second time," Chris said.

"And where is your car parked?"

"Down the street. The spots in front of the house were taken when we got home."

Chris saw where Novack's mind was going. "So he had to have followed us last night," Chris said. "Otherwise, he couldn't have known I was here."

Novack nodded. "And he was watching when you discovered the box this morning."

Chris started pacing, frustrated. "But who the hell is he?"

"At this point, you're the only one who can figure that out."

"What do you mean?"

"All we can do, all the Feds can do, is follow the clues. But I've got a hunch this guy isn't going to leave many of them. So the best thing we have to go on is the fact that he picked you. It's unlikely that choice was a random one; if it was, we're in deep shit."

"So he hates me? Or he's getting revenge on me?"

Novack nodded. "Both would be my guess. So you've got to figure out who you've known in your life that would want to do that."

"There's nobody, I swear."

Novack and Willingham frowned together, as if their faces were synchronized. "Earth to Chris. Earth to Chris. Come in, please," Novack said. "Of course there's somebody. Among other things, there's a destroyed building and a hanging body to prove it. You just don't know who the somebody is yet, but you should spend every minute of every day figuring it out."

Chris nodded. "Okay. You're right."

"Another question," Novack added, "is whether you're going to write about this."

Chris had thought about that already, and said, "I think I should."

"Why?"

"Because it's news. If this was happening to someone else, and I found out about it, I'd write the story. Why shouldn't I just because it's happening to me?"

Novack shrugged. "That's your call."

"You think my writing about it hurts your chances of catching the guy?"

Novack thought about that for a few moments. "No,

but the FBI might have a different view of it. You can ask them when you talk to them."

"When do I have to talk to them?"

Novack looked at his watch. "Well, I'm going to call them in about three minutes, so figure ten minutes after that."

THIS WAS NOT GOING to be easy.

It's not that it would be mentally challenging; all the preparation had been done long ago. And it wasn't that there was any concern about possible failure, as success was certainly assured. It was just that there physically was a great deal more to do, and P.T. had to do it all by himself.

He smiled to himself at the thought that one of the things "psycho killers" can't do is delegate.

He walked along Lemoine Avenue in Fort Lee, slowly and seemingly casually. It was midday, so there were a decent number of people out, but this was not really a walking area. People in New Jersey generally drove to where they were going and the streets were crowded with cars.

He was carrying with him the power of life and death, but he knew that the same thing was true of everyone he passed. Any of them, if they chose, could pull out a knife or gun and kill someone unsuspecting. It would be an easy thing for them to do.

They all had the power to kill, but chose not to use it. That was one of the ways they differed from him.

His disguise of a goatee and different hair color

was probably not necessary; he was sure he knew where the increasingly prevalent cameras were well enough to avoid them. The American people were being spied on every single day, but they seemed to pay it no heed. The fact of that amazed and sickened him.

As P.T. approached a green Chrysler parallel parked at the curb, he reached into his pocket and slipped out the device. It was no more than two and a half inches wide and an inch thick and fit neatly into the palm of his hand.

He stopped and leaned down next to the car to tie his shoe and in an instant, deftly attached the device to the bottom of the car, inside the rear fender. He felt the magnet snap into place and knew that it was there for as long as he wanted it to be. Which would not be very long.

He got up and continued walking to his own car. He looked at his watch as he did so, and saw that it was almost lunchtime. He was getting a little hungry, but wanted to arrange for ten or fifteen more deaths before he stopped to eat.

It was hard to judge the public reaction to part two of Chris's story, which described his interactions with P.T. and thus connected the bombing, the arrest of the mayor, and the Oswald murder. Based on Internet comments and call-ins to radio talk shows, the prevailing feeling was probably confusion, which was quite appropriate.

The twenty-four-hour cable news networks decided

it was the story of the decade, or at least until another story of the decade came along in a week or so.

Since the entire story centered around Chris at this point, his life was dissected around the clock. Friends from high school that he hadn't seen in fifteen years were recruited to describe their impressions of him, and his father Edward's career was scrutinized, mainly as a way of comparing him to his son.

No one expressed any doubt that Chris was being truthful; certainly, there was nothing in his past to indicate that he could be a mass murderer. But the bloom was rapidly fading from the rose of his recent status of super reporter.

A good example of this was an interview that CNN did with Wallace Cook, a *New York Times* reporter of considerable renown. Wallace and Chris went to journalism school together and had kept in touch over the years. Wallace had always tried to be helpful to Chris, even alerting him to job openings that Chris might be interested in pursuing.

But in this interview, Wallace was critical of Chris's recent actions. In addition to crediting his success to luck rather than journalistic skills, Wallace opined that Chris "might have been so taken with his sudden fame that his journalistic instincts may have suffered for it."

"Are you saying that he was oblivious to the danger?"

"I think he might not have realized the level of evil that he was dealing with," said Wallace, before qualifying his attack with another slap, claiming that Chris's behavior was "somewhat understandable" given his lack of experience.

Chris was hurt by his friend's words, but realized there was some truth to them. By his own admission, he didn't owe his scoops to instinct or talent, but rather to the fact that P.T. planted the stories right in front of his face. Whether he should have reacted differently or not was not something Chris was completely sure about, though looking back he couldn't pinpoint anything he would have changed in the moment.

Wallace's interview exposed the fact that even with the recent turn of events, most of Chris's competition were still jealous that he was the chosen one. No matter how this played out, he would always have the advantage of fame, which brought access, which brought credibility and success.

THE FBI'S EXAMINATION OF Chris's phone records got them nowhere.

There were in fact calls made to the office and cell phone at the times Chris reported and they were all made from the same phone number. The problem was that the source phone number did not exist. It was a fake, and the use of it showed P.T. to be technologically accomplished.

It was another in a series of frustrating dead ends and Agent Quinlan was worried. He knew that P.T. would be caught; he was far too active a criminal not to make a mistake, but that very activity was frightening. There was no way that he was going to pack up his weapons and go home. Other shoes were going to drop, and drop soon.

The most confusing part of a very confusing case was where Chris Turley fit in. It was possible that he was simply a randomly chosen vehicle to get P.T.'s story before the public. Yet it hardly seemed necessary; blowing up a building was the kind of thing that attracted media attention by itself. There would not be a need to put a reporter on the scene; every media outlet in the country would be all over the story.

And where did the mayor's arrest fit in? It seemed incongruous for P.T., at least when compared with his other exploits. It also seemed designed to make Chris Turley a media star, yet it was hard to see what P.T. gained from doing so.

Perhaps P.T. was someone with an individual vendetta against Turley. Why, then, build him up to be a media sensation? And why blow up a building or kill Oswald? How would that hurt Turley? It was more likely that P.T. picked Turley for a reason that was not personal, perhaps because of some article he once wrote or some comment he made on television.

But Turley was knee deep in it now, and if Quinlan was to be successful he would have to use him to get to P.T. Turley might be amenable to that, or he might not. His attitude would determine how much pressure had to be applied.

Quinlan was in his office when he got the call from Novack, telling him about the latest contact from P.T. "When did this happen?" he asked, annoyed that the FBI's taps on Chris's phone had not been set up yet.

"About three hours ago," Novack said, bracing for the explosion.

"And you're just calling me now?" Quinlan's voice was surprisingly calm.

"Right. It took me that long to interview Turley, get all the details, and have our forensics people analyze the box and phone."

"So you have your own forensics people?" Quinlan asked.

Novack would have preferred yelling from Quinlan, rather than the icy sarcasm he was getting. "Well, they're not really forensics 'people.' It's a forensics 'person.' And he's not really a forensics person, he's a high school chemistry teacher. But he's really smart, and he watches every version of *CSI*. I think *Miami* is his favorite."

"My sense is you think this is funny," said Quinlan.

"And my sense is you think I spent my last twenty years as a night watchman. Now if you want to work together, stop the condescending bullshit. Because I'm the one Turley trusts."

"Go fuck yourself, Novack."

Quinlan didn't know it, but that brought a smile from Novack. "That's more like it."

Novack detailed his conversation with Chris for Quinlan and also agreed to have the phone and box turned over to FBI experts. Quinlan asked to have all the reports sent to him, as well, and Novack was happy to comply.

"Is Turley at the scene now?" Quinlan asked. "I want to talk to him personally."

"I think he is. You want me to meet you there?" Novack asked. "I mean, now that we're pals?"

"I think I can handle it on my own, old buddy."

Chris took Quinlan's call on his cell phone and agreed to wait for him at Dani's. He hadn't been planning to leave for a while anyway, since they had a lot to talk about.

"The FBI agent is coming over," Chris said.

"If I had known we were going to have so much company I would have made more pancakes."

"I'm sorry about this," he said. "I should not have come here and brought you into this."

"I'm into it now," she said without apparent anger or resentment. She was just stating a fact.

"Yes," he said. "You are. It might make some sense for you to go somewhere until this is over."

"You mean hide?" she said.

"I understand it's not fair," he said. "But we don't know who this guy is, or if there's any limit to what he will do. And if he's trying to hurt me, he could do that by hurting you."

"This is my home." She said it with a mixture of anger and defiance and Chris was impressed by it.

He nodded. "Let me talk to Novack; maybe we can get you protected."

When the doorbell rang they both jumped, then smiled self-consciously at their reaction. Chris looked through the window, saw that it was Quinlan and Serrano, and let them in.

Chris and Dani took them through the events in the same detail they had given Novack. The agents asked a lot of questions and one of them made Chris remember something he had previously forgotten.

"He made a reference to my father," Chris said. "I don't remember the exact words, but he said I was like my father. And that I would find out how. I can't believe I forgot that," Chris said, annoyed with himself.

"You're under a lot of pressure," Quinlan said. "Anything else about your father?"

Chris shook his head. "I don't think so."

Quinlan was familiar with Edward Turley; he grew up watching him. "When did your father die?"

"About five years ago."

"And does P.T. mentioning him ring any bells for you? Maybe you and your father had common enemies?"

Chris thought about it for a few moments. "No. Nothing. As far as our work, my father was in a different league."

"You going to write about this?" Serrano asked, his tone revealing that he thought it was a bad idea to do so.

"I'll talk to my editor, but I think so. I think I should."

"Why?"

"Because it's news. Because it affects people and they have a right to know."

"What if it makes it harder to catch him?" Quinlan asked. "What if it eggs him on to kill more people?"

"Are you saying either of those things are true?"

Quinlan shook his head. "I don't know if they're true, but I don't know that they're not."

"And maybe if I stop writing, it'll piss him off, and he'll start doing even worse things to get attention."

"Worse than blowing up a building?" Quinlan asked.

"It's not possible?"

Quinlan nodded grudgingly. He wasn't going to lie about it. "It's possible."

THE FIRST SNOWFALL OF the season came two days later.

That was relatively early; in recent years the New York area had a few times gone past the first of the year before a measurable snowfall.

Clark Hendricks couldn't have been more delighted. He had always loved snow; it conjured up long-ago memories of snowball fights and school closings. And since Clark had just celebrated his seventy-second birthday, it had been a while since it mattered to him one way or the other whether school was going to be closed.

Clark and his wife, Betty, had retired three years ago, after selling the drugstore they owned and operated for forty-one years in Wayne. It had provided them with a good life and an even better retirement.

Unlike their contemporaries, who headed south for the winter, Clark and Betty did the opposite. They never liked hot weather, so they headed north for the summer, renting a house in Maine. During the winter they holed up in their home in Lincoln Park, keeping it stocked with food and firewood.

This particular snowfall reached the magic number of six inches, which meant that there was enough to justify Clark's initial use of the snowblower he had recently purchased. It was state-of-the-art and looked like a golf cart; Clark could sit on the seat on top and blow the snow as far as he wanted, up to twenty feet.

Betty came into the den and saw him looking through the window at the snow falling outside. She came up alongside him. "Looks like about five inches," she said.

"The guy on television said six."

"No way," she said, smiling. "Looks like five at the most. You want me to call Harry?" Harry Sanders was the man they and most of their neighbors had been paying to plow their driveways for the last few years.

Clark knew she was having fun at his expense. "Not necessary. I'm going to try out the snowblower."

"I thought the manual said it requires six inches?" she asked.

"Which is a happy coincidence," he said, "because that is exactly the amount that has fallen so far."

She kissed him on the cheek. "I'm so excited for you," she deadpanned. "Dress warmly and be careful."

"I will," he said, heading for the closet to get his winter jacket and gloves.

The snowblower was in a large shed about thirty feet from the house, where Clark also kept his tools and lawn mower. Clark hadn't used any of them in years since they hired someone to take care of the lawn while they were away for the summers. He had thought about moving it to the garage, but hadn't really expected a snowfall this early.

He trudged through the snow to the shed, loving every single moment of it. There was something about falling snow that was incredibly invigorating, and for about the five millionth time he wondered why he had never seriously taken up skiing.

The snow felt very light and powdery, and the wind was blowing it around quite a bit. Clark knew it might limit the effectiveness of the snowblower, and he might have to use it again later, especially if much more came down. That was fine with him.

Clark got to the shed, opened the large door, and went inside. The snow-blower was right at the entrance, key in the ignition as he had left it, poised to make its debut. When his neighbors saw him and it in action, they might ask him to work his magic on their driveways. Which would also be fine with him.

Not as spry as he used to be, Clark mounted the machine with some difficulty. He almost fell off twice in the process and was glad that Betty had not come out to watch. But finally he made it to the top, from where he would rule the snow-covered world.

Clark turned the key and lived another quarter of a second. The blast sent the walls of the shed outward, and an incredible wall of flame shot straight up, as if it were impatient to devour the falling snow.

In the open air, the noise was not as loud as one might expect, but the concussion was powerful enough to blow out five windows in the house.

In the first moments, Betty was more bewildered than frightened, but she ran outside to see what had happened.

And then she screamed.

CHRIS WAS GETTING READY to leave for his office when his phone rang.

"Did you hear about Clark Hendricks?" P.T. asked. "Boy, that really puts things into perspective, doesn't it?"

"Who is Clark Hendricks?" Chris asked.

"Was. Who *was* Clark Hendricks. May he rest in peace."

Chris was jolted by what P.T. said, but tried to sound calm. "Okay. Who was Clark Hendricks?"

"Elderly gentleman . . . I never got to know him, but he seemed nice enough. Betty is certainly going to miss him."

"Did you kill him?"

"In a manner of speaking. But at the end of the day, you killed him."

"How did I do that?"

"By being you, Chris. By being you. It's in your genes."

"Why are you doing this? What do you have against me?"

P.T. chose to ignore the question. "You have the power to end this."

"You're not making sense."

P.T. laughed. "That's okay, there's plenty of time for you to understand."

Chris was aware that the FBI was by now certainly listening to every word they were saying, so he tried to prolong the call, in case that was necessary to help them trace it.

"Why are you killing all these innocent people?"

"Innocence is a state of mind, Chris. It means nothing in the real world."

"Of course it does. Why do you say that?"

"You know, I think you're trying to keep this conversation going so that the FBI can trace the call. In the process, you're wasting my time."

"I want to understand what you're hoping to accomplish," Chris said.

P.T. laughed. "I'm doing more than 'hoping.' Anyway, don't you think you should head down to Mr. Hendricks's house? The other media whores are going to beat you to your story."

"I want to talk to you. I think we should meet."

Click.

The call was patched through to Agent Quinlan, who heard some of it in real time and the rest on tape. There seemed no longer any doubt about two things. First, P.T. was real, and not someone that Chris Turley had created. And second, his choice of Turley was not random; it was highly personal.

Quinlan actually learned about the death of Clark Hendricks through the phone call. The explosion had happened only three minutes before the call was made, and local police and fire were just arriving on the scene.

If not for the call, it would have been a while before Quinlan was notified. Initially, it would have been premature for the locals to call the FBI; the detonation was first thought to possibly be the result of a terrible accident, such as a propane tank explosion. There was no obvious reason to link it to P.T., and it was ridiculous to imagine that ideological terrorists would target the shed of Clark Hendricks.

Quinlan and other agents rushed to the Hendricks house and ordered the local police to cordon off the scene. Novack arrived at about the same time. Quinlan asked him, "Are you the only cop in this county? Is there nothing you're not assigned to?"

"I'm not here officially; I just heard about the explosion and thought it might be connected. Since you're here, I was obviously right."

Quinlan nodded. "Yeah. Our boy called Turley and confessed."

"Did he say why?"

"He said it was Turley's fault."

Quinlan started walking towards the shed. "You mind if I hang around?" asked Novack.

Quinlan thought for a moment and said, "Come on." He led Novack to the scene; they were going to need all the brainpower they could find.

"Lawrence, it's about my father. I know it." Chris had gone to see Lawrence Terry at the office as soon as he got off the phone with P.T. He hadn't bothered to call Quinlan or Novack first, since he knew the FBI was listening to his calls.

"That doesn't make sense, Chris."

"It does to him. He's made it personal, Lawrence. And he's mentioned my father twice, as if we're both to blame."

"So somebody has a grudge against your father, waits until seven years after he retires and five years after he dies, and then starts killing innocent people for revenge? While giving you the inside on the stories?"

"Don't ask me to explain it, Lawrence. But what he's been doing has taken a long time to plan. And maybe he would have done this to my father if he hadn't died. And maybe he gave me the stories so I would be famous, and therefore more like my father."

"Chris . . ."

"Isn't that possible?"

Lawrence was going to argue, but instead just nodded. "Of course it's possible, Chris. And I certainly don't have another explanation. But that doesn't make it true."

"You know much more about my father's career than I do. I need you to think about who my father could have hurt this badly."

"Chris, do you know how many stories your father covered over all those years? And he wasn't writing about the weather; he was exposing people who didn't want to be exposed. He hurt plenty of people badly and most of them deserved it."

"Most of them? Some people didn't deserve it?"

"Listen to me," Lawrence said. "Your father conducted journalistic warfare. He attacked people that needed attacking. But in any war, there is collateral damage and innocent people could get caught up in it."

"P.T. said that innocence is a state of mind. That it means nothing in the real world."

"He's obviously a psychotic asshole, and you're quoting him like he's Plato? The overwhelming number of people your father hurt, even destroyed, had it coming. But so what? You think P.T. has to be someone who was wronged unfairly for him to be pissed off? That's crazy."

"I'm going to go through my father's files," Chris said. "Can I call you when I have questions?"

"Of course. Where are they?"

"We put them in storage when my mother went into the home. I'm going to get them out this afternoon."

"Write your story first."

Chris nodded; he had given this a lot of thought. He was going to keep telling the public the truth until shown a reason to do otherwise by Quinlan or Novack. If Clark Hendricks could be killed, then no one was safe. Because in P.T.'s world, innocence was simply not a factor.

And people had a right to know that.

CLARK HENDRICKS, 72:
THE LATEST VICTIM OF A SERIES OF
SENSELESS, SICKENING ACTS OF VIOLENCE
by Chris Turley

The man who refers to himself as "P.T." called me again today, informing me that Clark Hendricks, a retired pharmacist living in Lincoln Park, had been killed in an explosion at his home.

This call was made three minutes after the tragedy had occurred, well before it was reported in the media, and even before emergency personnel had arrived on the scene.

There can be only one explanation: "P.T." committed another murder.

After telling me of Mr. Hendricks's death, "P.T." continued to babble on about how these killings were all my fault, and how I have the power to stop them.

When I told him that whatever his grievances were with me, innocent people should not suffer for them, he scoffed that "innocence is a state of mind." And when I asked to meet with him, he hung up on me.

I have no idea who "P.T." is, or what is behind his bizarre, horrifying behavior, but I am working with authorities to try and figure it out.

Until then I will keep informing the public of developments, and keep doing all that I can to help bring this nightmare to an end.

NOTHING THAT CAME BEFORE even approached the furor that greeted Chris's latest story.

That P.T. could have taken the life of an innocent, seventy-two-year-old retiree with no apparent enemies in the world drove home to the public just what kind of a man was in their midst.

The randomness of the act, on top of the previous murders, was the aspect that was the most chilling. Most people have techniques to keep themselves safe, especially from violent crime. They don't go to seedy sections of the city at night, they don't pick up hitchhikers, they avoid cash machines in certain areas at off hours . . . and when somebody does one of these things and is victimized, it seems understandable and therefore less frightening.

This situation was dramatically different. If Thomas Oswald could be killed while Christmas shopping in a busy mall, if Clark Hendricks could be blown to bits in his own garage, then no amount of self-protection would be sufficient.

Such was the sensation that Chris's story created that it even changed the economics of the newspaper business, or at least that of the *Bergen News*. Circulation of the physical newspaper barely increased, because everyone with a computer was so anxious to read it that they did so online as soon as it was posted.

The paper made up for this situation by increasing the online advertising rates it charged, and they pretty much could have named their own price, since it was estimated that the previously infrequently visited site now was drawing more visitors than *The New York Times*, *The Washington Post*, and *USA Today* combined.

Scott Ryder, the tech guy who ran the newspaper Web site, was running around like a crazed zombie. He told Lawrence that it was like "planning a concert by the high school choir, and then having Springsteen show up to perform instead. Who the hell would handle crowd control?"

Law enforcement was taking great pains to try to calm the public, even saying that there was not yet any physical evidence to tie the latest incident to the previous ones. P.T., in his conversation with Chris, could have been taking credit for something he had nothing to do with.

While that was technically true, the authorities were deliberately avoiding the fact that it had been P.T. who'd made the call to Chris well before the explosion had been reported in the media. It was obvious that the only way he could have known about it, and known the identity of the victim, was if he caused it. While Chris had mentioned this in his story about the killing, law enforcement spokesmen were subtly implying that he could have been mistaken about the timing.

If the public was foolish enough to believe the police assurances, which they were not, then they would have been even more upset. If P.T. was not the killer, then it would have meant that there were two random, murderous lunatics out on the street, which would not exactly have been reassuring.

Chris was refusing all interview requests and trying to block out the furor around him, which was not the easiest thing to do in light of the fact that the press camped out in front of his house around the clock.

He called Dani a few times and she was holding up pretty well. Novack had stationed a patrol car in front of her house for protection and both she and Chris were grateful for that. She had taken a paid leave of absence from her job, which Lawrence had willingly gone along with, especially since she agreed to write a couple of feature stories from home.

"I'd love to see you," Chris said during one of their calls, "but I don't want to draw you any further into this lunacy."

"Let's not let him dictate how we live our lives," Dani said.

"Easier said than done."

"Hey, I'm not saying we should go dancing. I'm saying you should come over, and I'll make dinner, and we'll have a glass of wine and talk."

"You have no idea how good that sounds, except for the part about you making dinner."

"I knew it. You didn't like my pancakes."

"What gave it away?"

"You threw them out when you thought I wasn't looking."

"Oh. Well, I would be happy to fake eating them again, if I could get to spend time with you. But every time I leave my house, the national press corps goes with me."

"Can you sneak out without them seeing you?"

"No, I don't see how. But I have another idea that might work."

"Make it work," she said. "I'll whip up some batter."

Chris called Bruce Harlow and asked if they could meet at the newspaper office. Harlow agreed, though he couldn't contain his curiosity. "What's this about, Chris? You want to document what's going on? It's an instant bestseller." Harlow was implying that Chris might want to start keeping extensive records of his ongoing experience with P.T. and that perhaps Harlow could cowrite a book with him.

Fully aware that the FBI was listening to his calls, he decided not to answer Bruce's question. "Let's talk when we meet, okay?"

They agreed to meet at the office in twenty minutes and Chris went to the garage, got in his car, and drove out of the driveway. He was learning that it was not necessary to stop when the press people assembled there were in the way, that they could be counted on to move when his car barreled towards them.

Chris arrived before Bruce, and while he was waiting for him he went to Scott Ryder's office. As always, Scott was hunched over his computer, trying to keep the overburdened Web site up and functioning.

"Hey, Scott, let me ask you something. You know anything about masking voices?"

"Masking voices?"

Chris nodded. "I want to know if there is any technology that would let this lunatic change the way his voice sounds. You know about stuff like that, don't you?"

Scott nodded. "Voice transformers. Sure, they're very advanced now. You just talk into the machine and it comes out any way you want."

"So if this guy wanted to change the way he sounds, he could do it? Maybe from a voice I would recognize to one I wouldn't?"

"Are you kidding? He could really be a teenage girl, and you would have no way of knowing it. You want me to get you some literature on it?"

Chris shook his head. "Not necessary. I'll take your word for it. And I can look it up online."

Bruce arrived a few minutes later, and they went into Chris's office and closed the door. "You look like you've had a rough day," Bruce said.

Chris nodded. "I've had better."

"I can imagine. I haven't run into a single person who can talk about anything other than you and that lunatic."

"I've got a feeling it's going to get worse before it gets better," Chris said.

"So how can I help?"

"This is just between us for now, okay? I don't want the FBI digging into this stuff until I have reason to believe I'm right."

Bruce nodded his agreement. "Whatever you say."

"I think there's a chance this is about my father. P.T. . . . the guy who's been doing this . . . seems to be focused on him."

"What do you mean, 'about your father'?"

"I'm not completely sure; I'm just swinging wild. But maybe he had a grudge against my father for something and he's getting his revenge against me."

"Can you tell how old he is by his voice?" Bruce asked.

"It's hard, and it could be computer masked anyway. Scott Ryder just told me they have machines that change your voice as you talk into it. According to Scott, it could be a female and I wouldn't know it."

Bruce frowned. "Goddamn technology."

Chris nodded. "Anyway, if it's his real voice, then he's around my age, certainly nowhere near my father's."

"So you're asking me if there's anybody I learned about while I was doing the book that would be capable of this? Somebody your father hurt really badly?"

Chris nodded. "Yes. Anything come to mind?"

"Chris, we haven't talked about this stuff, and I think that was a good idea. But you must know that your father badly damaged a lot of people, most of whom had it coming. That was his stock in trade; he exposed what he considered wrongdoing and corruption and hypocrisy. Sometimes it wasn't pretty."

"I know that."

"Then you also know that the list of people who might have held a grudge against him could fill fifty typewritten pages, single-spaced, printed on both sides."

"I need you to narrow it down for me. Not everyone on the list would be the type to do something like this. I'm not interested in CEOs who manipulated stock prices. They get their revenge with lawyers, not bombs."

"But the list would extend out."

"What do you mean?"

"Well, let's say he sent one of those CEOs to prison. So the people he employed would then be out of work. Maybe their kids would have to drop out of college. Any one of those people, if they were deranged enough, could blame your father for their lot in life."

"I know that," Chris said. "But I have nowhere else to begin."

"Okay. I'll get right on it."

"You going to start with Hansbrough?" Chris asked.

Bruce nodded. "Everything started with Hansbrough. You know that."

"You'd be amazed by how little I know. But thanks, Bruce. I appreciate it. Now I have one other favor to ask."

Bruce agreed to the other favor, which involved driving to Dani's with Chris huddled and hiding in the backseat of his car so the press didn't see him leave. It went off without a hitch, and within twenty minutes he and Dani were sipping wine in her den.

He was actually a little taken aback at how glad he was to see her. It had been a while since he had felt this way about a woman this quickly and it might never have happened to this degree. He wondered if it had anything to do with the stress he was under and if he was just feeling unusually needy.

It would be nice if that stress ended so he could put his feelings to the test.

And so people could stop dying.

DORIS RANDOLPH WAS GROWING more worried by the day.

Thinking back, it was hard to remember a time when she wasn't worried about her grandson, Peter. Maybe there was such a time, but it would have been before that horrible day many years ago, when her own son, Gerald, had walked out onto that highway.

Coming on the heels of his mother succumbing to cancer, Peter was never the same. Sullen, unpredictable, and sometimes prone to violence, he had twice been institutionalized in his teenage years.

After that he had rebounded, even to the point where he had joined the marines. Doris worried even then, but it was a worry tempered by a hope that he had turned the corner.

He had not, and after a year he found himself in a military prison for badly injuring a man in a bar brawl, one of a number of fights he had gotten into. When he was released he was thrown out of the corps. The marines had decided to wash their hands of him, but that was something Doris could never do. So Peter came to live with her.

She was his mother and his father; she was all he had. She could never abandon him.

It was easier when her own husband, James, was alive. He could handle Peter much better than she ever could; he could connect with him. His death a year ago left still another void in Peter's life, which she felt ill-equipped to fill. Especially since Doris couldn't afford to give up her job as an office manager.

But now she had a more pressing concern. Peter had always blamed his father's death on Edward Turley and his hatred for him was intense. Gerald had been the general manager of a small manufacturing firm with defense department contracts, and when the Hansbrough mess broke, he was implicated in it.

Gerald was never charged with wrongdoing; his suicide made that a nonissue and he maintained his innocence until his death. But he felt a public humiliation and believed that people considered him a traitor. It was more than he could take.

Now it was impossible for Doris not to notice Peter's obsession with the murder spree that was dominating the headlines. It seemed centered on Edward Turley's son, and though he didn't speak about it, Peter seemed to have transferred his hatred from father to son.

Every day when she left for work, and again when she got home, Peter was huddled over his computer, devouring any and all information he could get on the murders. She knew it was unhealthy and it frightened her.

She wanted him to talk to someone, a professional who could help him. Her medical coverage at work would pay for half of it and she'd manage the rest. But he wouldn't hear of it; they had argued. Bringing it up again would just set him off.

So Doris continued to worry, knowing that she could do little to impact the situation, and that she had no one she could turn to.

And at night, lying in bed, she could feel that worry start to border on panic. What if he was more than just obsessed with the murders? What if he was on some level involved in them?

So far she had been able to drive those thoughts to the back of her mind and she successfully buried them by recalling happier days. Days when Peter was part of a loving family, with a mother and father who doted on him.

But he wasn't called Peter back then, and that was the source of Doris's fear. Gerald had called his little boy "Petey."

Not to be confused, Doris prayed, with "P.T."

NOVACK QUICKLY MADE A decision to narrow his focus.

Quinlan and the FBI were dealing with the horror of a lunatic on a murderous rampage, apparently killing at random to support an agenda that was not at all clear. Despite their apparent lack of success so far, they had far more resources to investigate it than Novack and the local police departments could ever muster.

But the anomaly in all of this was P.T.'s use of Chris Turley to set up the mayor in the sting at the hotel. It wasn't different just because no one died and there had been no violence involved; it was different because it absolutely could not have been random, or a lucky guess.

"And P.T. knew what the mayor was doing that night," Novack said to Willingham.

"Which means?"

"Which means he had some special access, either to the mayor or to Charity. The number of people who had that access can't be that great."

"But P.T. might not have had that access. He could have gotten the information from someone who did."

Novack nodded. "That's true, but it still narrows

the field considerably. And that's the field we should play on."

Novack and Willingham set about the tedious task of questioning everyone at Englewood Town Hall who had any connection whatsoever to the mayor or his office. No one would admit to having any advance knowledge about that night in particular, or the mayor's extracurricular activities in general.

Those lack of admissions did not surprise Novack or Willingham; their hope was merely that someone might point them in the direction of someone else who knew something. But even that didn't happen, and the two days they had spent questioning the township employees yielded nothing.

One of the people they interviewed was Craig Andrews, the deputy housing commissioner and close friend of Chris Turley, who'd gone to look at cars with Chris just before the building explosion. Like the others, Craig claimed no advance knowledge of the mayor's activities.

Unlike the others, he was lying.

One of the many unsettling aspects of recent weeks for Chris was the fact that he had not been able to visit his mother since he'd brought Dani there. The visits had become a comforting part of his routine, and Chris missed being able to go there, but he certainly didn't want to turn the quiet existence that she and the other patients had into a media circus.

With Christmas quickly approaching, Chris missed his mother even more. She had always made the holidays a special time, even when her husband was not there to share in it.

Chris called her one evening and a nurse held the phone to her ear. He only talked for a few minutes, just told her that he loved her and that he would see her soon.

She didn't answer him; he couldn't even be sure that she heard him.

But it made him feel a little better.

The FBI had an expert in practically everything. That fact never ceased to amaze Nick Quinlan; he was sure that if he called and asked for an expert in aardvark psychology, they would send someone right up to his office.

The expert he was talking to at the moment was Eric Mandel and his field was voice recognition. He could compare and match up voices and was said to be able to listen to as little as two sentences and then know within fifty miles where the speaker had lived during his or her formative years.

He talked of "voice prints" and "timbre" and said the former were nearly as definitive as fingerprints in establishing identity. He also claimed a ninety-seven percent accuracy rate as to whether spoken sentences were truthful.

But at the moment, Mandel was being annoyingly vague, going on and on about "magnification" and "transfer" and "pitch" and a bunch of other terms that Quinlan couldn't have cared less about.

When Mandel paused to take a breath, Quinlan

jumped in. "What I want to know is whether the voice we hear on those phone calls is the speaker's actual voice."

"I can't be sure. If it's disguised and is computer altered, it's extraordinarily well done. It is in every sense a human voice, but I cannot say with certainty if or how much it has been altered."

"If it's a fake," Quinlan asked, "is the real voice likely to be similar?"

Mandel shook his head. "No, not at all. I mean, it could be, but it could just as easily be drastically different. It could be a teenager, or a woman, or anyone."

"So you heard two different voices in that conversation, but they both could have been the same person?"

"Yes. It would have to be orchestrated, of course, but it could certainly be done."

Quinlan had asked the question since the phone record showed that the number P.T. made the calls from did not exist. He had thought that the latest call exonerated Chris, but what Mandel was saying meant that wasn't necessarily the case. It could conceivably be true that Chris and P.T. were one and the same.

Not likely at all. But a possibility and not to be completely discounted.

Bruce Harlow took the first step in order to go back through his notes on the aborted biography of Edward Turley by requesting them from cyberspace storage on the company computer system, which he was told could be accomplished by the next morning.

Chris was floundering, Bruce thought, and had no

real reason for thinking the current crisis was related to his father's work. But if it would help Chris, whether he found anything or not, Bruce would go through his notes, even though doing so would remind him of a painful time.

P.T. had to constantly tell himself not to get overconfident. The only reason things were going as smoothly as they were was because he meticulously prepared for every eventuality.

Turley, the cops, the public . . . everybody was reacting pretty much exactly as he had expected they would, which made things even easier.

But there was so much more to accomplish and P.T. knew that even the most perfectly designed battle plans always changed after the enemy was met. This war would not be any different.

Now, for instance, there was a situation to be dealt with. P.T. had expected it, he just hadn't thought it would come up this soon. But he would handle it and then pick up where he left off.

He would be ready for whatever they threw at him.

TWO DAYS WENT BY without violence or any contact between Chris and P.T.

Chris did not find the respite to be particularly anxiety reducing, since he had no doubt that it would all resume, on P.T.'s timing and terms. He tried to keep busy by doing some research on a three-part story he had long planned about the New Jersey Supreme Court, but concentration was almost impossible.

There was only one story that mattered now and all he could do was wait for the next chapter to be written.

It was an annoyance to Chris that he had to remain in a mostly reactive mode. But there was nothing he could do about it. Absent an arrest, the media ball was clearly in P.T.'s court.

For Bruce Harlow, going through all the material related to the researched but unwritten Edward Turley biography was a daunting task. It consisted of seventy-one separate computer files, each relating to a specific part of Edward's overall history, be it a job, a story, or a personal relationship.

His belief was that it would be a waste of time.

There would be no smoking gun to find, just a long list of people who Edward had placed under the searing media spotlight, many of whom couldn't handle it. But whether any of them could have sworn some kind of bizarre, deadly revenge on the world, particularly involving Edward's son, was not something that Bruce or Chris would have any way of knowing.

Of course, if he turned the list over to the FBI, they would have the manpower to track each person down and maybe make some progress.

Not that Bruce had anything else important to do these days. Cathy, his wife of fifteen years, had left him four months earlier, citing a sudden uncertainty that marriage was for her. She said this in the form of a message left on his answering machine while he was at work, from a location that she neglected to share with him.

Her uncertainty likely had dissipated since then, as he had not heard a word from her since. He knew it was over and felt he was in the process of dealing with it emotionally, though every time the phone or doorbell rang he felt a pang of hope that she was coming back.

Bruce went into his study, turned on the classical music that he always listened to when he worked, and turned on his computer. He spent almost an hour just going through the files for the purpose of organizing them. There was a huge amount of material, a painful reminder of all the work put in on a book that had gone nowhere.

Two separate files were devoted to Hansbrough,

which was clearly the biggest story of Edward Turley's career, a career that was filled with big stories.

Hansbrough was Roger Hansbrough, a man whose army career began as a captain in Vietnam, where he was awarded the Silver Star for valor. That medal was the beginning of a rise up the ranks all the way to two-star general, with the promise of more. Knowledgeable people felt that secretary of the army was definitely within his reach, and even chairman of the Joint Chiefs was not out of the question.

General Hansbrough was ultimately in charge of army procurement, which meant that it was his job to oversee the arming, clothing, housing, and feeding of the soldiers. He took over the job in 1990, and it assumed an even greater importance a year later, as Desert Storm approached.

The war was obviously going to be fought in adverse weather conditions, with sandstorms and intense heat a given. There was also the expectation of unconventional methods to be used by the enemy, including roadside bombs and sniper fire. Most feared of all was the possibility that Saddam Hussein might unleash biological or chemical weapons on the advancing troops.

The U.S. Army was not properly equipped for all of these eventualities, a situation which General Hansbrough was called upon to rectify. Congress opened the financial spigot; money was not an object in the urgent task of getting the soldiers what they needed on a timely basis. And it all went through Hansbrough.

In the heat of the situation, controls were lax and the temptation for Hansbrough proved too great. He accepted bribes from defense contractors eager to carve out a place on the gravy train and, even more significantly, he looked the other way as quality suffered.

An informant initially put Edward Turley on the story, but he grabbed on to it and would not let go. By the time he finished, Hansbrough was court-martialed, the first U.S. general in more than a hundred years to suffer that indignity.

But the story did not end there. Every contractor who cut corners on armor, weapons, and other necessities for the troops came under Turley's microscope and more than twenty people at various levels went to jail.

The rest of the media jumped on the story, as well, and the country, swept up in a wartime patriotic fever, was rightfully outraged by these criminals. Turley received enormous credit and acclaim for exposing them and it cemented his already extraordinary reputation.

Now Chris believed it possible that one of those people was out there killing, in a warped attempt to get revenge for what Edward did. It was clearly a reach, but one that Bruce was willing to take the time to pursue.

The fact was, the upside to doing it was more than just helping Chris and possibly finding a killer. Bruce knew very well that if he found something and the crime was solved, he could name his price on a book deal.

Stanley Cates knew he had a bargaining chip the size of South Dakota well before Novack called. As a defense attorney, he represented a number of women who shared Charity's profession, and he usually pleaded the cases out for a fine and sometimes limited prison time, depending on the number of offenses the accused had in her past.

He had even represented Charity herself on three separate occasions, but this time was very different. First of all, the connection to the mayor obviously made it a very special case, one that the public would be intensely curious about. But now that the incident was at least loosely tied to the lunatic out there killing people, it gave it a still higher priority.

The authorities would want to know exactly what Charity knew, especially who could have been aware that she was seeing the mayor that night. Obviously, P.T. was one of those people who had that information, since he gave it to Chris Turley.

Cates wanted P.T. to be caught as much as anybody else, but he still had a client to defend. Charity would tell the cops whatever she knew, if anything, but only when he had a deal in place to drop the charges. It would be the easiest deal he ever made.

Cates and Novack had always had a pretty good relationship, mainly because they both avoided bullshit whenever possible. So when Novack called asking to meet with Charity, Cates told him the situation straight out. "You can talk to her, but then she walks," he said.

"Defense attorneys are my favorite people," Novack said.

"Careful. Some day you might need one. So, do we have a deal?"

"I'll get back to you."

"Good," Cates said. "We're due in court in a few days. You can come along with the assistant prosecutor, have him drop the charges, and then we'll meet in an anteroom right there. Of course, I'll have to clear this with my client, but that shouldn't be a problem. That work for you?"

"See you then," said Novack and he hung up.

BRUCE HARLOW STARTED GOING through individual files and taking notes at about 7:00 P.M., right after dinner. He fell asleep while doing so at about 8:30, and an hour later was awakened by the doorbell. This time the pang of hope that Cathy was returning was strong, since it was unlikely that anyone else would be stopping by at that hour. He lived in a wooded area in Pomona, a Rockland County community on the New Jersey side of the Hudson River, and the nearest neighbor was more than five hundred yards away.

By the time Bruce got to the door, his hope had diminished in the face of logic. Cathy had a key and therefore would not be ringing the doorbell. Unless, of course, she thought he might have another woman over. Her thinking that, Bruce knew, was even less likely than it being true.

Bruce pulled back the curtain on the small window in the front door, saw who it was, and opened it.

"What are you doing here?" were his last words as the poison dart hit him in the neck.

P.T. didn't bother answering the question. Instead, he closed the door behind him and stepped over Bruce's body. He gathered up Bruce's computer and the notes he had begun taking, then picked up the phone.

He dialed 911, and the operator answered in an incongruously bored voice, "Nine-one-one, emergency."

P.T. didn't say anything, just put the phone down without severing the connection. That way the police would trace the call back to the house and come see if anything was wrong. A murder would definitely qualify as something wrong.

P.T. wanted Bruce's body to be discovered quickly, so he could move the process along.

Timing was everything.

Novack called Chris at midnight to ask him if he knew Bruce Harlow. Chris was in bed, making notes for the story he was planning to write the next day.

"Yes, he writes for the paper. Why?"

"He's dead."

The news was like a punch in the chest for Chris, and for the moment he found it difficult to take a breath. "How?"

"Same as Oswald, a poison dart. You know anything about this?"

"I know it was my fault."

This time Novack didn't question Chris on his own. He told Chris to come to Harlow's house and then he and Quinlan would question him together. Neither man had a problem doing that; it was long past time to worry about turf wars and they were beginning to trust each other.

An upset Chris dressed quickly, so much so that he

forgot to put socks on. He went out to the car, but came back in to get his cell phone, just in case P.T. called him. It was infuriating to him that P.T. controlled him in that way, but there was nothing he could do about it.

Chris made the thirty-minute drive to Bruce's house in less than twenty minutes. He took the Palisades Interstate, which led him past the exit where he'd found Oswald's body hanging from the tree. Remembrances of how P.T. was destroying his life were popping up all over.

When he arrived, Quinlan and Novack were waiting for him with their questions. Chris told them about his approaching Bruce and asking him to go through his notes on the book, in the hopes of getting a lead on who P.T. might be.

Quinlan's irritation was obvious. "So now you're playing detective? Who are you, one of the Hardy Boys?"

"I thought it was a long shot," Chris said. "If he found anything, I was going to come to you with it."

"That's big of you."

"Chris," Novack said, "you come to us with everything. You understand?"

"I didn't want my father dragged through this if I was wrong."

"Your father's dead, asshole," Quinlan said. "And so is Oswald, and so are the people in that building, and the old guy on the snowblower. And maybe Harlow could've helped us figure out who's doing the killing, but now he's dead, too. And all because you believed your own media bullshit and tried to be a hero again."

Chris was angry at being spoken to like that, but his anger was tempered by his knowledge that Quinlan was right. "Did you find his notes?"

Quinlan frowned as Novack said, "No notes, no computer, nothing."

"Shit," Chris said.

Novack nodded. "You got that right."

Since Harlow's house had become a restricted crime scene area, Chris was able to get out the back way without the press following him. Bruce's death was the capper to what was already an overwhelming weight he was feeling.

Somehow, though he had no idea why, people were dying because of him. There had been other deaths, and Chris had been involved because P.T. had brought him into it. But the death of his friend Bruce Harlow was directly, unambiguously his fault.

The impact of this realization was almost too much for him to bear. It was so unlike anything he had ever experienced, ever felt, that he had no idea how to summon the tools to deal with it. He didn't even feel like he could afford the time to mourn; every ounce of his focus had to be devoted to understanding why this was happening. Only in that way could he hope to prevent still more murders.

Almost without realizing that he was doing it, he drove to Dani's home instead of his own. He first checked in with the officer sitting in the squad car in front; the officer was familiar with him and had been told he could come and go as he wished.

He went to the front door and rang the bell. After a few minutes the curtain was pulled back and Dani saw he was there. She opened the door.

"Chris . . ."

"Bruce Harlow is dead."

Her hand went to her mouth. "Oh, no."

"I'm sorry . . . I just didn't want to be alone."

She looked at him and said, "I know the feeling." Then she hugged him and pulled him inside, closing the door behind them.

Chris decided not to write a story tying Bruce's death to P.T. It wasn't because he had no proof; the chance that Harlow's death was a coincidental murder was so remote as to be off the charts. He also didn't remain silent at the behest of Quinlan and Novack, though they clearly preferred it. Those were decisions that it was proper for Chris to make himself.

Rather, he didn't write it because to do so accurately would be to reveal to the world that this nightmare somehow involved his father. It would set off wild speculation and finger pointing among the public and Chris felt that unintended consequences might result.

The truth, though Chris didn't even want to admit it to himself, was that he was protecting his father.

THIS WAS NOT GOING to be a fun day for Stanley Cates.

As the defense attorney for Charlene Manson, aka Charity, the hooker who was in Mayor Stanley's room at the Claremont Hotel, it was just last week that he successfully argued for her to be released on bail.

But on this day, he and his client were supposed to appear in court before Judge Henderson on some procedural matters. He would be there, but he was quite certain that his client would not.

Cates had been trying to reach Charity for the last four days, to no avail. He had managed to contact some of her friends and coworkers, who claimed to have no idea where she was. They feared for her safety, but Cates was sure she had just run off. It wouldn't be the first time it had happened to him.

He had his own safety to fear for. Judge Henderson was nicknamed "Hatchet" by attorneys who practiced in his court, and it was not a term of endearment. Nor was it a sign that he treated attorneys with deference or kid gloves. Unfortunately, the only person the judge would have available to be angry at for Charity's absence would be Cates.

The prosecution, citing the overriding public importance of the case, had argued for a prohibitively high bail, but Cates had successfully prevailed on Hatchet for a bail of $50,000. It had been posted and Charity had been out that afternoon.

The assistant prosecutor, Norman Trell, entered the courtroom, along with Novack. Trell looked over at the defense table and noticed that Cates was alone, the defendant nowhere to be seen. Their eyes met and Trell's look was one of sympathy. He had been the subject of Hatchet's anger in the past and wouldn't wish it on anyone, not even an opposing defense attorney.

Novack's expression was somewhat less sympathetic and Cates realized that Hatchet was not the only person who was going to be pissed at him. And Novack was the type who stayed pissed.

There seemed to be a delay in Hatchet taking his seat behind the bench and it stretched on for fifteen minutes. Finally, the bailiff walked over to both Cates and Trell and told them that Judge Henderson wanted to meet with them in his chambers.

Cates assumed that Hatchet had found out Charity was not in attendance and wanted to destroy her lawyer in private. When they got back there, Hatchet was sitting behind his desk, not wearing his robe.

"Gentlemen, I've just received a phone call." He turned to Cates. "Your client's body was just recovered from the Passaic River."

An interesting media phenomenon was developing in the ongoing P.T. story. The *Daily News* had revealed that the FBI and police believed that the murder of Bruce Harlow was directly tied to the case, but Chris did not confirm it. As a result, the accuracy of the *News*'s story was widely doubted.

Chris was, by this time, considered by the public to be the only authoritative source on the case. If he said something, it was taken as gospel. If he didn't, it was considered to be of questionable credibility.

No one could remember a precedent for one reporter or media outlet having cornered the market for credibility. The most obvious comparison, that of Woodward and Bernstein of *The Washington Post* on Watergate, really didn't fit the bill. Many other media outlets advanced that story; the *Post* simply led the march.

When it came to P.T. and the murders that were dominating the airwaves, Chris Turley was the proverbial horse's mouth.

But days had gone by, and the horse's mouth had nothing new to report. Charity's death was kept under wraps by the authorities and Chris was not even informed of it. Quinlan was of the school that said information was to be gathered but not shared, unless there was something to be gained by sharing it. He saw no upside in confiding in Chris.

The net effect of all this was to make the public think that there had been at least a lengthy pause in P.T.'s efforts, even though the truth was that two people had died during that time. This perceived gap fueled speculation that the killing spree could be over, that perhaps P.T. had gotten his fill.

One story out there was that Carlos Ramirez, a Patersonian who four days before had been arrested and jailed on a charge of domestic violence, was in reality P.T., and that the murders had stopped because he was behind bars.

It was a measure of the combustible nature of rumors surrounding the story that this particular one was started by Carlos's wife, Carmela. She told a courthouse reporter for the *Bergen Record* that she believed her husband to be P.T. She had no evidence for this, which did not deter the reporter in the slightest.

The truth was that Carmela was tired of getting slapped around, and she reasoned that if Carlos was suspected of being a murderer, he would spend more time in jail, and therefore, more time away from her.

It was quite effective. Even though Novack and Quinlan completely discounted the possibility that Carlos was P.T., the arresting officers did some extra due diligence and discovered an outstanding assault warrant against Carlos in Miami.

Carmela was off the hook for three to five years.

"ALL OF A SUDDEN you've gone shy on me, Chris?"

The call from P.T. was on his home phone this time, jolting him awake at 6:00 A.M., two days after the discovery of Charity's body. Chris experienced an instant feeling of dread mixed with exhilaration, and he quickly searched for a piece of paper and pen to take notes. Then he decided not to bother, since all his conversations were being recorded by the FBI anyway.

"What does that mean?"

"Two people have died, yet you haven't seen fit to write about them? That's a little disrespectful to their memory, don't you think? And what about the public's right to know?"

Chris was confused by P.T.'s referring to two murders. One must be Bruce Harlow, but the other was a mystery to him. "Two people?"

"You mean they don't tell you what's going on? You're out of the loop?"

"Who are the two people?" Chris asked.

"One was your writer friend, who by the way was a better writer than you by a long shot. He could paint a picture with his words, Chris, while all you do is string sentences together. I'm going to miss reading his work."

"Who else?"

"The mayor's little girlfriend."

"Charity?"

"Charity," P.T. confirmed. "Now why didn't you write about your friend's death?"

"I didn't want to."

An edge crept into P.T.'s voice. "Is that right? You think you're calling the shots here?"

"I'll write what I want, when I want to."

"So you're taking a stand on this?" P.T. asked.

"The statement speaks for itself," Chris said.

"Fair enough. Now I'll try a statement that speaks for itself. Because of your attitude, someone is going to die tomorrow morning at eleven forty-seven. And that person's death will be on your head."

"Wait a minute . . . there must be a way . . ."

P.T. cut him off. "Suicide is painless, Chris."

Click.

Chris hung up the phone and immediately called Novack. He didn't bother calling Quinlan, since if he hadn't heard the call live, he would be notified about it any minute.

Within thirty minutes, both Novack and Quinlan were in his kitchen drinking coffee. Those thirty minutes had given Chris the time to grow more and more upset.

"What the hell am I going to do?" Chris asked.

"You're not going to do anything," Quinlan said. "And you sure as hell better not write about this."

"Are you out of your mind? Someone is going to die, and I even know what time it's going to happen. People have a right to know that and protect themselves."

"All you're going to do is cause a panic," Quinlan said. "And for what? How the hell are people going to protect themselves?"

Chris was adamant about his decision. "That's up to them. They can hide in their basements. They can leave the country. They can go to church and pray for their safety. Maybe none of it will work, but they deserve the chance to try."

It was something that both Quinlan and Novack had thought about on the way over there. Chris was right; the public did have a right to know the danger that was out there, especially since it was so specific. But that was a decision that would be made at a level way higher than either of them.

"I think you may be right about that," Quinlan admitted. "But leave it to us to tell them."

"I left it for you to tell them about Harlow, and look where we are," Chris said. "And Charity . . . for God's sake, why couldn't you even tell me about her? What about my damn right to know?"

"We are not partners here, Turley," said Quinlan. "Our job is to protect people's lives; your job is to sell newspapers. The way it works is you tell us everything and we tell you what we think you should know. I would have thought you understood that by now."

"I'm writing about this," Chris said.

"Be careful, Chris," Novack said.

"Of what? I'm not going to sit here with my thumb up my ass while somebody dies tomorrow because I didn't warn them."

"Their government will warn them."

"Maybe, maybe not. But I'll do it either way."

"Novack's right," said Quinlan. "You'd better be careful. I still have you as a suspect in this. I can have you arrested and showering with twenty-five felons by this afternoon. And when they strip search you, there'll be no place to hide your goddamn type-writer."

"You do what you have to do," Chris said. "But if you lock me up, P.T. will start killing people until you let me out. It's all about me, and he's not going to let you take me out of the picture."

He paused and looked at them both. "It's all about me," Chris continued. "And it's all about my father."

Not surprisingly, when Chris spoke to Lawrence he strongly endorsed Chris writing the story. He even speculated that if they did not run it, the paper could be liable for a lawsuit from the family of someone killed by P.T. at 11:47 the next morning.

Chris decided to leave out P.T.'s "suicide is painless" comment. He appeared to be suggesting that Chris commit suicide, but Chris didn't think including that advanced the story in a meaningful way. The focus of Chris's piece would be on the threat.

Once Chris was finished, Scott Ryder made sure the article was up on the Web site immediately, and a special afternoon edition was published to get it out on the street.

If the public was to be adequately informed, time was of the essence.

P.T.'S MESSAGE:
"TOMORROW AT 11:47 A.M., SOMEONE ELSE IS GOING TO DIE"
by Chris Turley

He called me this morning to convey the threat, and he made it clear that he considered it a retaliation for my refusing to write about two other murders that he committed.

One of those victims was Bruce Harlow, a superb writer and colleague of mine at this newspaper. The other was a prostitute who went by the name of Charity, and who was with Mayor Alex Stanley in his hotel room when he was arrested.

I had not written about Mr. Harlow's murder because I was not aware of any concrete evidence implicating P.T. in the murder, and I was not aware of Charity's death at all until P.T.'s phone call.

But P.T. was not interested in my explanations; he pronounced my behavior to be the cause of a murder he vows to commit at precisely 11:47 A.M. tomorrow.

I have no idea who his intended victim is,

what the method will be, or whether in fact he intends to go through with it. But I felt compelled to voice this warning because there seems to be no line that P.T. will not cross.

THE REACTION TO P.T.'S threat basically took two forms.

First was a widespread fear and borderline panic, as people resolved that they and their loved ones would stay home at the appointed time. Of course, since Clark Hendricks was killed in his home, there was no guarantee that doing so represented any kind of immunity.

It was estimated that, in the six hours following the publication of the story, more than one million people left the metropolitan area, and hotels in states like Massachusetts, Pennsylvania, and Delaware were said to be experiencing a huge influx of short-term guests.

Second was the defiance of a smaller segment of the public, who outspokenly said that they would not live in fear and that P.T. would not be allowed to control their lives. There were even those who organized hasty "P.T. parties," public gatherings designed to show off their fearlessness. It was impossible to determine how much of this was bravado, but there would certainly be very few people who would be completely comfortable at 11:47 that morning.

The number and size of such parties was also limited by two other factors: The fact was that it was a normal workday and people generally couldn't just walk away from their jobs. Also, there weren't that many fearless people around willing to tempt fate in such a manner.

The official government advice was, not surprisingly, a compromise position that satisfied few. It admitted that P.T. was a real danger, and that his warnings were to be taken seriously, but it also suggested that people go about their lives while taking prudent precautions. Anything strange was to be reported to the authorities immediately and special tip lines were set up to receive the calls.

By now there were a hundred and eighty agents assigned to Quinlan's FBI task force, none of whom had as yet turned up a single solid lead that might help them find P. T.

All overtime and vacations were canceled for every local police force in New York and northern New Jersey, and every available officer was out on the street. None of them had the slightest idea what they were looking for.

Like Chris, all they could really do was wait to see who was going to die.

And hope that P.T. would make his first mistake.

Vince Gregory fit squarely into the "I'm not going to let that bastard run my life" camp. It wasn't anything new for him; he was taking plane trips right after 9/11 and never let those colored terror alerts change his behavior one iota.

Vince had a business lunch planned that day at

noon. It was important to him, as it was with a major client of his office supply business. But he received a call at 9:00 that morning canceling the lunch, with the client claiming a "head cold that he couldn't shake."

Both the client and Vince knew the reason was non-sense and the client didn't even throw in a fake cough or sneeze to lend credibility to his story. He had made a decision that it was safer to be at home, Vince knew, perhaps curled up in his cellar, hoping P.T. would target someone else.

Not Vince. He'd go to lunch by himself and he'd have his choice of tables.

Not that he didn't take precautions. He carefully searched the inside and outside of his car for previously planted explosive devices and found nothing. There was a limit to how meticulous the search could be and it certainly was possible that he missed it.

But it was a chance he was willing to take.

The restaurant was in Edgewater, a half-hour ride from Vince's home in Wyckoff. The ride on Route 208 and then Route 4 was much faster than normal, as mid-day traffic was as light as he had ever seen it. It was about a week until Christmas; in past years these roads would be filled with holiday shoppers. Vince smiled to himself; there must be a lot of "head colds" going around.

He turned off Route 4 into Fort Lee at 11:42. There were maybe a third as many people around as normal. Most of them were looking around warily, casting frequent glances at their watches. Some others seemed unconcerned and possibly unaware; Vince figured those people must have been dropped in from Mars that morning.

At 11:45, Vince turned on to Lemoine Avenue. He wasn't sure if his watch was even right and he wondered if possibly it was slow and P.T. had struck already. He turned to a news station, where he knew they would be monitoring events religiously.

The announcer said it was "eleven forty-six, just one minute to go." Vince couldn't help but feel a twinge of nervousness, though he knew the odds against him being a target were astronomical.

He stopped at a light and the radio announcer intoned that the "moment of truth" had been reached. Vince looked over at the bus stop next to him and saw an elderly woman sitting, waiting on the bench for the bus. Next to her was a newspaper vending machine, with an ad emblazoned on it for the *Bergen News*, showing a photo of Chris Turley, their star reporter.

Vince didn't really have time to appreciate the full irony of that, because the scene he was staring at completely disappeared in a huge fireball. The bench, the woman, the newspaper machine . . . all of it was engulfed, and Vince's car was thrown about fifteen feet, rolling over and coming to rest upside down.

The car's windows on the passenger side exploded inward, and Vince's face became a mass of blood. Miraculously, his eyes were spared in the barrage.

Vince tried to get out of the car, but soon realized he was pinned down and needed help. It felt like it took a month for that help to arrive, but it was really only a few minutes.

During those few minutes, he realized that his bravado was a thing of the past. He had not been the target; that honor was reserved for that poor, old woman. But it had been close enough that he would never tempt that fate again.

P.T. would undoubtedly threaten to strike again, and when he did, Vince would feel a head cold coming on.

THE BOMBING AT THE bus stop elevated the story from national to international.

Friendly governments around the world expressed sympathy and offered help, though obviously there was nothing for them to do. Unfriendly nations professed it to be a sign that the American system was morally bankrupt and crumbling.

Pundits proclaimed it to be a new chapter in the war on terror. This was homegrown and not ideological, and it was grim proof that a well-armed person or group, without conscience, could create disproportionate havoc in the populace.

The governor of New Jersey was resisting those who were suggesting he call up the National Guard. The truth was that there was no significant help that they could provide; this remained essentially a police effort.

New businesses cropped up overnight. People who claimed to have dogs that were trained to uncover explosives were charging a hundred dollars to have their dogs sniff cars and two hundred for homes. Service stations and body shops were also selling their services to make sure that customers' cars were "clean."

In two cases, explosive devices were actually found

on cars. The FBI's experts found them simple but very well designed; it was obvious that their adversary knew quite well what he was doing.

The materials used to make the bomb mechanisms were common, had many nonlethal uses, and were sold in all hardware stores. Those stores were canvassed and records were obtained of all purchases of those items made by credit card. If the purchases were made with cash, there was, of course, no record kept and no trace possible.

People were not only scared, they were also understandably angry. Of course, P.T. bore the brunt of that anger, but citizens looked for other outlets, as well. The FBI was not doing enough, they felt. With all their resources, they couldn't catch one guy?

Chris represented another target. What had he done to create such fury? And how could he possibly not have any idea who was behind it?

More than seventy-one thousand "tips" came in to hot lines set up for that purpose. They were broken down into various levels of credibility and were followed up in fashion. So far nothing had come close to panning out.

Chris's life had basically been shut down. He went from home to office and back, and did nothing except write a story each day and wait for P.T. to call.

He continued to worry about Dani, but didn't want to visit her because of the additional attention it would bring to where she lived. They spoke on the phone, but since they knew they were being listened to, those conversations were strained.

"I wish I could see you," he said during one of their calls, before explaining why he didn't want to go to her house.

"I feel the same way," she said, then yelled, "You hear that, FBI? We want to have sex!"

He laughed; she seemed to have a consistent ability to make him do that. "I've got an idea," he said. "Why don't you stay here?"

"You're asking me to move in with you?" she asked, a touch of amusement in her voice.

"Why not? With all the police and reporters outside, this is the safest place in the country. Why shouldn't we be together?"

"Works for me," she said.

"Great." They agreed that she would pack some suitcases and come over, sneaking in the back way while he was at the office and therefore fewer reporters would be on hand.

By that night, Dani had moved in and once again, Chris was stunned at how good it felt to be with her. They went to bed early and made love. Afterwards the conversation inevitably drifted back to the current crisis.

"I don't know how you're able to handle this kind of pressure," Dani said. "I don't think I could survive it."

"I think that's the point," he said.

"What do you mean?"

"I don't know how P.T. sees this ending up," he said. "But I don't think my survival is part of it."

FBI Agent Samuel Morris arrived at the Charles Anthony Insurance Agency, identified himself, and told the receptionist that he needed to speak with Doris Randolph. Morris was an agent based in the St. Louis office, one of many recently brought in to beef up the already bloated task force.

The receptionist called and told Doris the FBI was there to speak with her and Doris felt a jolt of fear shoot through her.

They were after Peter.

She told herself to remain calm and invited Agent Morris back to her office. "How can I help you?" she asked.

"I just have a few questions relating to an investigation we're conducting. Your son was Gerald Randolph?"

She nodded. "Yes, that's correct. He's deceased."

Morris already knew that, which was one of the reasons he considered this interview a waste of time. A dead man made an unlikely suspect, but the directive had gone out that everyone with even a tangential association to someone "wronged" by Edward Turley was to be questioned. "When did he pass away?"

"More than twenty years ago. Why are you interested in Gerald?"

"I'm sorry, but I understand he took his own life?"

"Yes."

"I realize this seems intrusive, but it's quite important. Can you tell me why he did so?"

"Gerald was very depressed; he was an unhappy soul. We tried to bring him out of it. Perhaps today, with the proper medication, he could have—"

Morris interrupted. "Are you familiar with the name 'Edward Turley'?"

"The journalist?"

"Yes. Did Gerald ever mention him?"

"Not that I can recall."

Morris thought that highly unlikely, but let it pass. This woman was trying to protect her son's memory. "Edward Turley broke a major scandal about defense contractors; your son was one of the people mentioned in some of those stories."

"My son did nothing wrong."

"But were those stories a factor in his depression?"

"I don't believe so. No," she lied.

"Did Gerald have any siblings?"

"No."

"Any children?"

She stiffened slightly. She wanted to say no, but if they knew enough about Gerald to have looked her up, they probably knew about Peter. She nodded. "He had a son."

"Where is he now?" he asked.

"He lives in California."

Agent Morris asked a few more questions, then thanked her and left. He thought she seemed nervous, but that was a common occurrence in people being questioned by the FBI. He would file a report, but would do or say nothing that would call special attention to it.

When he left, Doris struggled to keep her emotions under control. She was upset that she'd lied to the agent, but not because she feared retribution.

She was upset because she felt compelled to lie, which could mean only one thing.

She was not positive that her grandson was not a murderer.

CHRIS SPENT HOUR AFTER hour going through his father's old records and files, having gotten them out of storage.

It was an incredibly difficult task. Even understanding much of it was a challenge, since the notes Edward had taken were meant for himself and therefore were often cryptic and incomplete.

Additionally, in making the notes Edward focused on the positive aspects of his work; he was not chronicling those whom he hurt to the point where they might have a grudge against him. And his career was so long and all-encompassing that the possibilities were endless.

Working in Chris's favor was his access to the archives of the *Bergen News*. Anything he found that interested him he could call Scott Ryder and ask him to cross-reference with the paper's records. Scott would get back to him with chapter and verse on everything that had been reported about the subject since he crossed paths with Edward, and this allowed Chris to eliminate and not waste time on a number of candidates.

Dani proved to be invaluable to this process. She

was a tireless and efficient researcher and covered more ground than Chris. She also was careful, and rather than summarily dismissing a person as unlikely, she would check with Chris before doing so.

But hanging over their heads, every moment of the day, was that it had been two days since the last bombing, and P.T. had not called again.

The tip came in to the FBI hot line at three o'clock in the afternoon.

"I know who P.T. is. I'm sure of it." It was a woman's voice and when the agent on the other end tried to get her name, as was standard procedure, she resisted. "I want to remain anonymous," she said. "I'm afraid."

"No problem," the agent said agreeably. "Just please tell me your information."

"There's a man named Wallace Timmerman . . . everybody calls him 'Wally.' He's the man you're after."

"What makes you say that?"

"He knows all about explosives. He works for a construction company, and he does the demolition work on buildings."

"Is that all?"

"He hates the reporter, Chris Turley. Keeps saying that he deserves to be the next to be blown up."

This was becoming a common refrain and did not impress the agent much. For some reason, Chris Turley was becoming the target of a great deal of public anger, as if this entire thing was his fault. "Do you know why he hates Mr. Turley?"

"I do, but I'm not sure I should say," the woman said.

"That would be information we would need for follow-up," the agent said patiently.

She sounded very hesitant, as if weighing every word. "Well, about ten years ago, there was a big scandal . . . a child pornography ring which went clear across the country . . . quite a few people were arrested."

"And?" the agent pressed, since many other calls were waiting.

"And Mr. Timmerman was a schoolteacher, but he was caught up in this ring."

"How does this relate to Mr. Turley?"

"Well, it doesn't, not exactly. But the man who broke the story was Edward Turley, his father. He put Mr. Timmerman's picture on television and then they arrested him. He was in jail for a year and his wife left him. So he's hated Mr. Turley ever since, just because of his father."

The suspicion that P.T. might have held a grudge against Edward Turley, as well as his son, was not public knowledge. That gave this tip high-priority credibility and it was immediately flagged and sent up the ladder to be investigated further.

The file on Wallace Timmerman reached Frank Serrano's desk in just two hours. The speed reflected the incredible urgency assigned to every aspect of the P.T. investigation, but the most significant fact was that it got to Serrano at all. Most investigative tips on this case reached a quick and disappointing dead end.

This one didn't.

The basic facts of the woman's story were confirmed, and after reading the details, Serrano considered it significant enough to bring to Quinlan's attention.

Quinlan was skeptical, mainly because, despite Bruce Harlow's death, he still had doubts about an Edward Turley connection to P.T. He shook his head. "This is bullshit."

"You've got a drawer full of better leads?"

"I've got nothing," Quinlan said. "When can you talk to him?"

"I've got four other interviews to conduct. I can do it tomorrow afternoon, or I can send other agents over to do it."

"No, you do it. But first I'll ask Turley if this guy's name rings a bell."

Serrano nodded. "Okay. Let me know."

Quinlan had been calling Chris with some frequency. It came from a belief that somewhere in the recesses of Chris's mind there had to be the answer. He had to have had some contact with P.T., something that could have triggered this mayhem, and Quinlan felt that by prodding, he could get Chris to access it.

Quinlan reached Chris at his office and, as usual, dispensed with the pleasantries and jumped right in. "The name Wallace Timmerman mean anything to you?"

Chris was taken by surprise, since Wallace Timmerman had come up in the research of his father's files. "Yes. He got caught up in a child pornography ring my father exposed. He went to jail."

Quinlan was surprised. "You answered pretty quickly. You remember this guy very well?"

"No, I didn't remember him at all. I've been looking back at my father's career, and I ran across his name."

"Any other names you've run across?" Quinlan asked, his irritation showing.

"You'll be the first to know if I come across any real possibilities," Chris said.

"And you don't think Timmerman fits that bill?"

"No way."

"Why not?"

"There's no history of violence, and by all indications he's been turning his life around. Why after all these years would this be coming out?"

"If this is all because of a grudge against your father, then it's by definition years old," Quinlan pointed out.

"I know, but there has to be a recent trigger. I didn't see that with Timmerman. But I'll think about it some more."

At that point, Scott Ryder walked past Chris's office and Chris signaled for him to come in and wait while he finished the call. "How long do I have?" Chris asked Quinlan.

"First thing in the morning," Quinlan said.

They hung up and Chris turned to Scott. "A couple of days ago I asked you to go through the archives for information on Wallace Timmerman."

Scott nodded. "The porn guy."

"Right. Can you dig some more on him?"

"I gave you all we have here, but I can check some other databases."

"Are there others?" Chris asked.

Scott smiled, amazed at Chris's lack of understanding of the cyberworld. "There are always other databases. When do you need it?"

"I have to give the FBI whatever I have no later than first thing in the morning."

Scott nodded. "You got it."

Like everything else involved in this investigation, the FBI opted to take extra precaution in the questioning of all potential suspects, and Wallace Timmerman was certainly no exception.

Frank Serrano would conduct the interview with another agent accompanying him, and three other agents would provide backup outside in case anything went wrong.

In the morning, an agent posing as a friend of Timmerman's went to his office at the construction company, and determined that he had taken the day off, allegedly to go to a doctor's appointment. Still another agent was dispatched to Timmerman's house in Leonia, and he would alert Serrano when the subject was at home.

The interview would be conducted at Timmerman's house, providing he were willing. If he refused, that would be seen as a significant sign, and Serrano would concoct a reason to bring him in for questioning. Quinlan would then conduct the interview himself, or watch Serrano do it through a two-way mirror.

Chris got to his office at eight o'clock in the morning and was surprised to see Scott Ryder waiting for him. "You got something on Timmerman?" Chris asked.

Scott shook his head. "Nothing that I didn't give you before. Since he got out of jail he's been a model citizen."

Chris nodded. "I'm not surprised. Thanks for checking."

"No problem," Scott said, but instead of leaving, he just stood there.

"Was there something else?"

"Maybe . . . I saw something that might be worth mentioning."

"Mention away," Chris said.

"Well, in going through everything, there was one guy that caught my attention. You ever hear the name 'Gerald Randolph'?"

Chris thought for a moment and said, "I don't think so. Who is he?"

"He was a general manager of a defense contracting plant that was caught up in Hansbrough. Not a major figure, apparently, but your father specifically referred to him a few times."

"So?"

"So his life fell apart. His wife had died of cancer not long before that, and then he lost his job, spent his savings on lawyers, and wound up losing his house."

Chris shook his head in sadness at the story. "Shit."

"It gets worse," Scott said. "He killed himself by taking a New Year's Eve walk out onto a highway. That's why I'm mentioning him, because P.T. mentioned suicide to you."

"I don't understand. How could he possibly be our boy if he's dead?"

"When he walked out onto the highway, his son was watching," Scott said.

"How old was the son?"

"I'm not sure, the sources I looked at were vague about it. But definitely under ten. His name was Peter."

This was something that interested Chris, since it would provide a possible explanation for why years went by before revenge was sought. The kid needed time to grow up first.

"See what else you can find out about him, okay? I don't want to go to the FBI with this until we know more."

Scott nodded. "I'm on the case."

"Thanks, and if Lawrence gives you shit about how much time you're spending on this, tell him we're working on a story that will win him a Pulitzer."

Scott laughed. "That should do the trick."

SERRANO GOT THE CALL at 1:00 P.M., telling him that Timmerman had returned home.

He was in a staff meeting that was to end at two o'clock, so he sent word to the other agents that they would plan to arrive at Timmerman's house at 3:00. In the meantime, the agent who had called would remain posted near the house, with instructions to follow Timmerman if he left before then.

At precisely three o'clock, Frank Serrano and Agent Fred Woods approached Timmerman's house, with three agents taking up positions behind them. The house was a modest two story on a private, tree-lined street in Leonia, with perhaps fifty feet separating Timmerman's house from each of his neighbors. On the garage was a rusted basketball hoop without a net, which looked as if it hadn't been used in a very long time.

Serrano rang the bell and he and Woods instinctively took a step to the side as they waited for the door to open. It did not, so he rang it again, and after another thirty seconds the door opened and Wallace Timmerman stood in front of them. He was a large man, at least six foot two, two hundred and thirty pounds.

"Yes? Can I help you?" he asked.

Serrano took out his identification and held it up, close to Timmerman's face. "Mr. Timmerman, I'm Agent Serrano and this is Agent Woods. We're with the Federal Bureau of Investigation, and we'd like to speak with you. May we come in?"

Timmerman closed his eyes and seemed to sag slightly, but quickly recovered. "What's this about?"

"May we come in, please?"

Timmerman nodded and opened the door wider. "Yeah. Of course."

He turned and they followed him in. Serrano was struck by how neat and meticulous everything was. It reminded him of his grandmother's house and seemed completely out of character for the gruff and sort of sloppy Timmerman.

"You guys want anything to drink?" Timmerman asked.

"No, thank you," said Serrano and Woods quickly seconded that.

They entered a small den and Timmerman said, "Is this okay?"

"Fine," Serrano said.

"Okay," Timmerman said, "so what d—" He was interrupted by the telephone ringing, and said, "Excuse me a second."

He picked up the phone on an end table next to a small sofa. "Hello?"

A voice on the other end said, "Mr. Timmerman, are the FBI agents with you?"

"Yes. Do you want to speak with them?"

"No, thank you. Good-bye."

By the time he put the phone down towards the cradle, there was no longer a phone. An explosion obliterated everything in the room in a massive fire, killing Timmerman and the two agents and almost bringing down the entire house.

Two of the agents outside were thrown to the ground by the force of the blast and one of them had his collarbone broken by flying debris.

Significant damage was sustained by the house on the right side of Timmerman's while the one on the left escaped with only some broken windows. One of the agents outside scrambled to his feet and called 911, while directing his partner to call Quinlan.

But they knew that there was no possibility that arriving help would do Agents Serrano and Woods any good. No one who was in that house could possibly have survived.

When Novack arrived on the scene, Quinlan had already been there ten minutes, surveying the damage. Emergency, forensics, and medical personnel were doing their work, but it was obviously a recovery operation; there was no one to be rescued.

"I'm sorry about your men," Novack said.

"Yeah," said Quinlan. "Me, too."

"Families?"

"Woods was single, but Serrano had a wife, plus a daughter from a previous marriage." He didn't bother to mention that the new widow was his own first wife. He dreaded calling her, but he wanted to tell her before she heard it elsewhere.

"Shit," Novack said.

Quinlan nodded. "Yeah." Quinlan considered all of his agents to be part of his family, and this was far from the first time that he had seen them die. But this was a particular agony, especially in the case of Serrano, who was almost literally family. Quinlan had brought him here, had requested him specifically, and now he was going home in a box.

"And Timmerman was P.T.?" asked Novack.

"Looks that way. The place blew just a few minutes after they went inside. A good bet is that something happened to make Timmerman think we were on to him, so the piece of shit decided to go down in flames."

"It couldn't have been planted by somebody else beforehand and timed to the agents' arrival?"

Quinlan shook his head. "Don't see how. We only heard about Timmerman yesterday, and we certainly didn't go public with it. I didn't even think it would pan out."

"Where'd you get the tip?" Novack asked.

"Anonymous. A female."

"So you gonna go public that P.T. is dead?"

Quinlan shrugged. "That's above my pay grade." Then, "You think we should?"

"No."

"Why not?"

"Because P.T. is smart and I don't see him going down that easily. Two agents ringing his doorbell would not send him into a suicidal panic; he would have anticipated much worse."

"There would be one positive if you're right," Quinlan said.

"What's that?"

"If he's still alive, it means I can strangle him."

CHRIS AND DANI HEARD the news while watching television.

They were watching old episodes of *Seinfeld*, which seemed to be the furthest they could get from the constant anguish and fear that news reports provided. But a special "breaking news" bulletin intruded on their sitcom escape with the revelation that an explosion was rumored to have killed two FBI agents and the owner of the house, whose name was not available. Informed speculation was that it was tied into the P.T. case, but no details or confirmations were available.

Chris called Novack but didn't get him, leaving a message asking him to return the call. Then, with nothing else to do, he and Dani sat down to wait for further bulletins.

Within an hour, the main facts of the story started leaking out, or at least the FBI's interpretation of those facts. Wallace Timmerman, registered sex offender, was the infamous P.T. When FBI agents went to his house, he decided to commit suicide rather than allow himself to be arrested and he killed two heroic agents in the process. The Bureau had not yet issued an official statement, but they weren't disputing what was being said.

There was no mention in any of the reports as to why Timmerman had gone on the killing spree, or any connection to Edward or Chris Turley.

Chris's phone was ringing incessantly, as friends and other media outlets wanted his reaction to the stunning news. He chose to screen the calls, and the only time he answered the phone was when he saw that it was Novack calling.

"How are you going to occupy your time now, hotshot?" Novack asked.

"I'll think of something. So Timmerman was P.T.?"

"Looks like it."

"Is it possible they're wrong?" Chris asked.

"Anything's possible."

"It just didn't feel like this would ever end."

"By next week you'll be back missing jump shots."

Chris and Dani spent two hours talking about what they'd been through and what had developed between them in the process. "Now that we've lived together, we can start dating," she said.

"You don't have to move out right away," Chris said.

"Yeah, I do. We need to get normal again, maybe not have the pace of our relationship dictated by a serial killer."

"But we can still have sex," Chris said, and when she didn't answer quickly, he asked, "Right?"

She smiled. "You mean right now?"

That's not what he meant, but he was quick to adjust. "That's exactly what I mean."

She shrugged. "Sure, why not? We can start dating tomorrow."

Later, after they had made love and Dani was asleep, Chris sat down to write.

Quinlan agreed with Novack that it was not certain that Timmerman was P.T., though he certainly believed that he was. The facts, flimsy as they were, pointed to Timmerman as the murderer, but the most compelling piece was still the fact that no one on the outside could have known that Serrano and Woods would be in the house that day.

But P.T. had demonstrated himself to be both resourceful and elusive in the past, and it seemed out of character to both of them that someone who had proven to be such an elaborate planner would go down so easily. This especially worried Quinlan, and he expressed his reservations to FBI Director Kramer.

Kramer did not share those reservations. The FBI had taken a lot of heat throughout this investigation, and this was an opportunity to get out in front and tell the public that, because of the work of dedicated agents who made the ultimate sacrifice, Americans could put the horror of P.T. behind them.

Quinlan tried to get Kramer to hold off, and when that failed, he pushed him to leave himself—and all of them—some wiggle room. "Don't make it so definitive," Quinlan said. "We don't know this for sure."

Kramer said that he would consider Quinlan's point

of view, but then went out and made a statement un-
equivocally announcing that Wallace Timmerman
was P.T. and that P.T. was dead.

THE P.T. STORY WILL BE WRITTEN
OVER TIME, BUT IT BEGAN WITH MY FATHER
by Chris Turley

Wallace Timmerman and two courageous FBI
agents, Frank Serrano and Fred Woods, were
killed yesterday in a massive explosion that destroyed Timmerman's house. The authorities
have made it clear that they believe Timmerman
to be the man known as "P.T.," who has been responsible for the horrible series of violent murders these last four weeks.

Though I became the unwilling and seemingly unlikely vehicle through which P.T. attempted to threaten and intimidate the public, I
have no special knowledge of the events leading
to his death. More facts will come out over time
and better reporters than I will reveal them.

But I have an inkling as to why Timmerman
chose to communicate through me. Fifteen years
ago, he was implicated in a child pornography
scandal that my father, Edward Turley, exposed.
It became the link between him and me, irrational
as it might seem, and I can only believe that he
thought he was getting revenge against my father,
and in turn against me, by connecting me to his
horrendous crimes.

I understand that little of what I am saying makes logical sense. His actions certainly do not, no doubt because of a sickness that I cannot begin to comprehend. But I will work to learn more, and I hope that all of his secrets did not die with him.

And as always, whatever I learn, I will write about it on these pages.

"HELLO," DANI SAID, AND then heard a familiar voice say, "Put your boyfriend on the phone."

Lying next to Dani, Chris came awake and could see by the look on her face that something was terribly wrong. And before she said a word, he knew exactly what that was.

She held out the phone to Chris. "It's him."

Chris took the phone and said, "You're alive."

"If I wasn't, I'd be turning over in my grave at the things you wrote today. You think I am a child pornographer? I have a sickness that you can't comprehend?"

Chris didn't know if the FBI was still listening or taping his calls, so he started jotting down notes of the call as he talked. "I thought Timmerman was you."

"You were wrong, and now people will suffer for it." Chris could hear an anger and intensity in his voice that was different from previous conversations.

"This is between you and me."

"Exactly," said P.T. "And you are the reason why I am doing what I am doing. You and your piece of garbage father."

"What did you have to do with him?"

"You're an investigative reporter, Chris, so investigate it. But I'll tell you one thing I had to do with him."

"What's that?"

"I murdered him. Right there in the supermarket." He laughed. "You and everybody else thought it was a heart attack, because you're all lazy and stupid."

"I don't believe you." Chris felt the room spinning around him, as the horror of what P.T. was saying started to register.

"I don't give a shit what you believe. You weren't there that day. Did you know he knocked over a bunch of melons when he fell? It was pretty funny."

"So you got your revenge; why do other people have to die?"

"They don't," P.T. said. "The day you take your own life, this ends. It's only fitting."

"I was right; you have a sickness that's impossible to comprehend."

P.T. laughed. "Just like you told all those readers, readers you only have because of me. Well, now you can tell them that everything that will happen today is your fault."

Click.

As soon as P.T. was off the phone, Chris called Novack on his cell phone.

Novack saw on his caller ID that it was Chris calling, so he answered the phone with, "You think I'm available to you twenty-four hours a day?"

"He's alive," Chris said. "He just called me."

"I'll be right over."

* * *

The FBI tap had not been removed from Chris's phone, not because they thought P.T. was ever going to call again, but simply because no one had remembered to order its removal. Because of that, Quinlan was notified about it within five minutes and heard the actual audio five minutes after that.

He picked up the phone and called FBI Director Kramer. It was not a conversation he was looking forward to.

"I went on goddamn national television to say this guy was dead," Kramer said. "And I did that because that's what you told me."

Both men knew that Kramer's version was not an accurate one; Quinlan had cautioned him against making such a definitive announcement. But there was no sense in bringing that up now, so Quinlan did not. "We believed Timmerman was P.T.; there was no way to be sure."

"That's a big goddamn help. This guy is going to start killing people again."

Quinlan knew that was true, but he also knew that P.T. would be out there killing whether or not they had announced that he was dead. "We've got another problem," he said.

"What the hell is that?"

"P.T. knew that our agents were at that house, yet we had only decided the day before to interview Timmerman, and we didn't set a time until a couple of hours before this went down."

"So he has a source on the inside? In the Bureau?"

"We need to face the possibility of that." Quinlan had also told Chris about Timmerman, but he couldn't have known when the interview was going to take place. Yet P.T. set off the bomb within five minutes of the agents' arrival, and the agents stationed outside would likely have noticed if anyone was there watching the house.

"Maybe you're P.T.," Kramer said.

"I wish I was."

"I'll tell that to the attorney general," Kramer said and ended the call.

Within ten minutes, everybody up the chain of the command, all the way to the president, was notified that P.T. was very much alive and they were all extraordinarily pissed off about it.

At the end of the day, somebody's head was going to have to roll for this fiasco, and Quinlan fully expected it to be his own. Which was okay; that was part of the job.

But he was going to catch the son of a bitch first.

ONE THING THAT WAS certain was that the public had to be told.

It would not be fair to have people out there thinking they did not have to continue taking self-protective measures and then have P.T. strike again. It was a public safety issue, as well as a potential political nightmare.

Quinlan pressed Director Kramer for immediate public disclosure, but the bureaucracy had a tendency to move at its own pace, which was not often swift. The word finally came down that Kramer himself would make a statement at 1:00 P.M.

Quinlan knew that Kramer did not want to be anywhere near this; he was far more comfortable announcing good news than bad. For him to make the public statement personally must have meant that the president or attorney general insisted on it. Which also likely meant that when Quinlan's head rolled, Kramer's head would be rolling right alongside it.

If there was any thought given to not going public with the new information, Quinlan knew that Chris Turley would make that moot. If past performance was any indication, he would be writing about the phone call from P.T. and the public would take his story as gospel.

Quinlan arranged to interview Chris at the FBI offices about the latest phone call and he invited Novack to join them. It's not that Chris had any information about P.T. that Quinlan hoped to glean—Quinlan heard the entire phone call replayed four times—but he wanted to know if there was any possibility that Chris could have let slip to anyone that the FBI was investigating Wallace Timmerman.

Chris brought Dani with him to the Quinlan meeting. The police protection had been withdrawn when it was thought that P.T. was dead and he didn't feel comfortable leaving her behind. Quinlan did not want her to be part of the meeting, though, so she waited in the anteroom outside his office.

"Somehow, P.T. knew that our agents were going to be at Timmerman's and when they were going to be there," Quinlan said.

Novack nodded. "Obviously."

He turned to Chris. "You were the only person outside the Bureau who knew we were looking at Timmerman."

Before Chris could answer, an annoyed Novack rushed to his defense. "Bullshit," said Novack. "What you really mean is that he was the only person you told. You've probably got a whole task force full of people who knew about it; any one of them could have been the source to somebody on the outside."

"They've all been interviewed," said Quinlan.

"And they denied it?" asked Novack, feigning surprise. "You don't think it's possible that one of them told their girlfriend that they were going to bring P.T. down that afternoon?"

Quinlan was not about to be distracted. "Who did you tell?" he asked Chris.

"I told Dani, but she was with me the whole time from then until the bombs went off," said Chris. "And Scott Ryder, our computer guy down at the paper. He does research in the archives for me."

"We'll need to interview him."

Chris nodded. "I'm sure he'll be fine with that. Are you planning to go public with the news?"

"At one o'clock."

"Okay . . . I won't post my piece on our Web site until after that."

"Thanks," Quinlan said sincerely. "I appreciate that."

"You both heard the phone call," said Chris. "So you know P.T. says he killed my father."

"I don't know the circumstances of your father's death," Quinlan said. "You think he could be telling the truth?"

"The son of a bitch hasn't lied to me yet."

"I'll check back through the police reports," Novack said. "But my recollection is it was determined at the time that he died of natural causes."

"That was then," Chris said. "This is now."

While Chris agreed to wait for Quinlan to tell the public that P.T. was still alive, P.T. himself had made no such promise. And he operated on his own schedule.

At noon, a car exploded in Stanford, Connecticut,

killing the driver and a passenger and wounding two people in an adjacent car. Fifteen seconds later, another car exploded in Lower Merion, Pennsylvania, leaving the driver dead and a pedestrian wounded. Fifteen seconds after that, a third car exploded on Jerome Avenue in the Bronx, killing the driver.

The murders represented the first time that the horror had reached outside of New Jersey into neighboring states.

Within ten minutes, television stations had interrupted their programs to report the breaking news that the explosions had taken place. FBI Director Kramer then hastily moved his press conference up to 12:45 to tell the public what they already knew.

The nightmare was not over.

And it was spreading.

THE PUBLIC'S FEAR AND anger returned to a full boil almost immediately.

The *Bergen News* switchboard was overwhelmed with calls and messages for Chris, few of them complimentary. In addition, he had seventy-one requests for interviews, not including local television and print outlets around the country.

Feelings about Chris were definitely turning towards the negative. Not only did many people think he must have done something to provoke P.T., but he had also told the public that P.T. was dead, the first time his information had proven wrong.

Chris was feeling tremendous pressure, even more than before, and he still had no clear plan for how to handle it. His newspaper articles, while being devoured by an anxious public, were clearly not enough. Love him or hate him, people wanted to hear more from Chris Turley.

Chris went in to meet with Lawrence Terry, who had been under tremendous pressure himself. He was shocked to see that seemingly overnight Lawrence looked as if he'd aged substantially.

Both men agreed that Chris was going to have to

publicly answer questions. Lawrence felt that he should do one nationally televised interview, with a relatively easygoing interviewer, perhaps Larry King again. He could spend a full hour answering questions, which would also include some phone calls from the public.

Chris disagreed, since he was not confident that an interview like that would be viewed by the public as sufficient. "What about a press conference?" he asked.

Lawrence was immediately enthusiastic. "That's a great idea. We can do it right out on the steps, in front of the building."

"It's twenty-five degrees out there."

Lawrence nodded. "All the better; those wimps will ask you fewer questions, so they can get inside and drink hot chocolate."

"Can we get this set up for tomorrow morning?"

"Absolutely. This is the goddamn story of the decade. And we'll get some of the employees of the paper to stand behind you on the steps, as a gesture of support."

"That's not necessary," Chris said.

"Are you kidding? It's an emotional grabber, all of them out there backing up their buddy . . . my goddamn eyes are filling up with tears already."

"Can you set up security in time? We don't want P.T. blowing up the entire press corps."

"You're right about that. We'll have to close off the street and get security in to sweep the area."

They agreed that it would take a while to make the necessary security arrangements and delayed the press conference until the next afternoon. They would announce it right away, though, which by itself would take some of the pressure off.

"Lawrence, there's something else," Chris said. "Something P.T. said in the last phone call."

"What's that?"

"He said he murdered my father."

"That's crazy." Lawrence shook his head. "No way. Not possible."

"Then it would be the first thing P.T. has said that wasn't true."

"Your father had a heart attack."

"But there wasn't an autopsy," Chris said.

"Of course not; it wasn't a goddamn murder." Lawrence was angry at the very thought of it. "Why the hell would there be an autopsy?"

"I'm telling you what he said."

"And I'm telling you it's a crock of shit."

Though Quinlan had told Novack and Chris that the leak about the Timmerman interview had not come from within the Bureau, he was far from sure about that. An intense investigation was immediately started to find out whether anyone in the Bureau was culpable. It was based in Washington so that Director Kramer could monitor it closely, and so that it could not be compromised by the people on the scene in New Jersey.

Somehow P.T. had found out that Timmerman was a suspect and that agents were at his house to question him. Whoever made the mistake that resulted in P.T. finding out about it had caused the deaths of two agents, as well as Timmerman himself. It was vital to find out who that person was; it might also lead them to P.T.

It was even possible that P.T. had called in the anonymous tip about Timmerman in the first place. The Bureau's voice expert said that voice translation machines could certainly change a male voice to female. If it was P.T. who had made the call, he would have therefore known that Timmerman would at least be interviewed.

Quinlan and his investigative team were also focusing on how P.T. could be so efficient in his attacks. The last three bombings had occurred almost simultaneously, many miles away from one another.

It was not possible that P.T. was on the scene in all three cases, so he was obviously detonating the devices from a remote location. Yet, in each case, the car was occupied when the bomb went off. How could P.T. have known that?

Quinlan's assumption was that he attached tiny GPS devices to the cars along with the explosives. The devices would then transmit information back to him, telling him when a car was moving. If it was, then the car had to be occupied, and a kill was a certainty.

Scott Ryder came into Chris's office after Chris's meeting with Lawrence. "You got a second?" Scott asked.

"Sure."

"The FBI wants to interview me. You know what that's about?"

"Damn, I'm sorry, I should have alerted you. They

are trying to find out how P.T. knew about Timmerman, so they asked who I told. I mentioned you. It's no big deal."

Scott seemed a little concerned. "So what should I tell them?"

"The truth."

"Really? Lawrence is always warning everyone about talking to the police, so . . ."

Chris said, "We're way past that. Just tell them the truth."

Scott smiled, clearly relieved. "Okay. Thanks." He started to leave, but stopped when Chris called to him.

"Hey, Scott . . . that guy you told me about the other day . . . the one whose father committed suicide . . ."

Scott snapped his fingers. "Right. Gerald Randolph was the father, Peter was the son. I stopped checking into it when they said that P.T. was dead."

"So you'll get back on it? You never know . . ."

"I will. Right away," Scott said, and he rushed off to do just that.

P.T. knew everything that was going on well before it happened. It made his job ridiculously easy, but was at the same time a tribute to his preparation. He was very proud of what he had already accomplished and certainly of what he was about to achieve.

He wished that he could brag about it to someone, but he knew that was impossible. It was crazy to trust anyone in this world; in fact, the ironic thing was that this whole operation was made possible because someone trusted and confided in him.

The truth was that he had no time for other people now anyway. He was going to be a very busy man.

It was time to take his plan to the next level.

IN DEFERENCE TO SECURITY CONCERNS, strict rules were instituted for the press conference.

One of those was the requirement that media outlets and their reporters would have to apply for press credentials and that the number available would be one hundred, in addition to the major networks.

Those hundred passes were given out within ten minutes of the announcement that they were available. The reporters who didn't get them were able to contain their disappointment, since they could watch it on television in indoor comfort, while the "lucky" recipients would be outside, freezing their asses off.

It was also decided that there would be only one camera crew that would provide a common feed to everyone. This was similar to how it was done in the presidential debates and the State of the Union addresses. The main difference was that the public was far more interested in this.

Chris spent the morning with Dani, who helped him prepare for the questioning. "What are you trying to accomplish?" she asked.

"I want to share whatever I know, which isn't a hell of a lot," he said.

"I don't buy it," she said. "And you shouldn't be trying to sell it."

"What do you mean?"

"If all you wanted to do was tell what you know, you could print it in the paper and put it on the Web site. You need to do more and I think you know it."

"Just in case I don't know it, please enlighten me," he said with some frustration.

"Okay. You need to make people understand that this is not your fault. People are scared, and when they're scared they don't think rationally. Some of them think that you must have done something that's brought this down on them."

"That's crazy."

"Of course it's crazy, but it's also reality. You've watched the coverage, you know what's going on out there. You need to convince people that you're on their side, that you did nothing wrong, and that you're not capitalizing on this for the sake of your career."

"How do I do that?" he asked.

"Be likable," she said, smiling. "Be yourself."

At four o'clock, fifty employees of the *Bergen News*, including a coatless Lawrence Terry, took their places on the stairs in front of the building. Chris came out moments later and stepped up to a podium in front of them. He did not have any notes with him.

"I have a brief statement to make," Chris said. "For the last few weeks, I have been receiving phone calls from a man who identifies himself only as P.T. He has claimed credit for the series of murders, mostly in the form of explosions, that have taken place during that time. I have absolutely no reason to doubt that he is, in fact, the perpetrator of these horrible crimes.

"I have written about all of these calls extensively, with the exception of the most recent one. In that one his tone was angrier, and he berated me for believing that he was really Wallace Timmerman, a registered sex offender. He also claimed to be upset that I referred to him as 'sick.'

"He went on to warn me that the deaths that would follow would be my fault, and that the only way to end this would be for me to take my own life.

"I have no idea why he chose me, other than I believe, based on things he has said and that I have written about, that it somehow relates to a grudge he holds against my father. I cannot imagine what that might be.

"Thank you. Now I'll take your questions."

He called on a print reporter from the New York *Daily News*, who asked, "How is it possible that your father could have done something to someone resulting in this overwhelming hatred, yet you have no idea who it is?"

"I wish I knew that, but I'm afraid we may not learn the answer until P.T. is caught," Chris said.

"What steps are you taking to figure it out?"

"I'm spending all of my time trying to figure it out. But this seems to be an irrational hatred, not rooted in logic. That makes it much harder." He pointed to another reporter. "Yes?"

"Whether you've done anything to provoke it or

not, when P.T. says that people are dying because of you, how does that make you feel?"

"It's the worst feeling anyone could ever have, believe me," Chris said.

"Do you think there is any truth to it?"

Chris thought for a moment before answering. "I can't say; it would involve reading his mind. But it's certainly possible that he is killing people to get back at me. At least that's what he claims."

The next questioner asked, "Is it true you've been peddling a book deal for ten million dollars?"

"That is not true," Chris said.

The follow-up question was, "So, are you saying that under no circumstances will you write a book and profit from this situation?"

"I am saying that I have not given it a moment's thought."

The questioner was insistent. "But will you commit today not to make money from writing a book about these murders?"

"I can't say it any more clearly than I just have. There are more important things to focus on right now."

The news conference went downhill from there. The questioners reflected the frustration, fear, and anger of their readers and Chris was ill-equipped to deal with it.

The bottom line was that he had no new information to offer, no way to promise that all this would soon be over, and they jumped all over him for it.

When Doris Randolph came home from work, she was not surprised to find her grandson Peter glued to the television set. Chris Turley was in the process of giving a news conference and she knew it would take a massive earthquake to prevent him from watching it.

"Peter, I stopped at the market on the way home. Can you help me get the bags out of the car?"

He just stared at the television without answering her.

"Peter?"

Again no answer, so she sighed and went outside to get the bags herself. He was clearly obsessed, lost in another world, and once again it frightened her terribly.

If she had known what Peter was looking at, and that he wasn't listening to Chris Turley or the questioners at all, it would have frightened her far more.

Because what Peter had just seen was the answer to everything.

NICK QUINLAN WAS SUMMONED to Washington to meet with FBI Director Kramer and the attorney general.

He was annoyed at having to make the trip; unless they were calling him down there to fire him, he needed to stay at the nerve center of the investigation. And there was no way they were going to fire him; that would remove a layer of blame that they were not about to peel away until this was all over.

Quinlan was kept waiting in an outer office for more than a half hour when he arrived and he thought his head was going to explode with the frustration. He also wondered where Kramer was, until he was finally led into the attorney general's office and saw that Kramer was already there. Obviously, there was a part of the meeting that Quinlan was not privy to.

"Thanks for coming down, Nick," the attorney general said. "I know how much you've got on your plate."

"And I sure as hell am not dealing with any of it sitting here" was what Quinlan wanted to say, but instead he went with, "Yes, sir. Good to be here."

Kramer said, "I've been bringing the attorney general up to date on this P.T. business, Nick, but he thought it would also be helpful for him to be able to question you directly."

Quinlan nodded. "Fine."

He proceeded to answer the attorney general's questions in a straightforward fashion, which meant honestly stating that the investigation had to date made little progress in identifying, no less apprehending, P.T.

Based on Kramer's frequent interruptions to temper the pessimism, it was obvious that he had painted a somewhat brighter picture for the attorney general. But Quinlan would have none of it; he wanted to make sure that he conveyed exactly what they were up against.

The meeting ended with the attorney general saying, "I want this man taken off the streets," which didn't exactly strike Quinlan as a revelation. But then he added, with a nod to Kramer, "I think your idea just might help us get there."

Alarm bells went off in Quinlan's head at that last comment; what could Kramer have suggested? Once they were out of the office, Quinlan asked him just that, and he said that they would talk about it on the way to the airport.

"We're going to place a story in the press," Kramer said.

"What kind of story?"

"We're going to reveal, on deep background, that

Chris Turley is a person of interest in this case, that we think he might actually be P.T."

"Why would we do that?"

"Well, first of all, you yourself said that it was possible."

"That was weeks ago."

Kramer took a file out of his briefcase and handed it to Quinlan. "Read this."

"What is it?"

"It's a new profile on P.T. that the team in Washington just cranked out."

"I will, but tell me what this has to do with Turley."

"Well, I don't want to simplify it too much; the damn thing is a hundred and forty pages of psychobabble. I only read the summary. But it talks about P.T.'s irrational hatred for Turley and the chance it could lead him to make a mistake. And we need him to make a goddamn mistake."

"So if P.T. believes that we think he is actually Turley, the guy he hates so much, he'll do something stupid?"

"Exactly."

"You mean, like go on a killing spree?"

"He doesn't seem too shy about that right now, does he?"

"This could make it much worse."

"Or it could force him into a mistake, like going after Turley himself. Killing Turley would be a sure way to prove they're not the same person. And if he tries it, we'll be waiting for him."

"Or maybe he'll come after one of us. We're the ones who are confusing him with Turley."

Kramer hesitated for a moment before he spoke; that idea hadn't crossed his mind. "That's why they're paying us the big bucks," he said, trying to force a smile.

"I just want to go on record and say that I'm opposed to this decision," Quinlan said.

"The attorney general and I want to move forward with it."

"It's your candy store."

THE MESSENGER BECOMES THE SUSPECT:
TURLEY IS UNDER SUSPICION IN P.T. CASE
by Andrea Keller

Informed sources within the FBI have revealed to *The New York Times* that Chris Turley, the New Jersey newspaper reporter who has claimed repeated contacts with the fugitive murderer known as P.T., is himself on the list of suspects.

Speaking on condition of anonymity, those sources say that the technology exists for each of the phone calls, which Turley has claimed were made by P.T., to have been staged. Turley could rather easily have been using a voice transformer to enable himself to voice both sides of the conversations. Another possibility, less likely in this scenario, is that an accomplice could be involved.

The source, who is very close to the investigation, said that "Turley shows up everywhere," and that a case against him is slowly but meticulously being constructed. "It could all fall apart," the source continued, "but right now he's high up on the list of possibilities."

"HOW THE HELL CAN she write this kind of garbage?" Chris asked.

Andrea Keller's piece in the *Times* had left him angry and upset, and as soon as he got to work he had stormed into Lawrence Terry's office, *New York Times* in hand, to vent. The public was already tilting heavily against him out of their own fear and frustration, and something like this story could put them over the edge. His personal safety, as well as Dani's, could be jeopardized.

"It's not garbage," said Lawrence.

"What does that mean? You think I'm P.T.? You think I've been calling myself on the phone and then blowing up buildings?"

"Of course not. But that doesn't mean the story is garbage. Look, I've known Andrea Keller for years; she's a terrific reporter. She would not be writing this if she didn't have it nailed down. She's got a real source on this. Probably two."

"So I'm a suspect?"

"Either that, or they want it to look like you are," said Lawrence.

Chris thought about that possibility for a few

moments. "I don't believe that Quinlan really thinks there's a chance that P.T. and I are the same person. I just don't buy it. So they must be trying to pressure me, to scare me into doing something for them."

"Any idea what that could be?" asked Lawrence.

"All along they've been asking me not to write my stories, but I don't think that would be enough to make them plant this crap. P.T. hasn't even called me again since the last one, so there's nothing for me to reveal."

"It might be a good idea for you to go out of sight for a while."

"Go into hiding?"

"Why not? We'll find a comfortable place, Dani can go with you, and you can file your stories from there."

"No, Lawrence, I . . ."

"Chris, we don't want some lunatic out there thinking he'll take a shot at you to save society. Come on, you can use the time away, can't you? You enjoy having fifty members of our profession camping out at your house and trailing you wherever you go?"

"I'll think about it, Lawrence. Thanks. And there's one other thing I can use your help with."

"Name it."

"I need to know if P.T. was telling the truth, if he murdered my father. I checked with the coroner; if he was poisoned, it should still be detectable."

"I told you, your father was not murdered," Lawrence said.

"I need to find out for sure."

"So you want to exhume the body?" Lawrence was clearly dubious about the idea.

"I think so. Can you have the paper's lawyers work on that? I know it's for me personally, and I'll reimburse you, but I don't have the time—"

Lawrence interrupted. "Done. Don't worry about it."

Chris nodded. "Thanks. If I decide to go ahead with it, I'll sign anything I have to."

"Is this what your mother would want?"

"Right now I have to speak for her, as well as my father. And I know one thing; if he was murdered, he'd want us to know it and catch the son of a bitch who did it."

THE LAST FEW WEEKS had been a time of increasing dread and fear for Craig Andrews.

It was not the same fear shared by the average person, who was afraid of becoming a victim of P.T. Craig was scared on a much more personal level; he did not know what to do, and he sensed he had very little time left to do it.

Craig's time working in Englewood Town Hall had become much more bearable since Mayor Stanley had left office. They had not gotten along at all, and Stanley made it clear that he was never going to be supportive of Craig's own political ambitions. Craig had actively been looking for a way to bring the mayor down, and his covert spying had resulted in his awareness of the mayor's planned meeting with Charity.

But just the knowledge wasn't helpful unless he found a way to put it to use, and he felt his friend Chris Turley could do something with it. But he didn't want Chris to know where the information was coming from, so he had e-mailed it to Chris anonymously.

Yet that day when they were car shopping, Chris had told a story about going to meet an informant who had something to tell him about political corruption. When that corruption turned out to be the mayor's meeting with Charity, Craig was bewildered.

Why was Chris claiming to have gotten the tip from P.T. in a phone call, when it had come from Craig in an e-mail?

That question became more and more frightening over time, as future phone calls from P.T. led to all those murders. Had those calls been real, when the one about the mayor was not? Could Chris have been fabricating all of them?

Craig had known Chris for a long time and considered him a reasonably close friend. It was totally inconceivable to him that Chris could be a serial killer; it just simply was not in the realm of possibility.

Craig's assumption had been that Chris lumped the tip about the mayor in with the other, very real calls that he'd gotten from P.T. Chris must have had a reason for doing this, though Craig could not imagine what that reason might be.

Craig had lied to the FBI when they questioned him about possible knowledge of the mayor and Charity, since to do otherwise could have ruined his political career. He did this knowing that lying to the FBI in the course of an investigation, especially one this serious, was a felony.

So he had been paralyzed over these weeks, not knowing what to do. He didn't want to go to the FBI and belatedly tell them the truth; that had the real potential of ruining his life. But he also didn't feel comfortable confronting Chris with it, though he realized that his reluctance was a sign that he had doubts about his friend.

Now, with the revelation in *The New York Times* that Chris was a suspect in the murders, he could no longer in good conscience do nothing. It was either talk to his friend or possibly contribute to destroying that friend.

If Peter Randolph had one regret about being a murderer it was the effect it would have on his grandmother when the truth was revealed. He always feared that it would happen someday and now he understood that it was imminent.

She was a good woman, and she'd taken him in when he had nothing and no one. He knew that she loved him and he knew that she was frightened of him. Not of what he might do to her, but of who he was.

Soon she would find out who he really was, and it was going to be horrible for her.

He consciously tried to force the feeling of resignation that he had into one of anger, but it was difficult. He had been dreading this time for many years, while knowing full well it was coming. He had to tell himself that he must have his revenge, not for him, but for his grandmother.

Peter had to convince himself that if he was going to be destroyed, he should destroy his tormenter, as well. He would go down to the *Bergen News* and deal with the man in person; it was the only possible way to protect his grandmother.

* * *

"Tomorrow's Christmas, Chris. Don't you just love this time of year?"

P.T. was reaching Chris on his home phone, at seven o'clock in the morning, which seemed his favorite time to call. Or was it, Chris wondered, that he had a real job and found it difficult to call during working hours?

"What do you want?"

"To wish you a last happy holiday."

"That's touching," Chris said.

"So the FBI thinks you and I might be the same person," P.T. said. "I'm not sure which of us should be more insulted."

"I am."

"Have you considered killing yourself? It's the only decent thing for you to do, and it would save me the trouble."

"You're a coward."

P.T. laughed. "Whatever you say. But I just wanted to tell you that nobody will die for the next two days; it's my Christmas gift to my fellow citizens."

"That's big of you."

"Have you decided what you're doing for New Year's yet, Chris? Because I have, and soon I'll be starting the countdown."

Click.

Chris had no intention of calling the FBI about the P.T. phone call. If they really felt he was a suspect, he was going to stop dealing with them and had already discussed with Lawrence the need for a criminal attorney to protect himself.

But he did call Novack, who he considered an ally of sorts, and related the conversation in detail. When he finished, Novack said, "He's playing with you."

"I know. He's trying to get under my skin. Maybe he thinks I'll kill myself."

"Is that something you're considering?" Novack asked.

"No."

"Good."

"Is it true that the FBI thinks I'm P.T.?"

"I don't know," Novack said. "No way Quinlan does. Maybe the people above him."

"I'm not talking to any of them anymore. And you can tell Quinlan that for me."

"That's a mistake," said Novack.

"I don't think so. What about you? Do you think I might be P.T.?" Chris asked.

"No fucking way."

"Thank you," said Chris.

"You're not smart enough."

Chris laughed and said, "You got that right."

THE PHONE CALL CHRIS received from Craig Andrews was strange and disconcerting.

He told Chris that he needed to talk to him about something urgent, but did not want to have the conversation over the phone. He also did not want to come over to Chris's house and suggested they do it at a restaurant or bar.

"There's no such thing as a private conversation with me in a public place," Chris said. "The media follows me everywhere. My life is public. The FBI is even listening to this phone call."

Craig hadn't considered that and it scared him. "What about your office? I could come there."

That was fine with Chris, so he agreed to meet Craig in two hours. When he got to the paper, he stopped in at Lawrence's office first, to find out if he had found a lawyer to recommend to Chris.

"I've got two guys, both of whom are great," said Lawrence. "But you should talk to them and decide who you're more comfortable with."

"Okay, thanks. I will as soon as I get the chance." Chris knew he should be more aggressive about getting someone to represent him; it just felt that by doing so he would be drawn deeper into an uncomfortable and ridiculous situation. The FBI considering him a suspect simply did not compute; how could they be listening to his calls with P.T. and possibly believe that?

"And you should know that the paper will pay for your defense."

"Thanks, Lawrence. Hopefully I won't need one."

Craig was waiting for him at his office when Chris got there. Chris noticed that Craig seemed nervous and dreaded what he might have to say. He assumed it was some personal problem and never imagined that it could have anything to do with the P.T. situation.

Craig closed the door behind them and sat across from Chris's desk. "Chris, there's something I've got to ask you straight out."

"Okay."

"Why did you tell the FBI that you got the tip about the mayor in a phone call?" Craig asked.

"Because I did."

"I know better."

"What the hell are you talking about?"

Craig took a deep breath before answering. "I'm the one who sent you the e-mail."

Chris's expression reflected his bewilderment. "What e-mail?"

"Chris, a couple of days before the bomb went off at the medical center . . . I sent you an e-mail, I used a fake e-mail address so you wouldn't know it was me, and I told you that the mayor would be at the Claremont Hotel with that hooker."

"Craig . . ."

"But you said that you were told in a phone call from P.T., and you've never mentioned the e-mail." For the first time his tone was firm . . . insistent. "I need to know why."

"Craig, I don't have the slightest idea what you're talking about. I never got any e-mail like that. A guy called me and told me he had information about a government official and I agreed to meet him. I went there after we looked at the cars and the bomb went off. Later on, I found out he was P.T. and that he was committing all these murders."

"Chris, I sent you an e-mail. Are you saying that for some reason you never got it, and then coincidentally this guy gave you the same information?"

Chris thought for a moment and then said, "I guess that's exactly what I'm saying. You can believe me or not, but that's what I'm saying."

"But it doesn't make sense," Craig said.

"None of this makes sense. But what would I have to gain about lying about it? I . . . wait a minute . . . you think I might be P.T.? You think I might be a murderer? That's why you didn't want to come to my house, but had to talk to me in a public place."

"Chris, I just don't understand what's going on."

Chris's bewilderment was rapidly turning to anger. "What the hell did you think would happen if you came to my house? That I would chop you up and put you in my freezer? You think I'm a goddamn mass murderer? Well, then, you should be taking this to the FBI, Craig. So get the hell out of here and go do that."

"I don't think you're a murderer, Chris. But I am

going to have to tell this to the FBI. I lied to them; I could go to jail for that."

"Fine."

"Chris, I don't understand what is going on." His tone by this point was pleading, hoping his friend would provide a way out of this mess, but realizing that he wasn't going to.

"Join the club," said Chris.

Chris wrote a story about his latest call from P.T. He deliberately did not include a response to the *Times*'s story about him becoming an FBI suspect. He felt, and Lawrence agreed, that to do so would simply sound too defensive and would not accomplish anything. If people were going to believe that he was a suspect, his denying it would not sway them.

His philosophy was to keep telling the truth and at the end of the day, people would accept it.

Or not.

Shortly before he was ready to leave for the day, Scott Ryder came in to report what he had learned about Peter Randolph.

"I couldn't find a hell of a lot. He's had his difficulties, been in and out of trouble a lot. A lot of it is sealed, because he was a juvenile at the time. He was in the marines, which obviously didn't work out too well, since he was dishonorably discharged."

"Where does he live?"

Scott gave him the address.

"Do you know if he was here or in the marines at the time my father died?" Chris asked.

Scott did a double take. "You think he might have been involved in your father's death? I thought he had a heart attack."

Chris didn't answer him, just repeated the question. "Do you know if he was here or in the marines at the time my father died?"

Scott put up his hand. "Okay . . . I know it's none of my business. I'll compare the date with what I know. I should be able to find out."

"Thanks, Scott. I appreciate it."

"You know, I'm good at this, but the cops, and especially the FBI, can find out a hell of a lot more about this guy than I can."

Chris's level of trust with the FBI at that point was such that he wouldn't go to them with anything. "I know, but for now I want to keep this in-house."

Scott nodded. "Gotcha."

It was an irony that would go forever unnoticed that two very different people, with very different interests, were standing across the street from the *Bergen News* offices at around the time employees would usually be leaving.

One of those people was an FBI agent, who was part of a contingent covertly following Chris Turley wherever he went, in case P.T. reacted to the bait and made a move after him.

The other was Peter Randolph, who had a very different agenda.

SCOTT RYDER KNEW HE was being followed.

He had known it since he left the newspaper office; the man following him was not particularly accomplished at it. It was not unexpected, and it didn't worry him. He was prepared for it, just as he was prepared for everything else.

Scott stopped on the way home at a local diner and had a quick dinner. He didn't see the man when he came out, but it was dark and therefore easier for him to stay out of sight. But he was still there; Scott was sure of that.

Scott briefly considered going home for the night, which would have delayed the inevitable until the next day. It was an appealing thought; he was tired and not really in the mood to deal with this situation. But he knew better than to put these kinds of things off; it was preferable to get it out of the way now.

Scott knew that the man would not approach him until he could do so in an area in which he would not be seen, so he stopped at the Garden State Plaza shopping center in Paramus. It was nearing nine o'clock, closing time, so most of the last-minute Christmas Eve shoppers were gone already.

Scott parked far away from the store, in the most secluded area he could without it appearing too obvious. He left his car unlocked, then went inside and walked through a couple of stores, pretending to be shopping.

After ten minutes, having failed to buy anything, he walked out of the mall to the parking lot, ambling slowly to his car. He got into the driver's seat, deliberately avoiding the temptation to look into the back. He just hoped he hadn't wasted all this time.

"Hello, Carl." The familiar voice came from the backseat. It sounded strange; it was the first time in years that someone had called him by his real name. Scott looked in the rearview mirror, but it was too dark to see much except the glint of light shining off the barrel of the handgun.

"My name is Scott."

"I know who you are."

"Of course you do, Peter. But I'm a new man now . . . literally. And how have you been? Long time, no see."

"We need to talk."

Scott laughed. "We've already talked. Don't you remember?"

"I remember."

"I was going to look for you," Scott said. "You saved me the trouble. How did you know I was here?"

"I saw you standing behind Turley at the press conference."

Scott nodded. "Good. I'm glad that worked."

"Drive the car," Peter said.

"Sure. Where to?"

Peter directed him west on Route 4 to Paterson,

then south on Route 20. They turned off into Eastside Park, which had upper and lower sections. Peter told him to park alongside the lower section, which is where the ball fields were.

They walked towards a pavilion stationed between the high school and Little League fields. There was some moonlight, but not much. On the steps of the pavilion, Peter told Scott to stop walking and he did so.

"Peter, what the hell are we doing here? If you wanted to talk, we could have gone for a beer. Kicked around old times."

Old times were not something Peter wanted to kick around, certainly not with Scott. Their entire time together was as cellmates at Camp Lejeune, the marine base where they were both stationed.

"How did you get out?" Peter asked. During their time together, Scott/Carl was awaiting trial on a murder charge, accused of breaking a civilian's neck in a fight outside a local bar.

"They dropped the charge . . . not enough evidence. Ain't that something?"

"I want to know why you're doing this to me."

"Doing what?"

"Don't talk to me like I'm stupid, Carl." Peter held the gun in front of him with two hands, pointing it at Scott.

Scott laughed. "Why not? You're dumb as dirt."

"You're out there . . . you're going to make me look like a murderer."

"You are a murderer."

"I told you what I did because you swore you

wouldn't tell anyone," Peter said. One evening in prison, Peter had opened up to Scott and talked about his father's suicide and his resulting hatred for Edward Turley. Then he admitted that he had murdered Edward by jabbing him with a poison needle in a supermarket. It was the first and only time he had told the story to anyone.

Scott laughed again. "What did you think, I was your shrink? Was I charging by the hour?"

"I'll tell them what I know, Carl; I swear I will. I'm not afraid of what will happen to me."

"Now how are you going to do that, Peter? I mean, with you being dead and all."

With an almost imperceptible motion, Scott flicked his wrist and tossed some change he had taken out of his pocket. It landed behind Peter on the pavilion steps and he turned to see what had happened.

When he turned back, Scott was gone.

Peter was frightened. He knew how to handle himself well enough against most enemies, but he also knew that Scott was in another league. Even among the marines, Scott was known to be as deadly an adversary as one could face.

But Peter had a gun and he doubted that Scott had one of his own. He had seen metal detectors in the lobby of the *Bergen News*, no doubt put there because of the intense security concerns around Chris Turley. Scott would not have risked trying to bring a gun into that building; nor would he have thought he'd have any need for it. He also had searched Scott's car while hiding in it and had found no weapon.

Peter heard a noise that seemed to come from the pavilion. He slowly walked up the steps towards it, the gun at the ready. He considered running away and avoiding this confrontation, but he knew that the gun gave him an advantage that he would not have next time.

And there would definitely be a next time; that much was a certainty.

So Peter moved forward, as quietly as he could, searching for any glimpse of movement in the moonlight. But there was no movement, and no sound. He thought for a brief moment that Scott had left, and on some level hoped that he had, but that would not be Scott's style; this was all going to end here.

Suddenly Peter saw a reflection of light and moved towards it. He heard no noise and detected no movement of any kind.

Which is why he was so stunned to feel himself being grabbed from behind, less than a second before his neck was snapped.

Scott reached into Peter's pocket and took out a set of keys, one of which he was sure had to be to his house. "Petey, you're making this way too easy."

CHRIS AND DANI SPENT an incongruously quiet and peaceful Christmas Day together.

They didn't leave the house and kept the shades down, so it was almost possible to imagine that there was not a horde of press outside. And they never turned on the television, so for brief moments they could almost forget the swirl of fear and controversy that surrounded Chris.

Lawrence had promised that he would call if anything took place that he should know about, but Chris did not expect him to do so. P.T. had said nothing would happen on Christmas Day and he had unfortunately proven to be a man of his word so far.

He also said that the "countdown" would begin soon, and that sounded all too ominous.

Dani made a surprisingly good Christmas dinner, though they ate it as a late lunch and watched an NBA game afterwards. He was surprised to discover that she was a pro basketball fan, a passion that he shared.

"I know so little about you," he said. "I've been rather focused on myself."

She smiled. "I would say you've had a pretty good reason."

"Tell me something about yourself that I don't know," he prodded.

"Okay . . . I'm leaving the paper. I gave Lawrence my two weeks' notice yesterday."

The news surprised him. "Why?"

"I don't want to be there anymore."

He nodded. "Obviously, but why?"

"That is the why," she said. "That's how I live my life; I trust my instincts and then I follow them. It doesn't matter to me where those instincts come from or whether any logical process helped form them."

"So your instinct is to leave the paper?"

"Yes. I need to do something more important." She laughed. "I cover the public lives of celebrities; it would be pretty hard to find something less important."

"I hope your instincts don't tell you to move out of this area."

She leaned over and kissed him. "If they do, I'll tell them to shut up."

"How do your instincts say this is going to end?" he asked.

"You mean with P.T."

"No, I mean with you and me."

"They don't think it has to end."

He leaned back in to kiss her. "Then keep trusting them."

With no P.T.-related news for almost two days, the press started focusing on different aspects of the crisis. There was no shortage of topics to choose from;

Chris estimated that P.T. could disappear for a year before the coverage would come close to stopping.

But as Chris knew all too well, P.T. was not about to disappear.

Local officials were quoted as estimating that retail sales for the Christmas season were down more than thirty percent in the metropolitan area when compared to the previous year. This was particularly dramatic since the rest of the country was estimating a ten percent increase. The lost revenue was clearly in the hundreds of millions of dollars, and it was mostly revenue that could never be recouped.

Feature stories were done on the psychological impact P.T. was having on the local citizenry. Comparisons were made to the sniper shootings in the Washington, D.C., area, but this current situation was deemed much worse. Certainly the toll in lives and property was far more substantial, so the resulting greater impact on the collective psyche clearly made sense.

Two local shock jocks ran a poll among their listeners and the question to be voted on was whether or not Chris Turley should commit suicide as a public service. That night they were forced by their management to issue a public apology to Chris and they were suspended for a week each.

Fifty-eight percent had answered yes.

Psychiatrists and therapists were reporting a number of cases of a form of traumatic stress disorder, similar to that experienced by soldiers in wartime.

They likened it to the psychological stress that soldiers in Iraq suffered from the constant fear of IEDs, and the knowledge that one could blow up at any time. Many members of the public believed, with some justification, that any moment, any step, could be their last.

They knew they could be P.T.'s next victim without ever having seen it coming.

Doris Randolph decided that Christmas Day might have been the worst holiday she had ever spent. That was no small statement, since the other contender for the title was when her son, Gerald, walked out onto a highway on New Year's Eve. But the feeling she experienced that day was devastation, while this time she was overcome with fear and dread.

When she had come home from work to celebrate Christmas Eve with her grandson, Peter, he was not there. This was certainly not very unusual, nor was his staying out all night. He had done that before and she had always assumed he had been with a woman. That was fine with her; he was an adult and didn't have to check in with her as if he were a child.

But when he did not come home all of Christmas Day and did not answer his cell phone, she began to fear the worst. What made it all so difficult was that she wasn't really sure what the worst was.

It could have been that something had happened to him or it could have been what he was doing to others.

She had briefly experienced hope that she was imagining things about Peter when the story came out that Chris Turley was suspected of being P.T. If that were true, and she prayed that it was, then Peter was innocent and his obsession with the case was a semi-understandable function of the fact that he believed Chris's father caused his own father's death.

But Peter's increasingly erratic behavior, and now his uncharacteristically disappearing for forty-eight hours, had brought back her fear in full force.

There was no longer any question in her mind; she had put it off for too long. She was ready to admit to herself that she had to go to the FBI and talk to them. Maybe it would be nothing and they could help her find her missing grandson.

Or maybe it would be something, and they could prevent more people from dying.

One way or the other, it would have to be better than not knowing where Peter was, or who he was.

AT 10:00 A.M. on December 26, P.T. claimed another victim, just by doing nothing.

Dexter Chambers, a homeless man reduced to living in his car, was faced with what for him was impending disaster. He had no gas and no money to buy more. And without gas, there was no way to keep his "home" warm.

He had faced this problem a number of times in the past and his solution was to siphon gas from parked cars without a lock on their gas cap. He was quite accomplished at it and could walk off with a gallon or more in a matter of a couple of minutes.

But when he tried it on a Buick parked on Andrews Avenue in the Bronx, just a few blocks from where P.T. had struck a few days earlier, he was spotted by a local resident. The man misunderstood what Chambers was doing, and in fact believed that he was planting an explosive device in the gas tank.

He screamed out his suspicions and soon a mob formed and chased the panic-stricken Chambers down the block. The twenty-seven-year-old Chambers was fast, and could outrun ninety-five percent of his pursuers. Unfortunately, when being chased by a mob, nothing less than being faster than one hundred percent is acceptable.

They caught up to Chambers and dragged him down. His protestations of innocence were ignored and they began to beat him. Somewhere in the confusion, a shot rang out, though no one would say where it came from. It left Chambers dead from a bullet in the head.

P.T. had caused his death, as surely as if he had pulled the trigger.

The next day, the governors of New York and New Jersey held a joint press conference, during which they announced that they were calling up their respective National Guards to help police the streets. It represented a reversal of their previous position on the matter and was done simply to make the citizenry feel more secure. They would not have a clearly defined mission because there still wasn't anything for them to do.

In the same press conference, they cautioned the public not to take matters into their own hands and to remain calm. The Chambers killing was a sobering indication of what fear could cause and they spent a great deal of time getting the word out that attempts at vigilante justice would be counterproductive and furthermore would be dealt with severely.

At the exact time that the governors were attempting to reassure their citizens, Cynthia Carter was washing her clothes in a Laundromat on the corner of Vreeland Avenue and Nineteenth Avenue in Paterson. The press conference was on a television set high up in the corner of the room, but the sound was turned off.

Cynthia was in a hurry to get to her waitressing job in downtown Paterson and thought the spin cycle on the washer would never end.

When it finally did, she chose the dryer all the way to the right, since it was next to a table on which she could fold her clothes when they were finished.

She made the wrong choice. At the moment she pressed start, the machine exploded, killing her and another patron instantly and injuring two others.

Within three minutes of the explosion at the Laundromat, and before it was even reported in the media, P.T. called Chris on his cell phone while he was at the office. He spoke one word before he hung up.

"Four."

Chris quickly turned on the television and within five minutes saw a report on the most recent killing. He then called Novack and told him about the latest call and the brief message P.T. had delivered.

"Four?" asked Novack. "What the hell does that mean?"

"He's counting down, Novack. That's exactly what he said he was going to do."

"Counting down to what?"

"To one. He's counting down to one," Chris said. "He's going to reach zero on New Year's Eve."

Chris decided not to write about the latest phone call, at least not right away. It seemed as if every time he spoke out, in print or on television, it turned more people against him. Maybe the people who hated him still had a right to know, but at the moment he didn't feel the responsibility to tell them.

Chris called Dani to tell her he was coming home. She had just seen the news about the Laundromat bombing and was shaken by it. He told her about his theory that P.T. was counting down. He could have waited to tell her until he got home, but he knew the FBI was listening in to the call and he wanted Quinlan to be aware of it, without contacting him directly.

He left the building, from which point he had to walk no more than thirty yards to the facility where his car was parked. As always, there were onlookers there hoping to catch sight of him, as well as members of the press. And as always, he just ignored them and kept on walking.

Suddenly, some instinct caused him to turn and when he did so, he saw a man about five yards away, racing at him with a large knife. The man's eyes had a crazed look that sent a chill through Chris, but Chris's basketball training and athletic reflexes served him well.

He dodged out of the way at the last minute and the knife barely grazed his cheek, drawing a small amount of blood. Chris rolled to the ground and then jumped to his feet, certain that the man was going to come at him again.

But he didn't, because in a split second five FBI agents in civilian clothes were on the assailant and had disarmed him and thrown him to the ground. They performed with amazing efficiency and, in what seemed like less than a minute, they had taken the man off in one of their cars.

One of the agents came over to Chris and gave him a handkerchief to apply to his face, though the bleeding was not substantial. "We'll get you to a hospital," he said.

Chris shook his head. "No, you won't."

"You're going to need to be questioned about this anyway," the agent said.

"Are you arresting me?" Chris asked.

"For getting stabbed? Of course not."

"Then you can kiss my ass," Chris said. "You can take one cheek and Quinlan can take the other."

And he walked off and went to his car.

Dani proved to be a better nurse than cook and she cleaned and bandaged his face expertly. He only screamed in pain seven times.

"You're a baby," she said. "I've seen paper cuts worse than this."

"Excuse me. A crazed lunatic attacked me with a goddamn machete and half of America wishes he had succeeded in killing me. Can I get a little sympathy here?"

"You want sympathy?" she asked. "What about me? I slaved over dinner and because you came home late, it's cold."

"What did you make?"

"Salami sandwiches," she said, laughing.

They started talking in more detail about what happened to him and he said, "Those agents were unbelievable; they were on that guy immediately."

"Immediately after you got cut."

"They couldn't have stopped that."

"Why were they there?" she asked. "To follow you in case you went off and blew up some buildings?"

"I've been thinking about that," he said, "and I doubt that's it. I think they were there in case something exactly like this happened."

"So now the FBI is protecting you?"

"In a way, but I've got a feeling that's a secondary consideration. My guess is they want to be there in case P.T. takes a run at me, so they can nail him."

"So do they suspect you or not?"

"I don't think so. I think they've set it up in a way so that they think I might be bait to draw P.T. in."

She frowned. "Our tax dollars in action."

"It makes some sense," he said. "There are a lot of lives at stake."

"Especially yours."

"Which is why I'm going to stop running and start chasing."

"What does that mean? What are you going to do?"

"I'm going to take my life back."

The first step in taking his life back, as Chris saw it, was making sure that he still had one. There could well be maniacs out there taking a number to see who could kill him first, and Chris needed some protection from them.

Since Lawrence knew virtually everybody in the metropolitan area, Chris asked him to make a phone call and set Chris up for an appointment at a gun shop in Hawthorne. Dani went with him, since she said that by going she could make sure Chris didn't shoot himself on the way home.

The proprietor of the store was Lou Davis, and the store sold guns, ammunition, and fishing equipment. He was an old hunting buddy of Lawrence's and promised to take good care of Chris.

"What kind of firearm are you looking for?" he asked.

"I have no idea."

"You looking to shoot targets, animals, or people?"

"Hopefully none of the above," Chris said. "But people could be out there trying to kill me."

Lou nodded, as if he heard that kind of statement every day. "You ever fire a weapon?"

"No."

"Then I hope those people trying to kill you aren't too good at it."

Lou decided that the appropriate gun for Chris was a .22, and he took him downstairs to a small shooting range in his basement so that he could try it out.

Chris thought he did pretty well, and said so. He asked Lou for his opinion.

"You should be fine," Lou said. "As long as you don't have to use it."

While Lou and Chris were downstairs taking target practice, Dani was upstairs picking out a pepper spray key chain for him. She handed it to him when they got home.

"What is this?" he asked.

"It's a key chain that blows pepper spray in the face

of an attacker. I figured you should have it in case you run out of bullets."

"That's really nice," he said.

Dani nodded. "I was afraid it might be too romantic a gift, and I didn't want to give you the wrong impression."

"No, it's sweet. I was hoping for a machete, or maybe a bazooka, but it's the thought that counts."

"One more wiseass comment like that and I'll try it out on you," she said.

"My lips are sealed."

IT WAS ONE THING to get aggressive, and another to know what to do.

P.T. had to this point literally laughed in the face of the largest law enforcement operation in modern history, and Chris was now resolved to succeed where they were failing.

The first problem he had to tackle, before he could even begin looking for P.T., was the fact that he was followed wherever he went, both by the FBI and by the press. He and Dani went down to the office to meet with Lawrence, and Chris said, "The other day, when you thought I should be staying out of sight, you said you had a place where I could do it."

Lawrence nodded. "Absolutely."

"Where is it?"

"There's a house in Mahwah; it's more of a cabin really. I own it."

Mahwah was a perfect location, up Route 17 between Oakland and Suffern, less than a half hour away. And it was very secluded, a heavily wooded area with houses very far from one another. "You own it?" Chris asked.

He nodded. "My uncle died and left it to me about

five years ago. We used to go there when we were kids. I fixed it up, and now I go every once in a while to get away from the world. And believe me, when you're there, you're away from the world."

"Has it got a phone and television?"

"What am I, Grizzly Adams? Of course it does. And a bar, and a computer, and a goddamn massage chair."

"Sounds great. Thanks."

"So now we have to get you there without being seen," Lawrence said.

"We've got another problem bigger than that. I've got to change my appearance, because I'm not just going to sit in the massage chair all day. I'm planning to be out in the world."

"Doing what?" Lawrence said.

"Finding P.T."

"So you want a disguise or something?"

"Nothing major . . . maybe a different hair color . . . some glasses. I just don't want the average person on the street to immediately recognize me."

"Or take a shot at you," Lawrence said.

"Thanks, Lawrence. You really know how to cheer me up."

"I can take care of this," Dani said.

"How?" Chris asked.

"One of the ways you get inside stuff on celebrities is to get in good with the people who work for them. I know some of the makeup people who work on their movies; they can make you look like the Incredible Hulk."

"Is there one of them you can definitely trust?"

She nodded. "Yes."

"What's her name?"

She smiled. "*Her* name is Frank; I lived with him for a year. We're still great friends."

"I really don't know anything about you."

She nodded. "I'm a mystery, wrapped in an enigma."

The FBI's interview of Scott Ryder was to determine if he could have been the source of the leak that agents were going to interview Wallace Timmerman. Agent Larry Sampson conducted the interview and Lawrence Terry insisted that one of the paper's lawyers be present. He wasn't taking any chances this time, and while Chris was of a stature to refuse, Scott wasn't.

Sampson asked a few questions about Scott's background, and he willingly told him about his hometown, where he went to school, his parents, and general background. None of it was true, but Scott knew that the FBI would never figure it out.

Scott had killed the real Scott Ryder three years ago, after determining he had the ideal identity to steal. He then massaged his victim's biography through some computer wizardry, and the result was that only the most intense investigation could ever hope to uncover any falsehoods. Scott knew that he was not considered anything resembling a prime suspect, so the resulting investigation wouldn't come close to penetrating his deception.

Once the background portion of the interview was finished, Sampson asked, "When did Mr. Turley tell you that agents were going to interview Mr. Timmerman?"

"He didn't," Scott said. "He just asked me to go on the computer and see if I could find out any more information about him?"

"More information?"

Scott nodded. "Right. Chris had been asking me about people who were connected to his father, and I helped check them out. We had already considered Mr. Timmerman, but then Chris wanted more information."

"Did you discuss this with anyone else?"

"Just Chris."

"You never mentioned Mr. Timmerman to anyone else?"

Scott shook his head. "Nope. Nobody."

"Do you have the notes that you took about Mr. Timmerman with you?"

"Yes."

"I'll need to see them," Sampson said.

At that point the paper's lawyer interrupted and said that he would deal with that matter. Sampson said that he was finished with Scott, so Scott left the notes behind so the two men could presumably fight over them.

Scott couldn't help smiling as he left. Sampson and the people he worked with had no idea that the man they just interviewed was the man they'd been hunting all these weeks.

And they never would.

CRAIG ANDREWS WAS GOING to the FBI, but he wasn't going alone.

He was going to hire a lawyer, and unless that lawyer gave him dramatically different advice than what he was expecting, together they would tell the authorities what Craig knew and was hiding.

It's not that Craig didn't believe his friend. He had known Chris way too long, and way too well, to think he could be committing these murders. He even accepted that Chris didn't see the e-mail that Craig had sent, alerting him to the mayor's tryst with the prostitute.

But this wasn't about Chris. Craig had lied to the FBI when they questioned everyone at town hall as to whether they knew what the mayor was doing in advance of it happening. There was no way to push that under the rug.

What was going on with P.T. was so momentous that every aspect of it would be gone over again and again. It would somehow be revealed that Craig lied; perhaps the e-mail would be discovered and traced back to him. And his deception, in a case of this import, could send him to prison and ruin him for life.

Better to reveal it now, voluntarily.

Craig had a 10:00 A.M. meeting scheduled with Nick Alexander, a prominent local criminal defense attorney. They had briefly discussed the situation over the phone, but Nick interrupted the conversation and suggested that it would be better to talk about it in person.

Craig was more than a little scared about how this was going to come out, especially since he could not foresee an outcome in which he would emerge unscathed. Nick Alexander, as good as he was reputed to be, could not possibly get this wiped away.

A good result for most people in this situation might be a reduced charge, with perhaps probation and no prison time. But for Craig, a man counting on a future in politics, even that would be a complete career killer. Once word got out that Craig had impeded an FBI investigation in the P.T. case, he would be a pariah to the public.

Craig also wasn't sure of the timing. Nick might want him to talk to the FBI immediately, maybe even that very morning. Could it be possible, Craig wondered, that by nightfall he would be in custody?

He did some paperwork and paid some bills, just in case he wouldn't be returning anytime soon. With only ten minutes until he had to leave for his meeting with Nick, he went out to the mailbox to check if anything had arrived that he needed to attend to.

He opened the mailbox and was blown apart by the force of the blast.

* * *

P.T. called Chris on his cell phone, which he knew Chris had with him in Lawrence's cabin. He briefly debated whether to call him on the cabin phone, knowing it would frighten and bewilder Chris that he knew where Chris's "hideout" was.

But he opted against it; it would have meant taking a chance, however slight, and there was no good reason to do it.

Besides, it would be a brief conversation, as P.T. didn't have much to say. In fact, he summed it up in one word:

"Three."

Chris had long ago stopped notifying the FBI about the phone calls; he knew very well that they were listening to them and there was nothing else for him to add. Besides, he no longer trusted them, and felt it necessary to protect himself.

So he turned on the television, certain that P.T.'s phone call meant that he had struck again, and that the networks would soon be breaking into their programming to announce the news.

Within twenty minutes, cameras were on the scene of the explosion, and before the name of the victim was even known or revealed, Chris recognized the house, devastated now to realize that it was Craig who had been killed.

Chris also realized that Craig's death had to be tied into his knowledge of the mayor's tryst at the hotel with Charity and the fact that he had sent Chris an e-mail telling him about it. P.T. must have found out that Craig was going to the FBI to reveal that information and somehow P.T. must have felt threatened by that fact. It was another piece of a puzzle that continued to bewilder Chris.

But one thing he knew for certain, another person had died because Chris was alive.

And for the second time, it was a friend.

With Chris no longer reporting on the crisis, the public was for the most part receiving only the information that the FBI wanted them to receive. For that reason, they were unaware that P.T. was counting down, with three numbers and three days left until New Year's Eve.

The FBI in general, and Quinlan in particular, was being crucified in the media. That a single person could roam one of the most populated areas of the country, indiscriminately killing and bragging about it, seemed inconceivable. Yet it was happening.

Quinlan had a very different take on it. He was actually amazed that something like this had never happened before. And the fact that it was a single perpetrator, Quinlan knew, made the crimes that much harder to solve.

The United States military had faced a similar problem in Iraq, with soldiers getting blown up by IEDs planted in the streets. Even with close to two hundred thousand troops, in an occupied country, they had enormous difficulty trying to get it under control.

Israel had also faced the problem for years and had finally achieved some significant success by fencing off their country, so the attackers could not get in.

But the northeastern United States could not be fenced in, and it wouldn't help if it could, because the attacker was already inside. And he had done most of his work before the FBI even knew he was there or what he would be trying to accomplish.

There was virtually no limit to how many bombs P.T. could have planted before he was even in the public's consciousness. But if by some chance those pre-planted devices were to run out, there was nothing stopping P.T. from simply going out and planting some more.

In fact, Quinlan knew that P.T. was active; he was not just sitting back and letting his previous work speak for him. The proof of that was in the murder of Craig Andrews. Andrews had most certainly gone to his mailbox numerous times over the previous weeks and he would have noticed an explosive device if one had been there. Therefore, it must have been planted quite recently.

Quinlan sent out an army of agents to canvas Andrews's neighborhood, in the hope that someone had seen P.T. when he was there. Not surprisingly, no one did; P.T. was far too smart and careful to allow himself to get trapped in that fashion.

But the fact that he targeted Andrews, and therefore exposed himself to at least some jeopardy, is what particularly interested Quinlan. Andrews wasn't a random victim; he was killed for a reason. It was possible that the fact that he was Chris Turley's friend brought about his demise, as a further gesture of revenge and hatred by P.T. against Chris.

But Quinlan thought it was more than that, partly because P.T. made no reference to the friendship, taunting or otherwise, in his phone call to Chris. Perhaps on some level, Andrews was a danger to P.T., though Quinlan certainly had no idea how.

It was infuriating to Quinlan that he couldn't pick up the phone and talk to Chris about it. Because of the Director Kramer's lamebrained idea to spread the word that Chris was a suspect, he had understandably ceased communications with Quinlan.

Worse yet, he was now in hiding, and had eluded the agents assigned to follow him. Now, even if P.T. made an attempt to go after him, the agents would not be there to prevent it and capture P.T.

Chris would be found and surveillance restarted, but it was an inconvenience and a delay that just added to the problems that the case continued to present.

And delays were unacceptable, when every day brought another death.

CHRIS DECIDED TO FOCUS on Peter Randolph.

He did so for three reasons. First, the story that Scott Ryder related about Gerald Randolph's suicide on the highway, with young Peter watching, was awful enough that it could have provoked an overwhelming hatred and desire for revenge. Second, as far as Chris knew, the FBI was unaware of Peter, and Chris could therefore operate independently of them.

The third reason for checking out Peter Randolph was more obvious. Chris had no idea what else to do.

The problem, of course, was that he also had no idea how to go about his investigating. While most of America had considered him a hero for a week or two back when this all began, it was not in Chris's DNA to be physically aggressive. All he wanted to do was somehow assess whether Peter Randolph was a viable suspect and then he would turn him over to Novack to handle.

Chris drove to the Clifton address that Scott had given him. It was about three blocks from Nash Park, where Chris had played high school baseball. For some reason, he recalled in the moment that his father had never seen him pitch in one of those games, yet every time his father came home, he would ask Chris how his arm was doing.

Actually, Edward didn't use the word "arm," he would use "wing." He would say, "How's the wing holding up?"

Chris would always say, "Pretty good," but he remembered thinking that if his father would just come to a game, he could find out how the wing was doing firsthand.

Chris got to the Randolph house at 4:00 P.M. and from across the street saw no sign that anyone was home. He decided to sit in his car and wait for a while, mainly because he didn't know what else to do.

At 5:15, a woman parked in the driveway of the house and started walking around towards the front door.

Chris got out of his car and approached her. "Mrs. Randolph?" he asked, guessing that she was related to Peter.

She turned, a look of fear on her face, and Chris immediately sensed that this was a woman who had been afraid for a while. "Mr. Turley . . ."

She had recognized him instantly, a sad commentary on Dani's hair and makeup friend, but also an indication that she was very, very familiar with Chris. He had the feeling that she had been expecting him.

"You're not surprised that I'm here?" Chris asked.

"No."

"I want to talk to you about Peter."

She nodded in resignation. "Yes. Come in."

He followed her in, looking around warily in case

Peter was there. He saw no signs of him. "Is Peter home?" he asked.

She shook her head sadly. "No. My grandson has not been home for three days."

She offered Chris coffee and it seemed important to her that he have some, so he agreed. It allowed her to take some time to brew it and delay the conversation she knew was inevitable. Her body language made him believe that he had come to the right place at the right time.

"Mrs. Randolph, I don't know you, but I'm going to be very frank. I'm here because of the possibility that your grandson is involved with the explosions that have been taking place."

"You don't know that," she said.

"No, I don't," Chris said. "But I think that you do."

"No," she said.

"Do you know where Peter is?"

"No."

"Is it like him to be away this long?"

"No."

"Does he have a job?"

"No. Not since he left the army."

Chris was torturing this woman; he knew it and he hated himself for it. "Mrs. Randolph, did your grandson ever talk about my father or me?"

She nodded. "He hated your father and so did I. He drove my Gerald to his death. For nothing. For nothing!" The bitterness came pouring out and she took a moment to compose herself before she said, "My son did nothing wrong."

"Mrs. Randolph, I'm sorry if my father hurt you and hurt your son. Really, I am. But I can't change that. But if Peter is hurting people now, we have to stop him. You and I. I know you see that."

"He's a good boy."

"But he needs help. Help that you can't give him."

She thought for a few moments, then seemed to sag. "What do you want me to do?"

"To let the police come here and look through Peter's things. That should tell all of us what we need to know."

She hesitated, unable to say the words.

"Believe me," he said, "it is better to know the truth."

It took another half hour for Chris to get Doris Randolph to believe the truth of that statement and, in fact, she finally agreed only because she felt she had no other choice.

Chris stayed in the house as he called Novack from her phone. He would rather have done so from the relative safety of his car, since he was afraid that Peter could show up at any time. But he was also afraid that if he left, Doris might change her mind about cooperating. And if he used his cell phone, Quinlan would hear what was said.

"Where the hell have you been?" asked Novack when he realized it was Chris calling.

"Doing your job."

"Somebody's got to," Novack said. "What's going on?"

"Plenty. But before I tell you, I have a question. Do you keep Quinlan informed of developments in the case?"

"Except when I forget to," said Novack.

"Will you forget to this time?"

"That depends on what we're talking about."

"Not good enough. I need a yes, or we don't go any further. You don't go to Quinlan with this unless I say it's okay."

"Okay, but it better be good."

When Chris finished explaining the situation, Novack said, "It's good. Will she sign a release letting us search the place? Because we don't have enough for a warrant."

"She will."

"I'll be there in twenty minutes."

"And no Quinlan," Chris said.

"Quinlan . . . Quinlan . . ." Novack said, as if searching his mind. "Doesn't ring a bell."

Novack was there in fifteen minutes and Chris was surprised that he was alone. Chris introduced him to Doris Randolph and Novack gently took her through the procedure, telling her about the release she needed to sign to allow them to search.

She reluctantly agreed; there was no turning back now.

Once she had signed, Novack went out onto the front porch and gave a signal that brought an army of ten detectives and forensics people into the house. He had correctly gauged Doris's nervousness and decided there would be more chance for her to sign if he appeared to be alone.

Four patrolmen stayed outside, on guard in case

Peter should return. Novack let the detectives and forensics experts search the house, concentrating on Peter's room, as he engaged Doris in conversation. It was unproductive, as she was far too stressed about the people taking her house apart, and the fear that she had done something terrible to her grandson.

Her letting the police in could result in Peter going to jail for the rest of his life, or worse. Though she intellectually knew this could only happen if he were guilty of these horrible crimes, it still felt to her as if she were betraying him horribly.

In less than a half hour, one of the detectives searching Peter's room called for Novack to join them. Chris went with him to see what they had found.

In a drawer, under clothing, were ten GPS devices and material of the type used to contain the explosives that P.T. had been planting everywhere. In the desk was what amounted to a scrapbook of newspaper and magazine clippings, covering both the current murders, and the death of Edward Turley, five years before.

Chris stared at the press reports of his father's death, some of which had scribbled notations of approval written on them. At that moment, he had no doubt that Edward was murdered and that they were standing in the murderer's room.

"Novack, look at this." They went over to the closet and saw that hidden in the back were several shoe boxes. One of the detectives had opened the top box. It was filled with a material that the detectives assumed to be the clear liquid explosive that P.T. had been using, though that would certainly have to be tested.

"This is the goddamn mother lode," the detective said. "We've got the son of a bitch cold."

"Let's clear the building," Novack said, fearing that Peter could detonate the explosives while they were in the house. "Now."

"QUINLAN NEEDS TO BE told about this," Novack said. "I know we had a deal, but I'm breaking it."

What they had seen in the house was so jarring, and so incriminating, that Chris no longer had any interest in keeping the FBI in the dark. "I understand," Chris said. "Do whatever you need to do."

"This completely gets you off the hook," Novack said.

"Yeah. I'm outta here. Give Quinlan my regards." Chris started walking towards his car.

"Where are you going?"

"To write the story," Chris said. "That's what I do."

Quinlan and his people were at the Randolph house within twenty minutes of receiving Novack's phone call. Within forty minutes there were enough employees of the federal government on the scene to occupy a third-world country.

Included in the group was a psychologist to try to deal with Doris Randolph, who by this time was close to hysteria, even though no one had yet told her exactly what was going on or what had been discovered in her grandson's room.

Pictures of Peter Randolph, of which there were many in the house, were immediately sent to every police agency in the United States. Quinlan called Director Kramer and they agreed that steps should be taken to get the pictures before the public. Soon every pair of eyes in the country would be on the lookout for Peter Randolph, alias P.T.

Chris got back to the paper and didn't even take the time to inform Lawrence what had happened. Instead, he called Dani and told her and then sat down at his computer and began to type.

Scott Ryder approached Chris's desk as he wrote. "Hey, didn't expect you back for a while."

Chris didn't even look up. "We know who P.T. is. And you gave me the tip."

"Which one?" Scott asked.

"Peter Randolph. We've got him nailed for it."

"Is he in custody?"

"Not yet, but he will be. Now leave me alone; I've got to finish this."

"Sure, no problem," Scott said. "Congratulations."

He started to walk away when Chris said, "Hey, Scott. Good job, man."

Scott grinned. "Thanks. All in a day's work." Scott made arrangements for Chris's story to go up on the Web site the moment it was finished. He then went home and planted himself in front of his computer. A quick check of his GPS trackers told him that the car belonging to Salvatore Pinella of Camden, New Jersey, was in motion and traveling at fifty-seven miles an hour.

So he blew it up, killing Salvatore and his girlfriend.

Scott then turned on the voice transformer and called Chris at the office, who by this time had finished the story and was planning to go home.

All he said was, "Two."

P.T.'S IDENTITY REVEALED:
MASSIVE MANHUNT HAS BEEN LAUNCHED
by Chris Turley

A team of police officers, led by Detective Jonathan Novack, conducted a search of a Clifton home earlier today that resulted in substantial evidence that Peter Randolph is the serial killer known as P.T.

Found in Randolph's room were electronic devices consistent with those used in the bombings, materials that detectives were confident, pending testing, were dangerous explosives, and thick scrapbooks containing press materials related to coverage of the murders.

Included in the books were all the stories that this reporter has filed, as well as newspaper accounts of the death of my father, Edward Turley. It is believed that Randolph blamed Turley for the death by suicide of his own father, Gerald.

Randolph's whereabouts remain unknown, and police are cautioning that he remains extraordinarily dangerous.

CHRIS'S STORY BEAT THE FBI's formal announcement by two hours.

There was also a follow-up piece about the murders in Camden, but by comparison, the latter story barely registered. The terrorized public now knew who P.T. was and they knew what he looked like. And there was nowhere that Peter Randolph was going to be able to hide.

Tips flooded in by the thousands, overwhelming those whose job it was to receive them. If the callers to the FBI hot line were to be believed, Peter Randolph was everywhere.

At that moment, Scott Ryder, sitting at home in front of his computer, was the only person in the world who actually knew where Peter Randolph was. He was buried in a deep grave in the woods north of Oakland, New Jersey.

He would never be found, and Scott knew that Peter would go down in history as perhaps the most infamous criminal of the century. That he would never be captured would serve as fodder for historians and conspiracy theorists for decades. If they were still searching for Amelia Earhart now, they would never stop hunting for Peter Randolph.

And Peter's notoriety was going to continue to grow, because he wasn't nearly finished killing. Besides that, he was soon to become rich beyond his wildest dreams.

Too bad he wouldn't be around to enjoy it.

Dani and Chris spent the early evening watching the television coverage of the hunt for P.T. Since there was no real news to report other than that which had already been reported, the cable news networks filled their twenty-four hours of air with related items of no real consequence.

Chris was in the kitchen when MSNBC ran some footage that they'd gotten from a local New York affiliate. It was of Peter Randolph being randomly interviewed in the street by a roving reporter two years earlier, asking his opinion of the Mets firing of manager Willie Randolph.

Peter had looked like a deer caught in the headlights. "He's got my name," Peter had said.

The reporter looked bemused. "What do you mean, 'He's got my name'?"

"Randolph, that's my name."

"Well, then, Randolph," said the reporter, relishing the fact that he had found an idiot to make fun of, "I guess you're pretty mad about the firing."

"I don't care nothin' about it," said Peter, turning and walking away from the camera.

Dani watched the interview intently and when it was over yelled for Chris to come back into the room.

"What's the matter?" Chris asked.

"They just showed an interview that Peter Randolph did on the street a couple of years ago. A sports thing."

"So?"

"So I talked to P.T. twice on the phone. He had a much deeper voice than this guy," she said.

"I told you, they have those voice transformer machines," Chris said. "He could have made himself sound like anyone."

"Did they find the machine in the house?"

"I don't think so. Not while I was there."

Chris and Dani continued to watch the same network, which played the interview repeatedly, obviously considering it journalistic gold. There was no doubt that the voice was very different.

"If he had a voice transformer, why would he not have it in the house?" Chris asked. "He had everything else there."

"Maybe he didn't want his grandmother to overhear him making the phone calls," Dani said.

"She worked all day."

"You think it's possible that they have the wrong guy again?" she asked.

Chris shook his head. "No, all the evidence was there. It has to be him."

"You know, the guy in that interview didn't sound too bright. Wouldn't you say that P.T., as evil as he is, is smart?"

"Absolutely," Chris said.

"Smart enough to make everybody think that Randolph is P.T.?"

"I don't know," Chris said. "I'm not smart enough to figure that out."

Chris and Dani determined that, effective immediately, they were going to reclaim their lives. That included going back to work, starting to see friends again, and getting back to doing what for them were normal activities.

Neither of them mentioned this time that "normal" was Dani moving back to her own house. For now they were both comfortable this way and didn't want to do or say anything that would lead to a change. There would be time for reflecting on their relationship later. Or never.

Chris called Kip, the first time that they had spoken in weeks, and learned that Kip was planning to go to the funeral service for Craig Andrews, who was their mutual friend.

"You going?" Kip asked.

"I don't know if I should," Chris said. "I don't want my presence to be a distraction for his family."

"Hey, he was one of your best friends. He would want you there."

Chris wasn't so sure of that, since the last time he and Craig had spoken, the question at hand was whether or not Craig believed Chris to be a serial killer.

"Okay," Chris said. "I'll go."

"You want me to pick you up?"

"No, I'll drive myself, because I want to go see my mother afterwards."

The service was held in a large chapel on Route 17 and the room was overflowing with people. In that sense, it was typical of such political funerals; allies of Craig's were there because they were allies, while adversaries were there because they wanted to pretend they were allies.

It was a political dance, somber and serious, but with more jockeying for position than the Kentucky Derby.

The minister spoke glowingly of Craig, with a familiarity that is not always apparent at such services. He recited anecdotes of Craig's youth and talked about his outstanding personal qualities, as if he had been familiar with them for a long while. If he had spent time cramming for the service, it certainly wasn't obvious to anyone there.

"To his family, he was a source of pride and inspiration. To his friends, he was a beacon of trust and understanding. To his colleagues in the political world he occupied, he was an all-too-rare example of honor and decency."

The words made Chris think of their last conversation in which Craig claimed to have sent an anonymous e-mail, the intent of which was to destroy the mayor, his political rival. It would be a stretch to view that as a gesture of honor and decency, but Chris saw no reason to reveal that secret to anyone.

But that raised larger questions that Chris had so

far been unable to answer. If Craig was telling the truth, and why wouldn't he have, then how had Peter Randolph learned of the mayor's indiscretions? Was it possible that both he and Craig knew of them and independently decided to reveal the secret to Chris? Craig had realized that the coincidence of that would be astronomical, to the point that it was virtually impossible. That was why his trust in Chris had wavered.

Perhaps Craig learned of it from someone else, and that person either knowingly or unwittingly also conveyed it to P.T. In that case, the police should be looking for that connection, and perhaps Chris should reveal the apparent existence of the e-mail to Novack, or even Quinlan.

Chris scanned the room, aware that the person who represented that connection might well be there at that moment. If so, what was that person's motive, and was he or she aware that they were a source for P.T.?

But regardless of who that person was, or what their motive might have been, it was impossible to believe that both P.T. and Craig independently decided to give the same information to Chris.

It simply did not compute.

Chris had not seen his mother in weeks, by far the longest time that had ever elapsed between visits. It made him feel terribly guilty, but if Harriet Turley was aware that he had not been around, she concealed it well.

She showed no recognition of Chris when he arrived, nor when he gently kissed her hello. Instead, she sat in her chair and stared, talking occasionally to herself, speaking words that strung together rarely made any sense.

Theirs had always been a special relationship, one in which the son confided in the mother his personal secrets. Perhaps it was so because she acted so often as both mother and father to Chris, but it was a bond that he cherished and missed.

He needed to talk to her, but she was not there. She would never be there again.

Now, more than ever, there was so much to tell her; so much had happened in the last few weeks. And then there was the most shocking news of all, the fact that her husband may well have been murdered.

But Chris would tell her none of it, not because she wouldn't understand, but out of fear that somehow she would. She deserved to be protected from the world now; it was the least he could give her.

Chris thought of Doris Randolph and how she was suffering the agony of awareness. She would not live another day without feeling the pain her grandson's actions had caused.

As he sat with his mother, quietly holding her hand, Chris thought that Doris Randolph would envy Harriet Turley the darkness.

THE MESSAGE WAS RECEIVED by CNN at the exact moment that David Gregg was dying.

His death was a particularly ignominious one. Heading to Boston for the holiday weekend, he had stopped in a rest area on the Merritt Parkway in southern Connecticut.

While not everyone in that situation bothers to flush the toilet, David was unfortunately not that type of person. So he paid dearly for his consideration and cleanliness, as the flushing action triggered the explosive, which in turn made him P.T.'s latest victim.

The news directors at CNN hastily determined that the message from P.T. was real, which was easy to do under the circumstances. They then conveyed it to the FBI, and Quinlan asked that they not go public with it. He made the request without revealing that he had received a similar message, with additional wire transfer instructions that CNN was not privy to.

CNN refused his request to sit on the story, and within a few minutes it was posted on their air for all to see.

For weeks I have made my position completely clear. If Chris Turley were to die, no one else would have to. I am sorry that neither he nor anyone else chose to meet my very simple condition.

Instead, my home has been invaded and my mother terrorized. This has been done by people under the ridiculous impression that it is possible to capture or stop me.

Now it is too late, they have gone too far, and therefore I am going to speak in the only language understood by the corrupt government and equally corrupt media. The language of money.

If I do not receive one hundred million dollars by the last moment of the last day of this calendar year, the toll that I will exact in human life and treasure will make all that preceded it pale into insignificance. And then the price will rise.

Since there are those who will question the origin of this message, I am sending it at the exact moment that a traveler in Connecticut has lost his life because I have been ignored. He did not have to die, nor does anyone else.

So you have been warned. You can continue to cause your own suffering, or you can prevent it. It will be your decision.

The number is now one.

The message set off another furor, both in the media and the public square, about what should be done to stop P.T. The president of the United States felt compelled to issue a statement that "the United States does not negotiate with terrorists, homegrown or otherwise," which seemed to beg the point.

The fact was that P.T. was not negotiating, he was demanding, and he had long ago demonstrated the willingness and capability of backing up his threats.

There were competing arguments on both sides and they were taking place at the highest level. While the president sounded assertive and confident in his message, that was not how it played out behind the scenes.

As was the president's style, he played devil's advocate in a meeting with the attorney general, saying that, "I think we need to consider paying him."

The attorney general was adamant in his opposition, using arguments that were standard and time-tested. "I disagree, Mr. President. We have no guarantee that it would accomplish anything. He could easily continue to kill and demand more money."

"Or he could stop and go buy himself an island somewhere," the president said.

"Which would be an incentive for others to start imitating him, thinking that if they scare people enough, they'll get their own payoff."

"What's the real downside to paying him? Money? Are we deeming money to be more important than lives?"

The attorney general shook his head. "I think caving in would be a political disaster."

"Not if it makes the killing stop," the president said. Ultimately, he went along with the refusal to pay, while privately leaving open that possibility in the future.

There was much public speculation about the meaning of "one" at the end of the message. Chris had not publicly revealed his belief that P.T. was counting down to New Year's Eve. He knew it was a significant and ominous threat, but the authorities stated their belief that it simply referred to the date on which the money demand was deadlined.

Doris Randolph didn't know where to turn. Ever since Peter's disappearance and the subsequent search of her house, she had felt stunned and distraught. She didn't go to work, but spent all day watching television, hating what she was hearing about Peter and cringing that at any moment she would hear that he had been captured. Or worse. Much worse.

Doris was not a stupid woman, not by a long shot, and she understood that the evidence against Peter was overwhelming, yet she still had her doubts.

And now she had more than her doubts. She felt she had proof.

But she didn't know where to take it. The world had come down on her head; the police and FBI had labeled Peter as armed and dangerous, and it was clear that he would be taken dead or alive. Even her friends had deserted her; she had only heard from two of them since all hell had broken loose.

In the public's mind, her grandson made Hitler and bin Laden look like Penn and Teller.

Doris was afraid to leave her house; the press gathered in front intimidated her. Whenever she went outside, even to get the mail, they pushed towards her and yelled questions at her.

She felt instinctively that a person she could trust, and who might also be able to help her, was Chris Turley. She called him at the newspaper and though they at first said he wasn't available, they put her through when she identified herself.

"Mr. Turley, I need to speak with you," she said.

"What about?"

"Peter. I heard something today . . . Mr. Turley, my Peter did not do this. I have proof."

"What did you hear? No, wait a minute, don't say anything over the phone." Chris knew that his office phone was likely still tapped and was sure that hers would be tapped, as well. "Can you come here?"

"I'm afraid . . . there are so many people outside."

Chris felt terrible for this woman; she was a prisoner in her own home. None of what she was going through was her fault, yet it would ultimately define her life. And he could certainly identify with her being harassed by press in front of her home. "I'll come to you. I can be there in an hour."

"Thank you. I'm afraid I have little in the house to offer you. I haven't been able to go to the market."

"Don't worry about it. I'll see you soon."

When he got off the phone, he called Dani at home. "You up for taking a ride?"

"Where to?"

"To visit Peter Randolph's grandmother. I think it

would make her feel better if you were there. But we have to make a stop first."

Chris picked up Dani and they went to the supermarket on the way to the Randolph house, where they loaded up on groceries for her. He couldn't reduce her fear, but hopefully he could have an impact on her hunger.

Novack was annoyed. That in itself was not exactly a news event; he spent his entire waking life annoyed. And it fed on itself and multiplied; the very state of feeling annoyed was annoying to him.

The source of his current annoyance was his inability to connect Peter Randolph to Mayor Alex Stanley, or even to Charity, the hooker who visited the mayor that night. Most of the detectives in the department were still on that aspect of the case, since it was the only one officially under their jurisdiction, and no one had uncovered even the slightest bit of information that could explain how Peter knew what would happen that night.

Perhaps even more significant, every single neighbor of the Randolphs referred to Peter as a hermit who almost never left the house. Yet obviously P.T. had to have spent a great deal of time out and about, unless he was working with an accomplice, which seemed unlikely. There would have been no logical reason for Peter to have snuck out of the house on all those occasions, yet the neighbors said they almost never saw him.

On the other hand, these nagging doubts that Novack had were countered by the damning evidence found in the Randolph house and by the statement from P.T. broadcast on CNN. It amounted to a virtual confession by Peter Randolph; he even referred to his house being "invaded."

When Novack was in this mood, nobody wanted to come near him, but sometimes it was unavoidable. One of the officers assigned to him, a young patrolman named Fred McCaskill, entered Novack's office.

"Detective, I just wanted to tell you that I'm leaving for the day." Since they were on overtime mode, Novack insisted on being told when officers were leaving, so that he could make last-minute changes in their schedule if he needed them to stay around. It was not something that officers looked forward to.

"So Randolph has been captured?" he asked.

"No, sir. I don't believe so. No."

"So you're going to do something more important than trying to find him? Where are you going?"

"Home. And then I'm taking my wife to the movies."

Novack nodded. "Very commendable. A grateful public thanks you. Listen to the radio on the way home from the movie; that way you can find out if somebody else died while you were sucking down popcorn."

The officer was growing more nervous by the moment. "If you want me to stay, I . . ."

Before Novack could answer, Willingham came by

and extricated the officer from the conversation, sending him on his way. After he left, his partner said, "I see we're in a cheery mood?"

"Kiss my ass," Novack said.

"HE SAID I WAS his mother," Doris Randolph said as soon as they walked in the door.

"What do you mean?" asked Chris. "Who said that?"

"Peter. No, not Peter. In that horrible statement on the television, the one they said was from Peter. It said that I was his mother. But I'm not. I'm his grandmother."

"Maybe he made a mistake," Chris said.

"Chris . . ." Dani said, her tone telling him that he should know better.

"He would never make that kind of mistake," Doris said. "How could he? Would you? Peter didn't say that; someone else did."

"Maybe it was transcribed incorrectly. Maybe it really said 'grandmother.'" He didn't want to give this woman false hope that all of this was going to blow over and she'd have her grandson back.

"Can you find out if that's true?" she asked.

Chris nodded. "Yes, the original message was sent over the wire. I saw a copy of it; we even have it up on our Web site. Do you have a computer?"

She shook her head. "The FBI took it when they took Peter's."

"No problem," he said. He asked Dani for her cell phone, since it was the one the FBI was least likely to listen to. He called Scott Ryder at the office.

"Scott, I need you to do something for me."

"Sure. What's up?"

"Take a look at the message from P.T. that CNN circulated."

"What about it?" Scott asked. He was at the moment looking right at it, since it was on the front page of the newspaper Web site. Of course, he was familiar with it anyway, since he wrote it.

"Does it refer to his mother being terrorized, or his grandmother?"

"Mother. Why?"

"Gotta go," Chris said. "Thanks. I'll talk to you later."

Scott got off the phone and in two minutes online realized his error. He was furious at himself; it was the first mistake he was aware of since the beginning of the operation.

He knew that no serious harm would come of it; the belief that Peter Randolph was P.T. was too overwhelming to be changed by something as minor as this. Still, it was an upsetting thing to have happen, especially when he was so close to the end.

It was the least festive holiday season that anyone could remember. The number of Christmas parties and planned New Year's Eve parties was dramatically reduced, since people felt that P.T. would be more likely to attack a crowd, so as to achieve maximum impact. That was despite the fact that not since the medical center had he done anything other than target individuals.

The governors of New Jersey and New York released a report that they had commissioned together which said that even if P.T. were captured immediately, the economic impact he had already caused would be felt for at least seven years.

Tourism had slowed to a trickle; New York hotels that were ordinarily impossible to get into at that time of year were operating at an average forty percent capacity. Broadway shows that usually played to capacity were giving away tickets at half price, but that barely made a dent in the vast expanses of empty seats.

The producers of many shows were faced with the choice of closing down or trying to stay alive in the hope that P.T. would be caught soon. But few people had a real expectation of that.

Though tips were coming in by the thousands, the FBI, state, and local police were making no significant progress in locating Peter Randolph.

Quinlan did not believe that he was in the area at all; literally millions of eyes had seen his picture and were searching for him. And while it was true that he could be holed up somewhere, out of sight and with an ample supply of food and water, Quinlan doubted that was the case.

Peter would have had no reason to believe that his identity would be discovered, and though he could have had a hideout as a backup in case he was forced out of his home, it seemed more likely that he had fled the area.

The unfortunate truth was that he could be anywhere in the country, his deadly devices already planted and under his control. Quinlan did not believe that the countdown merely represented the days until the ransom was due; he felt that P.T. was threatening to pull off a major event on New Year's Eve or New Year's Day.

At Quinlan's suggestion, the word went out to substantially increase security at all major events, such as New Year's concerts and college bowl games.

While it was well above Quinlan's pay grade, he knew that a lot of consideration had been given to paying P.T. the money, but that the final decision was not to do so. Quinlan suspected that if the payment could be made with a guarantee of secrecy, the president would authorize it. But without that guarantee, it represented far too great a political risk.

Lawrence Terry was putting a lot of pressure on Chris to continue filing stories about the crisis. "This is our story," Lawrence said, "and we're letting it get away from us."

"The guy has stopped calling me," Chris said. "I don't know any more of what's going on than anyone else."

"What about this mother-grandmother thing?" Lawrence asked.

Chris was jolted by the question. "How did you know about that?"

"How did I know about it?" Lawrence asked. "What do you think I am, the janitor? I'm running this paper, and I keep on top of what the hell is going on."

Chris had told only Dani and Scott Ryder about his conversation with Doris Randolph. He doubted that Dani would have said anything, so he would have to speak to Scott about it.

He was annoyed with Scott if he was the source, but not terribly so. He hadn't told Scott to keep it confidential and Lawrence could be a rather intimidating boss. He may have known that Scott had received a call from Chris and demanded to know what it was about.

"I don't want to write about that yet," Chris said. "I don't want P.T. to know about it."

Lawrence slammed his hand down on the desk in anger, an uncharacteristic display for him, at least where Chris was concerned. The pressure was obviously getting to him, as it was getting to everybody.

"Who are you, Sherlock fucking Holmes?" He calmed down a little and added in a more controlled voice, "Chris, our job is not to worry about what P.T. knows. It's to make sure that our readers get to know. Okay?"

"Okay, I hear you. I'll get to it."

"Chris, there's a Pulitzer at stake here. It's the biggest story either of us will ever cover. Bigger than any story your father ever covered."

"Lawrence, I'll get to it."

"Good," Lawrence said. "Knock it out of the park."

"LET ME GUESS. YOU don't think Randolph is the guy" was what Novack said into the phone when he learned that Chris was on the line. Chris was calling from Dani's cell phone so that the FBI would not be taping the call.

"I have my doubts," Chris said.

"I know the feeling."

They agreed to meet at Novack's office to discuss their shared concerns. As Chris was leaving the paper, he ran into Scott Ryder. "Hey, Scott. Did you tell Lawrence I was asking about what P.T. said in the statement about his mother?"

Scott shrugged. "Sorry, Chris. He practically beat it out of me."

Chris nodded. "That's what I figured. Don't worry about it."

Once Chris got to Novack's office, the detective closed the door and asked, "Okay, what have you got?"

"You want to call your partner in so I can say this once?"

"No, he thinks I'm off the deep end on this one."

Chris related the reasons for his suspicion, including the failure to find a voice transformer at the house and the fact that the statement referred to Doris Randolph as Peter's mother.

Novack listened and said, "That's it?"

"No." He told Novack of his last conversation with Craig and of how Craig said he had sent an anonymous e-mail to Chris, alerting him to what the mayor was doing. The coincidence of P.T. and Craig giving him the same unsolicited tip was just too great to believe. "There's no way Craig Andrews was connected to Peter Randolph."

"That e-mail thing is something you might have mentioned earlier," Novack said.

Chris nodded. "I might have, but I didn't."

Novack, at Chris's prodding, shared his own reasons for his doubts about Peter's guilt. He talked about his inability to connect Peter to the mayor in any way, as well as Peter's neighbors' unanimous declarations that he almost never left the house.

"On the other hand," Novack said, "we found all that stuff at the house, and that statement was a goddamn confession. If Randolph isn't the guy, somebody has sure as hell set him up as well as someone can be set up."

"P.T. is smart," Chris said. "Did you see Randolph do that TV interview? He is not the sharpest tool in the shed."

"So where is he?"

"He's running. Hell, I'd run, too, if the whole world thought I was a mass murderer."

"He left three days before we got to his house," Novack pointed out.

"Look, I'm not saying Randolph is not P.T. I think he probably is. I'm just raising the possibility that this is not airtight, okay? And I think someone should be looking into it."

"That someone is Quinlan," Novack said. "He's got all the resources."

"He thought I was P.T.," said Chris.

"Get over it. And besides, I told you he was never on board with that. They rammed it down his throat."

"Can you set up a meeting?" Chris asked.

"I think so."

"You'd better hurry, because tomorrow is New Year's Eve. And I've got a feeling that after that it's going to be too late."

Scott Ryder took the rest of the day off from work, not unusual for this time of year. Half the staff was on vacation, and if any problems came up on the Web site, he could handle them from his computer at home.

It was December 30, and Scott knew that the countdown demanded he kill someone before the day was out. The truth was that he would rather not, as it would take him away from watching the coverage on television. Television watching had never been more fun; he would rather watch the talking heads blabbing about the P.T. crisis than the Super Bowl.

But Scott knew the importance of delivering on one's promises, or threats, in this case. Doing so tomorrow night would be even more important. Scott had no illusions that the money would be paid according to his timetable demand, so he would hit them harder than they had ever been hit.

And then they would pay, because they would know he meant exactly what he said.

Scott consulted his GPS monitors and saw that forty-five of the fifty-one were inactive. That percentage got higher every time he looked, most likely a reflection of the fact that people were growing more and more afraid to drive their cars.

As he always did, Scott put the possibilities into a hat and drew out the winning, or in this case losing, entry. He didn't know the name of the owner of the car, or for that matter whether or not it was the owner who was driving at that moment. All he knew was that the car was on the Cross Bronx Expressway heading west towards the George Washington Bridge, which was two and a half miles away.

He decided to play a little game with himself. If the driver turned off before the bridge, he would let him live and choose another car. If he got onto the bridge, Scott would blow up his car when he was approximately midway across.

The driver passed a number of exits, continuing to head for the bridge. Finally, there were just two possibilities remaining, either to get onto the bridge or take the Henry Hudson Parkway south.

Scott was fascinated as he watched the blip on the screen; this represented the ultimate video game. He didn't know the driver, but he found himself rooting for him or her to take the exit and be saved.

And that is exactly what happened. The car edged over to the right lane and exited onto the Henry Hudson Parkway. It was an amazing human drama that had just taken place, and only Scott got to watch and experience it. And he was happy with the ending.

Then, once again turning to the business at hand, he blew up a car on the Major Deegan Expressway, as it passed Yonkers Raceway. The driver was killed, as was the driver of a car behind it, which veered into the embankment.

Scott turned on the television for a few minutes, since he had to leave shortly to take a long drive. Within ten minutes the media had reported the explosions and identified the victims.

"Don't blame me," Scott said to the television. "Blame the guy on the Henry Hudson."

QUINLAN AGREED TO SEE Chris and Novack immediately.

Novack had described it as "important," and by this point Quinlan had a healthy respect for Novack's instincts as a cop. The fact that Chris was coming along only added to Quinlan's curiosity and willingness to take up some of his very precious and limited time with a meeting.

They went to Quinlan's office, but had to wait in an anteroom for a half hour. What they didn't know was that Quinlan was spending that time on another in a seemingly endless series of conference calls, which included Director Kramer and the attorney general, and which did nothing to move the case forward.

Quinlan could have summed up the entire call in one sentence; Peter Randolph was nowhere to be found and everybody was very pissed off about it.

When Quinlan got off the phone, he called Novack and Chris in. "Don't tell me anything that is going to make me feel worse," he said.

"Okay," Novack said. "I love your outfit."

Quinlan nodded. "Thanks. Now you can give it to me straight."

"We don't think Peter Randolph is P.T.," Chris said.

"Does that mean you're confessing?"

Novack cut in. "Chris doesn't think Randolph is P.T. I wouldn't state it quite so strongly. I would say there's a chance he's not."

"I assume you've got reasons?" Quinlan asked.

Chris and Novack proceeded to give the reasons they had discussed among themselves. Quinlan just listened for ten minutes, not interrupting.

When they finished, Quinlan said, "You're forgetting one thing."

"What's that?" Novack asked.

"Funding. Where did Randolph get the funding?"

"What are you talking about?" asked Novack.

Quinlan started to answer, but Chris interrupted. "He's right. He didn't make those explosives in his garage; he had to have bought the material from somewhere. And the other equipment, the GPS devices, the voice transformer, those things cost real money."

Quinlan nodded. "And Randolph hadn't held down a job since he got out of the army. His sixty-eight-year-old grandmother has been working in an office so they could make ends meet. So where the hell did he get the money?"

"Wait a minute," Novack said. "Are you saying you don't think Randolph is the guy, either?"

"I'm more with you," Quinlan said. "I have my doubts, but the evidence still points to Randolph. Having said that, P.T. has been jerking our chain since day one, so I don't completely trust the evidence. Especially when it was just sitting there for us to take. It might as well have been gift wrapped with a confession."

Quinlan's phone rang and he picked it up. "Quinlan." After a pause, he said, "Are our people on the way?" Then, "Keep me posted."

He hung up the phone and turned to Chris and Novack. "Peter Randolph's credit card was just used to buy gas on the westbound side of a highway outside Pittsburgh."

"Gee whiz," Novack said with obvious sarcasm. "What a wonderful, lucky break."

Quinlan nodded. "The guy makes the entire United States government look like idiots for six weeks and then he forgets to bring gas money? This really stinks."

"So what are we gonna do?" Chris asked.

"We?"

"Yeah, we. I'm more a part of this than you are. This guy has been using me, using my name, to kill people. Unless you still think that I'm P.T. and that I'm sitting in your office while I'm also driving past Pittsburgh. So what are we gonna do?"

"I'm going to keep looking for P.T., whether it's Randolph or somebody else."

"What about us?"

"I've got an idea," Quinlan said. "If Randolph is not P.T., why don't you go out and find the son of a bitch who is?"

Most publicly sanctioned New Year's Eve events were planned to go on as scheduled, since if politicians canceled them, they might be branded as wimps who caved in to a terrorist.

The most important celebration, the one that symbolized New Year's Eve around the world, was the dropping of the ball in Times Square. In a normal year, more than a million people would gather to freeze, drink, and cheer as the ball made its gradual descent and the clock struck midnight.

With the ongoing crisis, there was no really accurate way to know how many people would show up. The temperature was going to be in the forties, positively balmy by New York standards, with no precipitation. Under normal circumstances, a record crowd would be expected.

Of course, these circumstances couldn't be less normal and government officials were privately predicting less than three hundred thousand people. That was still a massive crowd, of course, and one that you wouldn't want in the vicinity of a bomb detonation.

The mayor of New York held a press conference to discuss the security arrangements for the evening. Of course, every time he was asked a direct question about specifics, he said that he couldn't talk about it because it involved security concerns.

But his overall message was crystal clear. The security in Times Square that night would be airtight. The mayor was willing to reveal that the area would be closed off for six hours in the late afternoon and evening and only then would people be let in, after going through special explosive detecting machines that were newly developed for airport use.

The mayor wanted everybody to be alert and to point out anything unusual to one of the enormous contingent of law enforcement officials that would be on hand. But he emphasized that he also wanted everyone to have fun and in the process show the world that New Yorkers didn't back down from anybody.

Of course, since there would likely be three-quarters of a million fewer people because of P.T., and assuming all those people weren't from Jersey, it was likely that some New Yorkers were smart enough to back down when the occasion called for it.

TWO FBI TEAMS IMMEDIATELY descended on the gas station where P.T.'s credit card was used.

It was three blocks from the highway, a small, two-pump station that did not have video camera surveillance. Forensics took fingerprints, but with all the people who came through there, it was basically a hopeless cause.

"You were right, Nick," said Agent Juan Cabrera, calling from the scene outside Pittsburgh. He had become Quinlan's closest confidant since Serrano's death and Quinlan had sent him out personally to assess the situation. "I think the guy was jerking our chain."

"I would rather have been wrong," Quinlan said. "But this is not a guy who makes stupid mistakes."

"So what do you want to do?"

"Well, either he used the card and doubled back east or someone else used it. Did the pump require a PIN number?"

"No."

"Treat it as if it were real; send the word out," Quinlan said. "Use as much local manpower as you can and get your ass back here."

"Will do."

An announcement went out to law enforcement and the public through various media outlets in the area that there was a possible sighting of Randolph. On the chance that he was actually heading west, big cities like Cleveland, Chicago, and Detroit were alerted to be extra vigilant, especially on New Year's Eve.

The political situation within the Justice Department being what it was, Quinlan had to tread carefully. He organized a group of eight agents, reporting directly to him, who were to operate independently and secretly, under the assumption that Randolph was not P.T. and that the real P.T. had likely killed him.

Down deep, Quinlan had a strong hunch that Novack and Chris were correct, and he couldn't remember the last time that one of those hunches was wrong.

Doris Randolph spent all her time glued to the television, not wanting to watch but powerless not to. She was therefore tuned in on New Year's Eve morning, when CNN received and broadcast another message they said had come from her grandson, Peter.

"There are eighteen hours to go in the year and my demands continue to be ignored," the message began. P.T. had not sent the same message to the FBI this time, since they already had the wiring instructions. He was far more interested in speaking to the public.

"Government officials, the people you elect and hire to protect you are boasting that their intransigence is a sign of political courage. On the contrary, it is an act of reckless disregard for your collective welfare.

"If they do not have the wisdom to reconsider, then tomorrow morning my price will have doubled.

"And after what the nation will have experienced in the interim, they will not hesitate to pay it."

When the message was complete, the CNN anchor launched into a discussion of Peter, as if it were certain that he was P.T.

Doris grew more and more upset every time she heard such things. Why could no one else see the truth?

Lawrence Terry was upset. Chris Turley, by now the most famous reporter in the country, had stopped reporting and Lawrence was watching the *Bergen News*'s dominant position in the P.T. case begin to slip away.

He called Chris into his office, a meeting that Chris had been dreading, knowing it would come eventually. He hated saying no to Lawrence, although he couldn't quite remember a time when he had actually tried it. The last time they had talked, Lawrence had intimidated him into saying that he would file a story, and he meant to, but he simply never had the time.

Chris felt that he and Novack were on to something and that the rest of the world was spinning its wheels looking for Peter Randolph. The real P.T. was out there, laughing at them, and about to do something far deadlier than anything that had come before it.

When Chris came in, the first thing Lawrence didn't do was offer him some scotch. It was an ominous sign that was not lost on Chris, who did not want a confrontation, but wanted only to pacify Lawrence and get out.

Lawrence opted for the reasonable, rather than angry, approach. "Chris, we are losing this story. With every minute that goes by, we are losing this story."

"I'll write something, Lawrence."

"That's what you keep saying. You're still drawing a paycheck, right? I mean, last time I checked . . . you still work here, don't you?"

"Unless you're firing me."

"I'm trying to get you to do your job."

"Believe it or not, that's what I'm doing. And right now I'm working on something that may turn out to be the biggest of all."

This, of course, piqued Lawrence's interest. "About P.T.?"

"Very much about P.T."

"Tell me what the hell you are talking about," Lawrence said.

"It's too soon to go with it, Lawrence. It's not anywhere near nailed down. Right now it's just a hunch, but Novack has the same hunch."

"I understand. Now what is it?"

"Do you promise not to have anyone else write it before it's ready?" Chris asked.

"You're really starting to piss me off," Lawrence said.

"I understand that, but you need to promise."

"Fine. Done," Lawrence said.

Chris decided to accept that; he knew he was unlikely to extract the word "promise." "Novack and I don't think Peter Randolph is P.T."

Lawrence's shock was evident. "Based on what?"

Chris went through the litany of their reasons and

Lawrence listened without interrupting. When Chris finished, he said, "I'm not buying it."

"I'm not selling it, Lawrence. But it's what I think."

"You can't write that. Twenty minutes after it hits the stands, they'll catch Randolph, he'll confess, and we'll look like idiots."

"That's fine. I told you I need to develop it more."

"His house was filled with incriminating evidence; even the Simpson jury would convict him."

Chris nodded. "I know that."

"And if he's not guilty," Lawrence said, "then where the hell is he now, on a cruise?"

"Maybe he's on the run because the entire world is after him. Or maybe he's dead, killed by the guy who set him up."

"You're way out there on this one, Chris. You're chasing a fairy tale, while every other news operation in the country is after the real story."

"You always told me to trust my instincts, Lawrence. You said I had my father's instincts; the only difference was the trust level."

"Not even your father's instincts were right every time."

"But mine have been damn good on this case," Chris said. "The only reason the cops even know about Randolph was because I told them."

Lawrence nodded. "And I gave you full credit for that."

"Actually, the truth is that Scott deserves most of the credit. He found out about Randolph and told me . . ." Chris stopped talking as the realization hit him.

"What's the matter?" Lawrence asked.

Chris was silent for another few seconds, playing it out in his mind, before responding. "Lawrence, Scott was doing research work for me online. He came to me and told me about Gerald Randolph being hurt by my father. I wasn't interested, because Randolph was dead."

"So?"

"So Scott said he flagged it not just because Gerald Randolph had a son, but because he had committed suicide, and P.T. had mentioned suicide to me."

"I'm not sure where you're going with this."

"Lawrence, at that point I hadn't told anyone that P.T. mentioned suicide to me. I didn't tell you, or Dani, not anyone. And I sure as hell didn't write about it. It's not something I wanted anyone to know. So how the hell did Scott know about it?"

"Maybe you told him and forgot."

Chris shook his head. "No, I . . . damn, maybe that's what happened to Craig's e-mail. Maybe Scott intercepted it. He knew my passwords from when he worked on my computer."

"What e-mail?" Lawrence asked, since Chris had never mentioned that to Lawrence or anyone besides Novack and Dani.

Chris ignored the question. "And all this technological stuff that P.T. is so good at; Scott could do that stuff in his sleep." The truth was coming at him in waves. "And he knew about Timmerman!"

Finally, Lawrence seemed to realize where Chris was headed. "You're saying that Scott Ryder is P.T.?"

"Not only that, Lawrence. My instincts are saying it."

"My instincts have been around longer than yours. And they're saying that yours are full of shit."

"He's not in today," Chris said.

"Well, then he's obviously a serial killer."

"Come on . . ."

"Chris, you recommended the guy for the job. He's been a model citizen."

Chris wasn't having any of it. "I've got to call Novack."

"Wait a minute; that does you no good."

"What do you mean?"

"Let's assume you're right, although I don't think you are. And let's further assume that we've only got hours left to prevent something big."

"Okay . . ." Chris said, prompting him to talk more quickly.

"We get the police involved, it'll tip him off. And they can't go barging in; believe me, there's not enough here to get a search warrant."

Chris nodded; Lawrence was clearly right about that. "Okay. You have a better way?"

"I think so. I'll call Scott and tell him we have some kind of disaster going on with the Web site and that he needs to get his ass down here immediately. Then you go to his house and check it out. Find something concrete that we can tell the cops about."

"What if he refuses to come in?"

Lawrence frowned; such refusals were unheard of. "He'll come in. And if the house is locked, just break a damn window. The paper will pay for it."

Lawrence picked up the phone, not really waiting for Chris to agree to the plan. He buzzed his secretary and said, "Kathy, get me Scott Ryder on the phone right away."

He put down the phone and picked it back up when it rang, thirty seconds later. "Hello . . . Scott, I've got Chris Turley here and we've got big trouble with the site." He listened for a few moments and said, "How the hell do I know? That's what I pay you for." Then, a few moments later, he said, "Absolutely. Good."

Lawrence hung up the phone and smiled. "He'll be here in fifteen minutes."

Chris stood up. "I'm on my way. If Scott doesn't come in, or you don't hear from me within the hour, call Novack."

"The hell with Novack," Lawrence said. "I'll call the damn chief. He owes me."

Chris started for the door when Lawrence said, "Just be careful."

CHRIS STOPPED IN DANI'S office to tell her where he was going.

She had come in to clean out her office and take home her personal things. "You're going to break into his house?" she asked.

He nodded. "Yes. I'd rather not, and if I'm wrong I'll apologize, but this is too important."

"Make sure he's out of there before you do."

"I will, but he told Lawrence he's on his way here."

"Let me come with you. Two of us searching is better than one."

He shook his head. "No, but if you don't hear from me in an hour, make sure Lawrence calls the chief of police."

She kissed him. "Okay, but watch out for yourself. Breaking and entering is not your strong point."

He smiled. "I'm multitalented."

"Just call me the minute you're out of there."

"I will. I promise."

Within five minutes of getting Lawrence's call, Scott Ryder left the house. This was an unplanned interruption, but not in any sense a big problem. Everything was in place and ready to go; for today, at least, Scott was just going to sit back and watch it happen.

He would do exactly what Lawrence said and it would be no problem at all.

Times Square was completely shut down as part of the security preparations for the New Year's Eve festivities. For the police it was an eerie feeling; the emptiness made it feel like it was four o'clock in the morning, when actually it wasn't even yet six in the evening.

The mayor, on the advice of the FBI, allowed the military to arrange to jam all cell and radio frequencies in the area. That would prevent remote detonations using cell phones or radio waves. It was believed that P.T. had been detonating his bombs through the use of a cell phone, though radio frequencies were also a possibility. This would effectively eliminate both.

The decision was made not to make an announcement about the lack of cell service. The celebrating crowd might be surprised and annoyed, but it was still considered better to keep P.T. in the dark about it.

The checkpoints would open at about 9:00 P.M., and the crowds and TV crews would be allowed entry then.

Chris arrived at Scott's Elmwood Park home, which was on the end of a cul-de-sac, which would create more privacy for what he was going to do. The only real problem he had was that he didn't know what he was going to do.

Chris didn't see Scott's car anywhere, at least not on the street. He didn't see it when he looked in through the garage window, either. That was certainly a good indication that he had gone to the office as Lawrence requested.

Chris, never comfortable with carrying the gun he'd bought, had left it at home, so it was not going to be much help now that he might need it. He went to the front door and rang the bell. If Scott answered, he would make up some story about thinking Scott was home sick and checking on him. It wouldn't be terribly persuasive, but it would be enough to get himself out of there.

No one answered the bell, so Chris rang it twice more, just to be extra sure. When there was still no answer, he tried the doorknob, on the unlikely chance that the door would open.

It did.

Scott had failed to lock it when he left. After quickly looking around to make sure he wasn't being watched, Chris opened the door and went inside.

He had been in that house a couple of times before, when he picked Scott up to take him to basketball games. But he really didn't know his way around, so he decided to just go from room to room, using his cell phone to take pictures.

Chris decided to allow himself fifteen minutes, assuming that there was no way Scott could deal with Lawrence that quickly and get back home. It was a small house, so that would be more than enough time.

Chris started in the kitchen, but there seemed to be nothing there that was in any way sinister. The closest thing to technology was an answering machine, but it looked like a standard model. Nevertheless, Chris photographed it and moved on.

Chris walked into the den and immediately knew he could safely cut his search short. There was a large computer console, feeding into three television screens, running silently and tuned to the three cable news networks.

At the moment, they were all covering the P.T. drama, which was no surprise, since that was pretty much what they did all day. Chris believed Scott was taping them to look at when he returned.

On a table were tools and a great deal of hardware. Chris was no expert, but he assumed that was where Scott put together the detonation devices. Chris didn't see any explosives, but he was not sure he would know it if he did.

But what made Scott's guilt an absolute certainty was the machine on a table attached to the telephone. Chris had no doubt it was a voice transforming machine, exactly like the one he had researched online.

Even though he had strongly suspected it, the realization hit Chris like a punch in the stomach.

Scott was P.T.

Chris quickly photographed everything in the room. He could look further in the house, but he felt there was no reason to take the risk. He had seen all he needed to see, now it was time to call in the professionals.

"Well, Chris, so nice of you to drop by."

Chris whirled to see Scott standing in the doorway, smiling, a gun in his hand.

"Scott, what are you doing? I just came by because I thought you were sick, and . . ."

Scott laughed. "Really? Did you bring me some soup?"

"Scott . . ."

"Turned out there wasn't such a big problem with the Web site or I might have missed you. Did you get some nice pictures?"

Chris's only priority at the moment was staying alive for the next hour. Between Lawrence and Dani, they would bring in the police when he did not return. He had to somehow prevent Scott from killing him before then and one way he could think to do that was to keep him talking.

"What have you got planned for tonight?" Chris asked.

"Well, it's New Year's Eve, so I considered going to one of those fancy black-tie parties. But then I figured, been there, done that. So instead I decided to blow up Times Square."

Chris tried to conceal his reaction to the magnitude of Scott's plan, but he was stunned by it. "Why?" was all he could say.

Scott laughed again. "Because it's there. And it's gonna be great. People are going to tune in to watch the ball drop, but instead they're going to watch it explode."

"What do you gain from this?"

"Money. Hey, you want to watch the show with me tonight? It's not Dick Clark anymore, which is a shame. I've wanted to blow him up for years. But it'll still be fun, and we can roast marshmallows, or make s'mores, or whatever the hell those things are called."

If Scott wasn't just babbling incoherently, then what he just said meant that he had no intention of killing Chris immediately. Which also meant there was a decent chance Chris would be rescued.

"I'll watch it with you."

"Great. Now let's get you tied up."

He took a large electrical cord and started to wrap Chris's wrists. As he was doing so, Chris asked, "Where is Peter Randolph?"

"Someplace where no one is ever going to find him. Did you know he killed your father?"

"I assumed he did."

Scott nodded. "Yup, stuck some poison in him right there in the supermarket. The guy was really messed up in the head."

Chris didn't have time to reflect on the irony of that statement. "What are you going to do with me?"

"Hey, I'm not going to do anything; we're basket-ball buddies. But Petey Randolph is going to kill you when the time is right."

"When will that be?"

"After they pay the money."

IT HAD ONLY BEEN forty-five minutes, but Dani was very worried.

Chris should have been out of Scott's house already and he'd said he would call her as soon as he was. When she hadn't heard a word, she went by Scott's office to find that it was dark and he was nowhere to be seen.

Dani went up to Lawrence's office and saw that his door was closed. She said to his secretary, "I have to see Mr. Terry."

"Do you have an appointment?"

"No," she said as she opened Lawrence's door and went in.

Lawrence was sitting at his desk, talking on the phone, when he saw her come in. "I'll call you back," he said into the phone.

She was obviously very stressed, so he said, "Dani, what's wrong?"

"Chris hasn't come back yet and Scott's not in his office."

Lawrence looked at his watch and said, "Shit." He picked up the phone and asked his secretary to find out if Scott was still in the building. He waited for a couple of minutes, then said, "Thanks," and hung up the phone.

"He's not here," said Lawrence. "But it hasn't been that long."

"Almost an hour," Dani said. "We should have heard from Chris by now."

Lawrence looked at his watch again. "You're right. Damn, I hope he didn't do anything stupid. I'm going to bring in the police."

Dani nodded. "Thank you. I'm going to go to Scott's house."

Lawrence said, "I'll go with you."

"Okay. I'll get my car out of the garage while you call the police. Get to Novack; he'll know what to do."

"I'm going to call the chief; he'll bring Novack in and probably a SWAT team with him."

The idea of that worried Dani; she feared that if they went barging in, Chris could be killed, either by Scott or in the crossfire. But she was out of her element and had to trust that they would know how to handle it.

She went downstairs to get the car and drove it to the front to meet Lawrence. She waited at least five minutes, which made her fear that he was having trouble getting the police to do what he wanted. In the meantime, she had still not heard from Chris, which was a development that seemed more ominous by the minute.

Lawrence finally came out the door, moving as fast as his seventy-year-old legs could carry him. He quickly got in the car and she pulled away.

"I hope you have the address," she said.

"I do. It's in Elmwood Park. Get on Route 4 west."

"Are the police on their way?"

Lawrence nodded. "If the idiots don't get lost. We're going to meet up with Novack two blocks from the house and figure out the best way to approach it."

They drove in relative silence the rest of the way, with Dani's panic mounting. It was no longer possible to rationalize not having heard from Chris in a way that wasn't frightening to contemplate.

They got off the highway and drove for another two minutes, with Lawrence directing her to make a few turns. Dani said, "Where are we meeting the police?"

"There aren't any police, Dani," Lawrence said. When she looked at him, he was pointing a small handgun at her.

Surprisingly, her primary reaction was anger, rather than surprise or fear. "You son of a bitch."

"I'm sorry, I never wanted it to come to this. The deaths were to be kept to a minimum; it would have been just as big a story. Chris would have been a superstar and we would have won a barrel full of Pulitzers. But Ryder went out of control; there was nothing I could do."

"So now you're going to kill me, and Chris?"

"I wish I saw an alternative, believe me."

She continued driving, her mind racing to come up with a way out of this predicament. She knew one thing—there was no way she was letting him take her to Scott Ryder's house. That meant certain death.

She started to give the car more gas, speeding up as they went down the street.

"What the hell do you think you're doing?" Lawrence asked.

"What are you going to do, shoot me, you piece of garbage? You do and we'll crash." As she talked, she continued to increase their speed.

"Slow down! Slow the damn car down!" He realized in horror that he had not even put on his seat belt when he got in the car. He tried to do so, but fumbled with it as he also tried to keep the gun pointed at Dani.

"Shoot me, asshole! Shoot me and both of us can die right here." As she talked, she pressed a control and instructions kept flashing on the dashboard. When it came to "deactivate passenger air bag," she pressed the button.

"I'll shoot!" he screamed. "Goddamnit, slow down or I will shoot!"

But she had no intention of slowing down. Instead, she took a deep breath and prayed that she wouldn't die. Then she veered off the road and deliberately rammed a telephone pole, making sure that the impact came on the passenger side.

Lawrence Terry crashed through the windshield, landing thirty feet away. He was dead before he hit the ground.

The damage to the car was total, as it crumpled on impact. Dani's air bag deployed, cushioning the blow, but she sustained a broken right arm and a broken left collarbone. She was dazed but conscious as she crawled out of the car and onto the street.

Passersby came over, trying to help, and she

screamed at the first person who came toward to her, "Do you have a cell phone?"

"Are you all right?" the man asked.

She disregarded his question and screamed even louder. "GIVE ME YOUR CELL PHONE!"

The man reached into his pocket and handed it to her. She dialed 911, and when they answered, she said, "I need to speak to Detective Jonathan Novack. It's a matter of life and death."

SCOTT RYDER WAS, FOR the first time since this operation began, in the dark.

The crash that killed Lawrence Terry happened three blocks from his house and certainly out of his line of sight. He heard the sirens from the police and ambulances rushing to the scene, but had no way of knowing it was in any way connected to his own situation.

The television networks that he constantly monitored also provided no clue as to what was going on at the crash site, since they wouldn't think this was anything other than a typical, though fatal, car accident.

But if Scott didn't know specifically what was happening, he certainly was starting to realize that he had a developing problem. Lawrence had called him when Dani went down to get her car and had told Scott that he was bringing her to his house. They should have arrived a while ago, a sign that Lawrence had very likely screwed things up.

But as always, none of this concerned Scott terribly. If anyone unwelcome arrived on the scene, Scott would see them through the elaborate camera setup that panned the entire area around his house.

And he would be ready for them.

* * *

Dani refused to go to the hospital, or to accept any pain medication from the paramedics, until Novack arrived and she could talk to him. That process took almost thirty minutes, during which she was in severe pain and even more severe panic over Chris's situation.

When Novack did arrive, she related the events to him as best she could. He believed every word of what she said and immediately called in reinforcements and a SWAT team.

Novack then called Quinlan to alert him to what was going on. Quinlan couldn't afford to be quite as trusting. To take his focus away from Randolph and get personally involved in this new situation was a risk, especially since they were now just five hours from midnight.

"You're telling me she was just in a car accident in which her passenger was killed and she's got a bunch of broken bones. I'd say her account could be clouded by some stress, wouldn't you?"

"It wasn't an accident," Novack said. "She rammed the car into a pole deliberately because Lawrence Terry was holding a gun on her. We found the gun in the wreckage. I'm just a small-town cop, but that would seem to add some credibility to her story."

The politically expedient move for Quinlan would have been to send a few agents to the scene to check it out and report back to him. Were he to go there himself, he would be taking a chance that while Peter Randolph was blowing up the world, the lead agent on the case was off on a wild-goose chase in New Jersey.

But Quinlan was never much for political expediency. "I'm on my way," he said and immediately ordered the full resources of the FBI to the scene.

By 7:30, Quinlan was at the crash site and, between federal and local, an incredible array of law enforcement assets were there and available.

Now all they needed was a strategy.

Scott saw the two men immediately through his security camera setup. They pulled up in a car, then parked and appeared to be consulting a map, pretending that they were lost. They were obviously agents sent in to check out the scene, and the fact that they thought he would be fooled by their actions was more than a little insulting.

By this point, Scott was not at all surprised to see them. He had expected to hear from Lawrence more than an hour ago, and the fact that he had not surely meant that something had gone wrong. Lawrence's involvement, both for strategic but especially financial reasons, had been crucial from the beginning, but Scott had feared it might come back to haunt him. And now it had.

"The cavalry just drove in, pretending to be lost," Scott said.

"What does that mean?" Chris asked.

"It means you just got more valuable, which in turn means you might live until tomorrow."

"I've got as good a chance as you," Chris said. "Lawrence has notified the FBI and they'll take you out."

Scott looked at Chris and smiled. "You're going to

die never fully realizing how stupid you are. Lawrence was in on this all along. I was after money and
you know what he wanted? To be a player again. How
pathetic is that?"

Scott's words were shocking to Chris. If it were really possible that Lawrence was on the other side, then
what could have happened to Dani? He had told her to
go to Lawrence if he didn't return.

And how did the police wind up outside?

There wouldn't be much information for the agents
outside to report back to their bosses. The cul-de-sac
was quiet; there was a light on in Scott's house, but no
real indication that anything was wrong.

Quinlan would have a decision to make—whether
to make a frontal assault or attempt to negotiate. Scott
was counting on them doing the latter, and he was confident they would, at least initially. They had to know
that Chris was inside; maybe he had told his girlfriend
and they wouldn't risk him dying in an assault.

That was Scott's major advantage; the other side
respected human life.

As the lead federal agent, Quinlan was in charge on
the scene. Hostage negotiators were on the way, but it
would be a couple of hours before they arrived. He
talked the situation through with Novack and they
agreed that they couldn't afford to wait.

Their first step was to send more agents in, not just
on the street, but around the house. They would hope

to learn additional information about the layout and the potential ways to go at the house and at the same time would get in position if an assault became necessary.

The fact that the house was on a secluded cul-de-sac was a mixed blessing. The location minimized the danger to neighbors or bystanders and made a potential escape try by Scott easy to prevent. However, activity in that area would by its nature be suspicious; this was not a busy street where there were likely to be cars or pedestrians.

The agents took their positions and one of them, Michael Farmer, reported back by radio to Quinlan.

"Sir, there's no sign of activity in the house."

"Any lights on?" Quinlan asked.

"I can identify one, probably three-quarters of the way back, in the center of the house."

"Stay in position and report any change. Remain positioned so as to avoid detection."

"Will do," said Farmer, unaware that Scott had long ago detected the agents and was monitoring their every movement.

New York's mayor was personally on the scene as security locked down the Times Square area. It wouldn't be opened to the public until nine o'clock, which meant that there was another hour left to check and recheck everything.

Even with the reduced crowd estimate, it would take close to three hours for the crowd to get through the metal detectors and screeners. There were also facial recognition devices at each of the makeshift entrances, all programmed to detect Peter Randolph.

The mayor had gone public with his confidence in the security arrangements and encouraged people to come down for the traditional dropping of the ball. That was his public position; privately, he was hoping for a much smaller, manageable crowd than had been forecast.

Even the ball itself had been checked and rechecked. Visual observation, explosive detection devices, and X-ray technology were all used. The process was difficult and by its nature inexact, but as a delicate crystal with equally delicate laser mechanisms, the ball could not be taken apart and reassembled on anything approaching a timely basis. In any event, it had been taken directly from its secure room at the glass factory to its perch on top of One Times Square, so it was considered safe.

Like every other public official in any way involved in the case, the mayor was far less confident than his public pronouncements indicated. He literally spoke to his police commissioner every ten minutes and every conversation was the same.

"Have you seen anything unusual? Anything that would cause you to worry?"

"No, sir."

"And none of your people have reported anything?"

"Mayor, we've got this under control."

"Call me the moment we don't," he said.

Finally, the commissioner called to say that they were ready for the crowd to be let in. "All you have to do is give the word."

The mayor took a deep breath. "Let them in."

CHRIS HAD A RINGSIDE seat to watch everything Scott was doing.

He was sitting in a chair, hands tied in front of him, against the side wall of the room. He was less than ten feet from Scott and had a clear view of him as he huddled over his computer console.

That close proximity presented a problem for Chris. He had determined that his only chance was to reach into his pocket and get his key chain, on which he had the pepper spray device that Dani had given him. Unfortunately, with his hands tied together, that would take a huge, awkward effort, one that would be readily noticeable to Scott.

Scott seemed to take some pleasure at Chris watching him in action. At one point, he got up and opened the bottom drawer of a dresser about three feet from where he was sitting. Chris could see inside; there were at least a dozen plastic pouches filled with some kind of clear liquid or gel.

"You see this?" Scott asked. "This is a plastic explosive as powerful as anything the army's got. There's enough in this drawer to level this entire block and knock out windows a half mile away. You see it?"

"I see it," Chris said.

"You want some?"

"No."

"You sure?" Scott asked. "I don't mind; I've got plenty."

With that, he reached into the drawer, took out a pouch, and flipped it casually underhand at Chris. Chris jumped back in panic, almost knocking himself and the chair over in the process, but the pouch just bounced off him and fell harmlessly to the floor.

Scott started laughing, clearly delighted with Chris's reaction. "You're a real profile in courage, you know that?" He laughed again and held up the pouch. "I mixed it myself; I made it so it would flame and burn white hot," he said with some measure of pride. "But it needs an electric charge to set it off. You could drop it off a building and nothing would happen."

He paused and laughed again. "Of course, those idiots think that by jamming the area, I won't be able to provide the charge." He shook his head in disgust. "Idiots."

Quinlan was given complete authority by the attorney general and FBI Director Kramer to decide what was to be done at the scene. What this meant was that they had signed off on an assault on the house without actually ordering it. This preserved their ability to place blame for a disaster squarely on Quinlan's shoulders.

There was still nothing concrete to go on, other than Dani's word as to what Chris had told her and the fact he was not anywhere to be found. But both Quinlan and Novack had no real doubt that Scott Ryder was P.T. and both were determined that he would be captured or dead before midnight.

When everybody was in position around the house, Quinlan decided that a negotiation should be attempted before aggressive action was taken. The likelihood was that Scott had no idea that they were out there, or even were on to him, and when he discovered his perilous situation, he might surrender. Unlikely, but possible.

Quinlan dialed Scott's home phone number from his own cell phone, and when it rang in the house, Scott said to Chris, "Get that, will you? Oh, sorry, you're all tied up."

He picked up the phone. "Hello?"

"Scott Ryder? This is Agent Quinlan of the Federal Bureau of Investigation."

"Agent Quinlan, it's a pleasure to talk to you. I'm a big admirer of your work. A fan, really."

"Scott, as we are speaking your house is surrounded by federal agents. We have reason to believe that Mr. Turley is being held by you against his will."

"Where did you ever get that idea?"

"Please walk out onto your front porch, with your hands raised above your head, and we can resolve this matter without anyone getting hurt."

"Hold on a second, will you?" Scott said. He put the phone down and walked over to a small console adjacent to the computer that had at least a dozen buttons on it. Chris watched as he pressed one of the buttons, then flinched as there was a deafening noise outside.

About fifty yards from the house, the ground under

two agents erupted in a fiery explosion, killing the agents instantly and throwing two others, thirty yards away, to the ground.

Quinlan and Novack were not in a position where they could see what happened; they were a block and a half away in a van that was serving as the command center. Camera coverage of Scott's house had not yet been set up, but they heard the explosion as if it were five feet away.

"WHAT THE HELL WAS THAT?" Quinlan screamed. When there was no immediate answer coming from anyone, he yelled again, "SOMEONE FIND OUT WHAT THE HELL IS GOING ON!"

Quinlan was still holding the phone and was surprised to hear Scott's voice come back on. "Sorry about that," Scott said. "I had to go kill two of your agents."

"You'll wish you hadn't, you son of a bitch."

Scott laughed. "I've got a hunch you won't find that kind of talk in the official negotiator's handbook." Suddenly, his voice took on a hard edge. "Now listen carefully, Quinlan. Any attempt to come at me is going to result in more dead agents. I've got the entire neighborhood wired. And if you did happen to make it inside, I've got enough explosives in here to destroy everything within a half mile. Understand?"

Quinlan had to struggle to get his temper under control. "So what do you want?"

"Just my money. I get my money and you get Turley. Oh, and one more thing. I'm the only one who can stop what is going to happen at midnight and right now I don't see any reason to."

"What is going to happen?"

"I look forward to talking about it with you, when I am assured that the money has been wired."

"There's no way we can get the money to you before midnight."

"Then that was bad planning, asshole. Because I gave you plenty of warning."

"I'll get back to you," Quinlan said.

"That will give me something to look forward to," said Scott, and then he laughed again.

QUINLAN HAD NO GOOD OPTIONS.

To start, he had no authorization or ability to pay the money, even if he were inclined to do so, which he was not.

But he also did not have the resources to mount an assault on a house that was as booby-trapped as this one was turning out to be. Two agents were already dead and there was every reason to believe that Scott was telling the truth when he said that more explosives were in place to protect himself from attack.

"We can't move in without armored vehicles," Quinlan said to Novack.

"This is Elmwood Park, New Jersey. There aren't a lot of tanks hanging around. Fort Dix would be the closest place that would have them."

Quinlan nodded. "But they're not getting here by midnight."

Further complicating matters was Scott's claim that the house itself was filled with explosives that could bring destruction as far as half a mile away. Quinlan knew enough about the detonations Scott had already set off to realize that that was a very credible claim and he also knew that a lot of people lived within a half mile of Scott's house.

"So what do you think?" Quinlan asked.

Novack shrugged. "I think we're in deep shit."

"We need to have this neighborhood evacuated," Quinlan said. "A full mile, to be safe."

Novack nodded. "My people are already on it. Unfortunately, the media has arrived."

"They get moved out like everybody else."

"Already being done," said Novack. "You try and rush that house, you're going to lose some people."

"I know. Problem is, we're going to lose people either way. It's just a question of which people, and how many."

"I don't think he'll blow himself up," said Novack. "People who want money generally don't want to die. It cuts down on the spending options."

"We're not dealing with a highly rational person, in case you haven't noticed. And you haven't said what you would do yet."

"I'd probably fill the place with gas and then rush it. And I'd do it quick. Turley has been saying for days something huge is going down at midnight and I think he's right."

"We haven't talked about Turley," Quinlan said. "There isn't much chance he can walk away from this."

Novack nodded. "I hate to say it, but he can't be a factor. There's too much at stake."

Quinlan said, "I'm going to call in a chopper. When this is over, we may have to get somewhere in a hurry."

"You're not as dumb as you look," said Novack.

"That's comforting. Let me know when the neighborhood is clear and then we go in."

Chris Turley obviously did not hear Quinlan and Novack decide that his life was not a factor, but he instinctively knew that it was the case. It had to be that way. Quinlan, and Novack if he was out there, would decide that Scott had to be taken out before midnight, no matter what. And midnight was a little over an hour away.

One way or another, when they came at the house he was going to die. They would storm in with no hesitancy and full power and the odds against him surviving such an assault were overwhelming. And if they didn't kill him, Scott probably would.

He would have to save his own life.

Chris was surprised at how calmly and rationally he was thinking. He wasn't feeling any panic, just an understanding of what he must do and when he must do it. On one level, he felt pride in his reaction; it would just be nice if he could one day tell someone about it.

Dani would be the person he would want to tell, but he realized with a wave of sadness that he was unlikely to ever see her again. All he could do was hope she was okay and the presence of the police on the scene gave him hope that she was. If she hadn't contacted them, he couldn't imagine who had.

And then he thought about his mother, and whether anyone would tell her that he was gone. The truth is that she wouldn't understand even if they did, and that was an ironic comfort to him.

Chris knew that Quinlan would have to take Scott's threats seriously and that it would take some time to prepare the assault. He didn't know how they would come; they might even have a plane fire a missile at the house. That is probably how he would do it.

It was eleven o'clock and he decided he would wait for the best opportunity in the next fifteen minutes to go for his key chain. If there was none, then at 11:15 he would do it and have to accept the consequences.

He couldn't afford to wait any longer than that.

Scott also knew they would come at him and that, one way or the other, he would be dead when it was over. That knowledge in no way changed his approach; he was going to do the best he could to prevail. They would know they were in a fight and they would be counting their dead for a long time when it was all over.

Scott figured that Quinlan had to be extra cautious after Scott described what he was up against, especially after the demonstration that killed two of his agents. If he were Quinlan, he would seek to incapacitate Scott before going in. Which could only be done one way.

Gas.

Scott was prepared for that, as he was prepared for everything else. He kept a gas mask in one of his desk drawers and he took it out and put it on the desk. Once he put it on, he would be able to function normally, no matter what they threw at him.

The crowd in Times Square, a paltry quarter million, was trying to make up for its smaller than normal number with extra revelry. These were the brave souls who were not going to let P.T. dictate how they would live their lives. It was New Year's Eve and they were damn well going to celebrate.

The crystal ball sat atop the building known as One Times Square. It was bathed in light, awaiting its yearly moment of celebrity. With the world watching, it would start its descent at 11:59 and would take exactly sixty seconds to make its way down.

Dani lay on a bed in her hospital room. She was still in great pain, but she remained glued to the television set, having refused to submit to the needed orthopedic surgery until she knew what had happened to Chris.

She knew that the media coverage was basically uninformed. They believed that the siege somehow involved P.T., but they knew little more than that. They did report the fact that evacuations were ordered almost a mile away, which left no doubt in anyone's mind that it was a very dangerous situation.

Dani did not expect that they would have any specific information to broadcast until after it was over. And that was what she was going to wait for, no matter what.

*　*　*

At eight minutes past eleven, a chopper landed on the deserted street, less than a block from where Quinlan was standing.

At 11:10, Novack walked over to him and said two words. "We're ready."

THE OPERATION WOULD BE a simple one.

Six SWAT team members, on command, would simultaneously shoot powerful tear gas canisters through six different windows. Then twenty agents would storm the house from all sides and shoot to kill.

Quinlan had more people at his disposal, but he felt that twenty would be adequate; there was no use exposing more to what was very serious jeopardy.

Quinlan himself would be one of the twenty, but he refused to allow Novack to participate in the initial assault. "This is a federal operation," he said.

"I'm going," said Novack.

"No, you're not."

"Then you'll have to shoot me."

"With pleasure," Quinlan said. He knew Novack would lose the argument, since Novack didn't have a gas mask.

As Quinlan started moving towards Scott's house, readying his own gas mask, Novack came up alongside him and said, "Quinlan, when you're in there . . . try and watch out for Turley."

Quinlan just nodded, raised his radio, and prepared to give the order.

* * *

Scott hadn't moved from his computer for the last fifteen minutes; he just sat there watching the screens for any sign of an attack, glancing occasionally at Chris to make sure he remained under control. Therefore, Chris had not had a chance to go for his key chain.

It was 11:15 and Chris knew he couldn't wait any longer. He had decided he would make the move suddenly, rather than slowly and carefully, because Scott was just too alert to not notice him for any length of time.

Chris moved both hands towards his right pocket, reaching inside for the key chain. Amazingly, he got his hands on it right away and was able to pull it out of his pocket.

He tried to twist it around in his hand, just as he sensed Scott was moving towards him. Scott's foot crashed into the side of his face, sending him back to the floor and the key chain flying somewhere across the room, well out of his reach.

At that moment, windows started crashing in and the sound and smell of gas escaping was instantaneous. Scott looked up and realized what was happening and he turned back towards his desk to grab the gas mask.

Seeing what Scott was about to do, Chris smashed into him from behind, pounding on his head and shoulders with his bound hands. His weight and the pounding knocked Scott to the ground and Chris jumped on him.

Scott struggled to throw Chris off, just as Chris struggled to keep him pinned down. His only hope was to prevent Scott from getting to his mask and then the controls that he could put to such deadly use.

The gas was getting to both of them, burning their eyes and causing an agonizing pain in their throats. Scott was screaming and gasping, while Chris just kept his mouth and eyes closed, holding his breath as he tried to stay on top of his enemy.

The door flew open and the two men on the ground knew that agents had broken in, though they could not see them.

In a final, desperate move, Scott threw Chris to the side and jumped to his feet. Blinded by the gas, he groped his way towards the desk, no longer heading for the gas mask, but instead for the controls that could blow up the house and the neighborhood with it. He reached the console just as a hail of bullets tore him apart.

Quinlan, just behind the agents who had killed Scott in front of his computer, grabbed on to Chris and dragged him out of the house and onto the porch. Novack was there waiting for them, but couldn't give Chris time to catch his breath or regain his sight.

"WHAT DO YOU KNOW?" he screamed. "WHAT IS GOING TO HAPPEN?"

Chris could barely get the words out as he scrambled to his feet, leaning on Quinlan. "I'll . . . tell you . . . on the way."

Quinlan, Novack, and Chris, along with five other agents, ran to the chopper and took off for New York. Chris had updated them on what was going on as best he could and there were decisions that had to be made immediately.

Quinlan was in contact with FBI agents in Times Square itself and with the New York City Police commissioner, who was stationed in the police command post on Forty-second Street.

"Is there any way to evacuate the area?" Quinlan asked, yelling to be heard above the noise of the helicopter.

"No," the commissioner said. "Not in the time we have left." He went on to say that the crowd was far too raucous to respond to gentle persuading, and a more vigorous push to evacuate could very easily set off a panic and stampede. "We'd lose a lot of people that way and we still couldn't clear the area."

"And we can't move the ball." It wasn't a question; Quinlan was just thinking out loud.

"The ball has been carefully checked," the commissioner said. "That can't be where the bomb is."

"It's there," said Quinlan.

Based on Chris's revelation that Scott was unconcerned about the jamming of cell and radio wave transmission, Quinlan and Novack were positive that Scott had set a timer to detonate the explosives. And they were equally sure that it was set to go off at midnight.

Which gave them five minutes.

There was not even a place to land the chopper. Obviously, it couldn't be put down in the street, since all streets were filled wall-to-wall with people. It also wouldn't work to bring the ball down early, in the hopes that people would think New Year's had come and gone and would leave the square. There was no time for that, nor was there time to bring in a military helicopter to cart the ball off to an area where the explosion could safely take place.

The military experts consulted expressed the belief that it would likely be worse to keep the ball from dropping and let it explode at the top of the building. The concussive effect on the street below would be devastating and there was a substantial chance that the blast would bring down the building.

Quinlan yelled to the pilot. "Go right to Times Square; hover above the crowd. I want to be able to see the ball."

The pilot did as he was told, and when the revelers saw it, they thought it was part of the show, since they had no sense that its being there represented any kind of danger to them. Besides, they were more interested in the crystal ball at the top of the building, which was slowly starting its descent.

Chris had watched and listened to all the consultations take place and when it was clear that no remotely acceptable solution had been reached, he stood up. "Shoot the damn thing!" he yelled.

When no one seemed to be paying any attention to him, he screamed, "Shoot it!" as loud as he could. His voice was still raspy and weak from the effects of the tear glass and his efforts would have seemed comical if the situation were not so dire.

"It'll blow up," said Quinlan. "It's better to let it get to the ground."

"No!" said Chris, desperately trying to be heard

above the din of the helicopter and the crowd below. "It needs an electric charge to set it off! Ryder said you could drop it off a building and it wouldn't explode. If you shoot it, you might be able to destroy the timer. Then there won't be any charge!"

Quinlan had absolutely no idea if Chris was right, but he made a judgment that there would be little downside to going along with him. He took out his handgun and yelled to the others, "On my command, empty your weapons into it!"

The five agents and Novack took out their weapons and leaned out the side facing the ball. At that distance, it would be impossible to miss.

Quinlan waited until the ball was halfway down the building; if it got much lower, there would be the danger of hitting people with errant shots or ricochets.

"NOW!" he yelled.

The men opened fire and the ball began to shatter with a series of mini-explosions as it continued its descent down the building. It was spectacularly colorful and bright, as if the slow-moving ball had converted itself into a fireworks display.

The sounds of the weapons firing blended into the helicopter and crowd noise, making it impossible for the people on the ground to know what was going on. Most of them assumed that it was some kind of amazing light show and they roared their approval.

The ammunition spent, the men in the chopper watched as the remnants of the ball approached the bottom. They had no way to know if the timer was intact, but they would learn soon enough.

The crowd, watching the clock on the side of the building, chanted down: "TEN, NINE, EIGHT, SEVEN, SIX, FIVE, FOUR, THREE, TWO, ONE . . ."

As midnight hit, the lights on the building came on in a beautiful, colorful display. Everyone in the chopper cringed in anticipation, but there was no explosion. The timer had been destroyed.

"Happy New Year," said Novack.

CHRIS TURLEY BECAME THE first nonjournalist to win the Pulitzer Prize for journalism.

That is because, by the time the award was announced, he had given notice to the *Bergen News* and opted not to pursue any of the one hundred and eleven job offers he'd received.

He had become the most famous reporter in the country, which is to say that he had become his father. It turned out that was something that ultimately didn't appeal to him.

Instead, he accepted a five-million-dollar offer to write a book about the P.T. affair. The idea of doing so was singularly unappealing to him; he had lived it once and didn't want to experience it again in any fashion.

On the other hand, it was five million dollars.

Chris and Dani decided that the living together thing was working pretty well, so they would keep at it for a while. As of this writing, that "while" is six months long, and neither of them seems inclined to mess with success.

Dani was justifiably considered a hero in her own right and has been fielding her own book offers. To this point, the highest bid has been two million dollars, which she considers highly insulting. Her agent thinks they can raise the price to two-million-five, which Dani figures is a half million dollars less insulting.

Investigators are still trying to dissect the life of Carl Gordon, Scott Ryder's real name. At this point, they have uncovered years of violent, criminal behavior and believe they have tied him to three other murders and a number of armed robberies.

Peter Randolph's body has never been found. His chances for a productive life ended the day when as a small boy he watched his father walk out onto the highway.

Agent Nick Quinlan's star continues to rise in the FBI and, depending on the results of the next election, he is considered a candidate for either director of the FBI or head of Homeland Security. At this point, the idea of taking a desk job like those is not particularly tempting.

Jonathan Novack is also considered a hero for his role in the P.T. saga, and has had three in-depth magazine pieces written about him.

He finds all the attention annoying.

Read on for an excerpt
from David Rosenfelt's next book

ON BORROWED TIME

Available in hardcover from Minotaur Books

THE MOMENT WE met is burned into my mind, and even now I replay it over and over. It's somehow vaguely comforting, and thinking about Jennifer gives her a presence. I've wanted to give her a presence for so very long.

It's not outright denial, but it's almost as good.

It was at a political rally for a candidate Jen was supporting. It's funny, but I can't remember who the candidate was, and I can't venture a guess, based on what I learned later about Jen's politics. In that area, she was always a contradiction: a social liberal who was fiercely in favor of the death penalty, and a fiscal conservative who never met a homeless shelter she didn't want the government to support. But whatever it was she was advocating at that or any other moment, that advocacy was fierce.

I'm a writer, so I had the political "get out of jail free" card; it was a violation of my alleged journalist credentials to even hint at my leanings. I wrote mainly magazine articles, most of them political or business-oriented, but I wasn't there for anything having to do with work. The truth is, I had just been wandering by and stopped to see what was going on.

So on that day we were who we are, or at least as I have always seen us: Jen as a participant in life, and myself as an observer of it.

It didn't take a particularly keen observer to notice her. She was light-up-the-room beautiful, even though she was wearing a New York Yankees cap. I hate the Yankees, always have, always will, but I quickly rationalized that I'd never really felt any animosity for their caps. So I went over to her and introduced myself.

"Hi. I'm Richard Kilmer. I'm a journalist."

"How nice for you," she deadpanned. Journalists were not necessarily her favorite people.

"Yes . . . I wanted to ask you a few questions. About the rally . . . the candidate. . . ."

She smiled, and it was the first time I had ever seen a smile that had nothing whatsoever to do with the mouth or lips. This smile was wholly in her eyes, and I later came to realize that this was part of her ability as a smile ventriloquist. Just by being in the vicinity, Jen could make everything and everyone smile, without letting on that she was doing so.

"I really don't know that much about him," she said. "But if you want your questions answered . . . Carl, come here a second?"

She called over a young man standing a few yards away. Carl was unshaven, balding, and maybe twenty pounds overweight. Not a horrible-looking guy, but not really my type.

"Hey," Carl said, proving that if nothing else he was a charming conversationalist.

"This is Richard Kilmer . . . a journalist. He's

looking for some information." She went on to tell me that Carl knew far more about this particular candidate than she did.

"What do you want to know?" Carl asked.

"Well, to be perfectly honest," I said, "I was more interested in the female point of view."

Carl frowned his disdain at me and walked away.

"You should have said so," Jen said, scanning the crowd. "Then let's see what we can find for you."

She was playing with me, no doubt looking for some female shot putter to stick me with. "I was interested in your point of view," I said.

"Let me guess," she said. "You're particularly interested in my point of view coupled with coffee, drinks, or dinner."

"That's uncanny," I said.

"Why didn't you say so in the first place?"

"I only use honesty as a last resort."

She thought about it for a few moments, as if weighing it. Then, "Coffee."

I HATED THAT LOOK.

It was a look that said, *You're full of shit, Richard. You know it and I know it, so let's move on, shall we?*

My problem with the look, and with Jen, for that matter, was that it and she were always right. In that case, I had just tried to tell her that we should drive to her parents' house in upstate New York on Monday, rather than Sunday. I had lamely claimed that we'd hit less traffic that way, but she knew it was really because I wanted to watch the pro football games. When it comes to football, I'm somewhere between a fanatic and a lunatic.

"You want to watch football tomorrow," she said. It wasn't a question, but rather a statement of fact.

"Football?" I asked. "Tomorrow? God, the week flew by; it never entered my mind. Where do the days go?"

She laughed, and asked, "What time are the Giants playing?"

"The Giants? The Giants? The name sounds familiar. . . ."

"Richard . . ."

"One o'clock. They're playing the Redskins at home."

She shook her head in amazement. "Redskins. How can a team have a name like that in the twenty-first century?"

I nodded vigorously. "Exactly. They are politically incorrect pigs. Which is the main reason I want them to be defeated tomorrow. Somebody has to take a stand on the side of decency, and they will leave Giants Stadium tomorrow having learned a moral lesson. And it's about time."

There was that look again. It was time to come clean.

"The winner makes the playoffs. The playoffs, Jen. That's three wins from the Super Bowl. I really want to see it."

"Then why didn't you just say so in the first place?"

I shrugged. "Honesty? Last resort? Remember?"

She smiled. "Tell me about it." That was sort of a catch phrase she used whenever someone told her something she already knew, which was pretty often.

Jen agreed that the game was not to be missed, so she called her mother and told her we'd be there on Monday. It wasn't a big deal, since we'd been invited for Christmas, which was Friday. Her parents lived in Ardmore, a small town about two hours from our apartment in Manhattan on the Upper West Side. We had a two-bedroom on the thirty-third floor of a building called the Montana, on Eighty-seventh and Broadway. If there is a piece of real estate in the world that should not be called Montana, it is that one.

Jen had told me a couple of weeks before that her parents were excited to meet me, that I was the first boyfriend she had ever brought home. As always, it was jarring to hear her call me a "boyfriend"; we seemed to be so much more than that. I think on some level that's why I bought a ring and planned to ask her to marry me the following week. If she accepted, and I anticipated that she would, I would instantly make the quantum leap from "boyfriend" to "fiancé."

In a matter of hours after first meeting Jen I had regressed from independent twenty-nine-year-old male, unwilling (or afraid, if some of my dates were to be believed) to make a commitment, to pathetic twenty-nine-year-old puppy, panicked that she wouldn't like me. My amazement that she did, that in fact she grew to love me, was not modesty, false or otherwise. The simple truth was that Jen could have had absolutely anyone she wanted, and she chose me. It was the kind of situation for which the word "hallelujah!" was coined.

Jen moved into my apartment four months after we met. We chose mine because it was bigger, and because I owned it, while she was just renting. In a matter of hours, the apartment went from a place completely devoid of personality to a real home. When Jen got finished with it, my impersonal group of rooms had become the kind of home the Waltons would beg to spend Thanksgiving in.

Jen even liked my friends, few in number as they were. Don't misunderstand, for the most part my friends are intelligent, successful people. They may have their faults, but there's not a terrorist in the bunch, and the world would be a better place if their level of goodness prevailed everywhere. But as a group, we have one flaw; we argue about everything. Everywhere. They are heated, sometimes stimulating, sometimes childish debates about a wide range of topics from sports to politics to people, and the truth is, most outsiders find it a little off-putting.

Since I had only arrived in town three months before meeting Jen, I had only had time to develop two close friendships. I had met both John Sucich and Willie Citrin playing basketball at the Y, and discovered we all had a love of politics, sports, and women. Not necessarily in that order.

Jen was an insider from day one, and one particular night was a perfect example as to why. We went out to the Legends Sports Bar to have dinner and watch the Knicks-76ers game. John and Willie brought along dates, who in my mind were named Somebody and Whoever. For both John and Willie, two dates was a long-term relationship, so I didn't spend too much time memorizing the women's names. I know it was dehumanizing, but I figured that if they didn't want to be dehumanized, what the hell were they doing with John and Willie?

That night we were arguing about the death penalty, a frequent topic. John and Willie were for it; I am so strongly against it that I once wrote a series of articles advocating my position. As always, they told me that if my sister were murdered I'd feel differently. I don't have a sister, but they'd probably killed her off fifty times. Jen was on their side; this was a woman who quite literally wouldn't harm a fly, but would apparently toast a convicted murderer or rapist without thinking twice.

I neither won nor lost the argument—in fact, the one common thread through all our arguments was that no one ever won or lost. Not a single time in my memory had anyone been convinced to change a position, no matter how stupid that position might be. But I could always tell when Willie and John were unhappy with how things were going, because they would say that they were fed up with my "Ivy League bullshit," as if my having gone to the University of Pennsylvania disqualified me from having a legitimate point of view.

Our second argument this night was about third basemen. It was and is my opinion that Mike Schmidt is the best all-around third baseman ever to play the game. John went with Brooks Robinson, while Willie picked Pie Traynor. Now, I'm sure Pie was great, but he was sucking dirt for about fifty years before Willie was born, so Willie's position was inherently uninformed. You could always tell the guy with the inherently uninformed position; he was the one who yelled the loudest.

Jen cast her vote for David Wright, a ridiculous choice so early in his career, but he was a Met and she always thought the Mets were the best. Somebody and Whoever were bored silly by the entire spectacle, though at one point Somebody said, "My brother likes sports."

Before long, Somebody and Whoever said their good-byes, while John and Willie stayed with Jen and me so we could keep the arguments going. When all the yelling was over, Jen announced, "Richard's spending Christmas at my parents' house."

"Whoa!" was John's response. "This is more serious than I thought."

"We're living together, idiot," I pointed out with my characteristic subtlety. "You didn't think that was serious?"

"Well, Richie, my boy, I'm afraid things are about to change."

"What are you talking about?" I asked.

John turned to Willie. "You tell him."

Willie sighed, as if he hated to have to break the bad news. "Rich," he said, "suppose you had a daughter who looked like that." He pointed at Jen. "Now suppose she brought home a guy who looked like that." He pointed at me. "You see where I'm going with this?"

"I'm afraid I do," I said.

Jen wouldn't hear of it. "They'll love him." She kissed me. "I love him."

A stupid grin on my face, I turned to John and Willie. "She loves me. Eat your heart out."